Stick to the Plan

A Forced-Proximity, Workplace Contemporary Romance

R.S. Barry

RILEY PAWS PUBLISHING

For my Mother and Grandmother, whom I lost last year.

They had me drive their drunk asses to *Magic Mike* for Mother's Day—I think they'd approve.

Irish Slang and Translations

Feck (fek): A mild expletive similar to "fuck" but considered PG

Eejit (e jit): Idiot

Gobshite (gob shite): Also idiot

*Slag (*slæg)*: A promiscuous woman

A ghrá (uh GHRAH): Love

An bpósfaidh tú mé?: Will you marry me

Aisling (ASH lin): Traditional Celtic girl's name, means "dream or vision"

Sinéad (shin AY): Popular girl's name in Ireland, means "God is gracious"

I Hate Mondays

BRIANNA

Shit, I'm late. Eight am staff meetings are yet another way to torture employees. My stiletto pump taps sharply against the tile floor of the elevator of C.A. Engineering Corp. Fucking move faster!

Stupid highway drivers; I would have been early if everyone hadn't slowed down to stare at the accident. I slip out of my jacket and dig out my tablet as I watch the numbers crawl by—preparing to bolt as soon as the doors open with a bing.

I walk past cubicles with short walls as the sun shines through tall windows. Despite the day just starting, the maze of desks is already humming. The lowered conversation tones mix with the clacking of keyboards and the occasional hiss of a coffee machine somewhere.

Without breaking stride, I drop my purse and jacket over the cube wall onto my desk and continue towards the glass doors of the conference room at the end of the aisle. One quick glance at my watch shows it is 8:05 am. Crap, he's going to skin me alive. There goes my chance at that promotion. No worries, I'll bust my ass for the next two years until the next one.

With one last deep, calming breath, I square my shoulders and open the giant door. Ten sets of suited shoulders turn towards me. Ten pairs of eyes fill with either derision, pity or, in one particular case, rage.

"Thank you for joining us, Barbie. What kept you, a sale at the mall?" Richard Stone, Senior Director of Research and Development, my boss, and a major *Dick*. He sits in his customary seat at the head of the twenty-foot glass and steel conference table. With his cropped blond hair, ice-blue eyes, and hard jaw, he looks as cold and intimidating as he acts in the boardroom.

Stay calm; he's trying to get a reaction out of you. "Apologies, sir. There was an accident blocking two lanes on the highway."

Richard glares at me with his icy stare for another ten seconds before turning back to the rest of the room.

"Now, as I was saying. There's a lot going on this week for C.A. Engineering Corp."

I quickly take the last remaining seat at the table. My chest expands with deep breaths to calm the fire in my belly. I adjust the hem on my knee-length pencil skirt under the table and cross my ankles.

Barbie!? I hate it when he calls me that.

The mall? As if all women only live for clothing and shopping.

Ok, so maybe I enjoy dressing nicely. Just because the "old boys' club" outnumbers me five to one doesn't mean I need to dress like a man! I don't see the big deal about a black skirt and a white blouse!

Opening my tablet case and smoothing my silk blouse, I force myself to relax the tight ridges forming between my eyebrows. In my peripheral vision, a handsome man about my age sits further down the table. He's wearing a gray vest and lilac button-down shirt. Fucking lilac! Johnson dresses like a freaking GQ model in a two hundred dollar shirt and I'm the Barbie Doll here? Okay.

At the other end of the room, Richard clears his throat and continues. "As you know, we have been in talks with Innovative Solutions, a small development firm based in Ireland, on a new joint project. The bulk of the team will be from this office, but a representative from I.S. will arrive today to act as point person. I expect all of you to welcome Mr. McLeary to C.A.E. and do everything you can to make this project a success. Now, I want updates on your current projects. Then I'll decide who will run point from our side. Johnson, you start."

One by one, they take turns giving status updates. Most have nothing new to report since last week. Some have unforeseen schedule delays. These unlucky souls have to verbally tap dance around the issues. Such is the lot of a project manager in a development industry.

You're handed a project with little to no details and told to go make it happen, quickly and cheaply. You develop a task list and timeline to accomplish the work, hoping you thought of everything and it all goes right the first time. The job doesn't come with a crystal ball, things rarely stick to the plan. You adjust and remove obstacles the best you can. It is stressful, challenging, thankless, often brutal—and I love every minute.

"Ms. Chance?" One blond eyebrow raises as Richard turns to me.

"The Sit Co project is complete; the customer received the product last week. I should have the closeout report submitted today. The Smart Screen project finished product testing last week. It passed all the functional tests, quality control checks, and received high marks in the user tests. Production begins this week."

"Sit Co is complete?"

I turn to face him directly, my emotionless mask firmly in place. "Yes, sir."

Richard flips through his notes and a crease appears between his eyes. "Two months ahead of schedule?"

"I found areas in the schedule that we could work in parallel to save time, and made it clear to the vendors that late merchandise was unacceptable."

For a moment I swear I see admiration in his eyes, but just as quickly, whatever the emotion, it's gone and Richard moves on to the next suit. One more update, and he adjourns the meeting. Almost as one, we all rise and exit the room.

"Ms. Chance, a moment," Richard says, his voice cracks like a whip.

Already halfway to the door, I pause. Damn.

"Of course, sir."

As my last peer files out the door, it closes behind him. Sealing me from freedom.

Double damn. Is this about being late? I quickly replay the meeting in my head—I wasn't too sassy, was I?

Richard purses his lips and taps his pen idly on the tabletop. "Very impressive work on the Sit Co project."

A compliment? Is this a dream? "Th... thank you, sir."

"You are a very thorough project manager. No detail gets overlooked, and your tenacity reminds me of myself at your age." His eyes glint and his lips curl into a smug smile. I can almost see why others think him handsome. "That, and your ability to complete projects on time and budget, is why I want you to take the lead on the Innovative Solutions project. Do well and you will be in consideration for the Director of Project Management position."

That promotion is everything I've been working towards for the last year. I want it so badly, I can taste it. "Yes, sir. Thank you."

"One more thing. There was an issue with the extended stay hotel; they lost the reservation for the exec from Ireland. Some conference in town has it completely booked. I'm under strict orders from the board to keep this McLeary happy and impressed. I'm not putting him up in some freeway motel."

A sinking sensation builds in my stomach. My gut is never wrong, and it's telling me I'm not going to like whatever Stone says next.

"I remember you bought that big house. You have all that room and no husband or kids anyway, McLeary can stay with you. Since you will be working closely with him, this will give you the best chance to collaborate."

"You want me to do what?" I ask.

This isn't a dream, it's a freaking nightmare.

"I want you to host our guest and ensure that he is happy. Frankly, I think he'd be a lot more comfortable at your house than a hotel. Plus, this way we can keep a close eye on him. Chance, this is important for the company." His expression shutters. This is his 'I have spoken' face. Oh shit.

"Sir, doesn't Mr. McLeary arrive today? I'm not prepared to have a houseguest at this short notice." Is he serious? This has to be some new form of torture he's conjured up for me.

"Take the rest of the day to prepare. Come back at five to pick up McLeary. The company will compensate you for any utility and food costs you incur. The board appreciates you going above and beyond. That is all." Richard lowers his eyes back to his tablet, summarily dismissing me.

My nostrils flare on three slow breaths. I turn on one icepick heel and head straight for the door, absolutely seething. Spine ramrod straight and vision tinging red, I retrace my steps of only forty minutes before past my desk and to the elevator. I ignore everyone around me. If anyone stops me, I'll explode and my 'cool under fire' reputation will be ruined.

I sweep into my house like a tornado. My anger just as deadly. So single-minded in my rage, I barely notice my small dog, Riley, jump off the couch and follow me to my bedroom. Finally giving into the fire burning in my veins, I kick off my heels towards the closet with a frustrated scream. Next, I peel off my skirt and blouse and throw them at the bed like they have personally offended me. Not even my favorite lounge clothes can comfort me.

"Asshole!" I scream at no one in particular. There is no way this is legal. Not married—real nice rubbing that in. Unmarried at twenty-eight wasn't exactly my plan, thank you very much.

My eyes wander to my naked ring finger. After almost a year, it still feels strange not seeing a diamond ring there. With a sigh, I turn to see Riley peeking out from under the bed. He looks worried more clothing will go flying. Seeing his anxious look, more of the violent rage dissipates from me. I reach down to scoop him up for a cuddle.

"I'm sorry, baby boy. Mommy's not mad at you."

Riley licks my cheek and nuzzles my chin. He understands in his doggy wisdom that I need cuddles, too.

"That man makes me so angry! He finally gives me some sort of recognition, then drops a house guest on me!"

I walk out of my room and down the hall. Absently scratching Riley's head, my steps take me deeper into the living room. A white leather sectional dominates the room, anchored by a dense blue area rug. It faces a gas fireplace and TV on one branch and a full wall of glass sliders. The view looks out into my courtyard pool and garden. Over the past eighteen months, I've painstakingly remodeled every inch of this place. Every detail in this house is a representation of me.

Well, a messier representation of me, anyway. A large stack of books pile by the couch. I don't think I have touched the guest room since Mom visited at Christmas. I know I left breakfast dishes in the sink too. Shit, what am I going to make for dinner?

I pull out my phone to look up recipes using what's in my fridge. While I have my phone out...let's check in on the girls. My running group message with my besties is the only thing that gets me through most days.

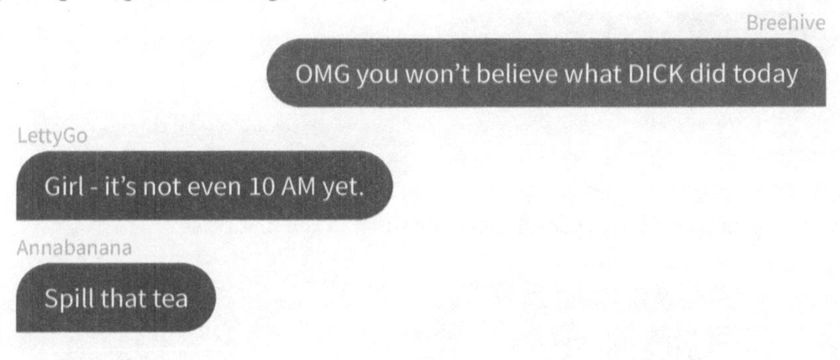

Breehive

He said he'd consider me for the promotion

Annabanana

Yay!

LettyGo

but...

Breehive

BUT I have to host a client from Ireland at my house

Annabanana

that man is insane

LettyGo

is he hot?

Breehive

DICK? Ew.

LettyGo

no jerk, the Irish guy

Annabanana

she never said it was a guy

Breehive

it is... he's an exec, so I'm assuming he's at least fifty...

LettyGo

not the question... is he hot?

Breehive

NICOLETTE! So not the point.

I chew my lip. There's a reason I messaged them in the first place.

Breehive

I know this must be totally illegal. Minimum, it's sketchy as hell. Is it wrong that I didn't say no? I'm home to clean up and make dinner...

Dots appear and disappear a few times. I gnaw at my lip some more, waiting.

Annabanana

Aw, honey, no. You have been working so hard. I understand not wanting to risk Richard being vindictive.

LettyGo

Richard - really? You can't just say DICK?

Annabanana

Har har. I can still taste Momma's soap when you two get started.

LettyGo

oh BLESS HER HEART

Annabanana

you're using that wrong

Breehive

GIRLS!

LettyGo

sorry. It's not wrong. Set boundaries and protect yourself. If he gets cheeky, I'll pop him one.

Breehive

thanks. Love you girls.

"Well, I guess I better get started," I say to Riley as I set him down. Cranking the radio, I put my latent anger to good use. Systematically moving from room to room, I scrub, dust, vacuum, and change linens. Satisfied that no one can find fault with my home, I check my watch: three pm. Plenty of time. Whistling, I head back to my room for a shower and change of clothes before I have to pick up my uninvited guest.

CHAPTER TWO

First Impressions

COLIN

The laptop bag digs into my shoulder, and my luggage drags across the industrial carpet behind me. I pause for a moment, enjoying the cold air blowing from the vents. My fingers itch to loosen my collar where the material sticks to my neck. Even in early spring, the humidity of central Florida is unbearable.

A woman sits at the large desk in front of the main elevator of C.A. Engineering. She looks up and gives me a cursory inspection as I approach, one eyebrow slightly raised. No doubt my tousled hair and wrinkled suit are to blame. I'd like to see how she looks after almost ten hours on a plane.

"May I help you?"

"Colin McLeary from the Innovative Solutions Dublin office t'a see Richard Stone." My Irish brogue sounds extra thick and gravelly from the night of travel.

Her eyes widen in surprise. She probably expected the Dublin executive to be older. Thirty is a little young for a vice president. Then again, maybe it really is just the rumpled suit.

"Mr. Stone will be with you in a moment, Mr. McLeary. He is finishing up the morning staff meeting now." She tilts her head towards the glass-lined conference room just down the aisle.

I smile at the assistant, thank her, and head towards the conference room to wait. The meeting seems to break up as I arrive, I watch the men file out as the lone woman stays behind. With nothing else to do, I study her.

Her back is to me. Long brunette hair sits in a simple tail. Her posture precise as she stands by the man at the head of the table. That must be Stone she's talking with and she doesn't seem to be enjoying the conversation.

She turns towards the door, every movement controlled but graceful. My breath catches as I see her face. Large blue eyes, high but delicate cheekbones, and a jaw that comes to a soft point. Her lips press together tightly, forming a white line around her prominent cupid's bow. Her looks are a striking mix of strength and femininity.

She instantly draws me in.

Sexy heels click against the floor, her gait smooth. Maybe I misread the situation. I take another look at her dark blue eyes. They sparkle with barely concealed fury. She passes me and I can't help but admire how her snug skirt hugs her curves with every step.

"You lost, son?"

Son? Seriously?

I turn back to meet the calculating gleam and slight sneer of the man in front of me. Instantly I know I'm not going to like him. Don't lose your temper, Colin, keep it professional. I stick my hand out for a firm shake as I introduce myself.

"Colin McLeary, VP Engineering from Innovative Solutions."

"Richard Stone, Senior Director Research and Development. Let's go to my office to discuss this joint venture."

With that, Richard turns and walks away. I fall in step beside him as he leads further into the building to a corner office. Two walls of windows back a giant desk with two chairs opposite. A large monitor hangs on the wall by a small table and four chairs. Shutting the door, he gestures to the chair in front of his desk, as he moves around the monstrous piece of furniture to the executive wingback chair behind it.

With effort, I hold in a sigh as I lower myself into the indicated seat. This guy has one hell of an ego and these mind games are tiring. So much for a warm welcome and friendly partnership.

Richard leans on his desk as he blatantly sizes me up over his steepled fingers. "Welcome to C.A.E. We hope you enjoy your time here. Since your visit is open-ended—I have arranged for you to stay in the home of one of our staff. I have assigned one of our top project managers to handle this project for you."

Nodding slowly, I run my tongue over my teeth and take a sharp intake of breath through my nose. There goes my hopes for hot tubs and room service.

If I wasn't under strict instructions to play nice, I'd make it clear how much of an ass I think he is. *Feck* me, I hate political games. I tap my finger on my knee twice before meeting his cold eyes with a firm look of my own.

"Thank you, but I wish to remain close to this project. Innovative Solutions has a keen interest in the success. I do not plan to release control until I am convinced C.A.E. will properly handle it."

Jaw ticking slightly, Richard quickly covers the movement with a smile that doesn't meet his eyes. "Of course. We hope to deepen our relationship with your company. I have cleared the office next door for you. I will take you on a tour of the facilities, and then you can settle in before your host collects you." Stone stands abruptly and heads to the door, barring any further discussion.

My watch says it's now 4:30 pm local time, and I am absolutely exhausted. I sit with my elbows propped on my temporary desk, pinching the bridge of my nose. All morning, Richard led me through the building. Prototype labs. Testing labs. Offices, interactive video-conferencing centers, and a sea of depressing cubicles that left me feeling vaguely claustrophobic.

I've shaken more hands than I can remember—the faces and names blurring together. A lunch meeting with the board, and then he dropped me in this office to settle in. No sooner had my butt finally hit a chair than an intern from IT arrived to set me up with a C.A.E. laptop and network credentials. I am finally alone and all I want is to get to wherever they have me staying, have a beer, and go to bed.

A knock on the door pulls me from my reverie. Standing in the doorway is a woman I haven't yet met. Her hair is the palest blond and curls around her shoulders, drawing the eye to a trim figure in a form-fitting white dress. An inviting smile is on her scarlet lips, and smoky makeup highlights her blue eyes that sparkle with interest.

"Mr. McLeary, I'm Rachel—Mr. Stone asked me to make sure you have everything you need." She walks closer with a clear swing of hips on high strappy heels and boldly looks me up and down. Her smile widens and becomes wolfish as she blatantly eyes me.

I keep my smile polite but stay seated with the desk between us, hoping my message is clear. "Thank you, miss, but I think I'm all set."

"I'm Mr. Stone's assistant. If there is anything you need, just let me know." Rachel leans over the desk, giving me a clear view of her generous cleavage, which is held up by some marvel of engineering. "And I do mean *anything*."

Well that is blunt. I feel a muscle in my jaw spasm. As a red-blooded man, I usually enjoy the attention of a woman, but her frank and unprofessional perusal is making me uncomfortable. And more than a little pissed off. "All the same, I'm sure I'll be just fine on my own. Good night." I let the smile drop further, praying she finally gets the message.

She doesn't.

Pulling out a business card from God knows where, she leans in even further and drops it on my desk. "Here's my card. In case you change your mind. Sir."

Her voice lowers to almost a caress, and she looks up at me through her eyelashes on the 'sir'.

Rachel is arguably attractive. All the same, I find myself comparing her to the mystery brunette from this morning. Rachel's eyes lack the same intensity of blue, her hair lacks the same richness, and she doesn't captivate me. I never saw the mystery woman on that *shite* tour. I caught myself looking for her at each stop.

A throat clears at the door, saving me from having to be rude. We both turn towards the newcomer.

As if conjured from my mind, there stands the mystery woman. Her clothes are different now, jeans and a blouse with a long open sweater thing. Her hair is now down and falling to her mid-back. She must have been offsite most of the day and is just now returning to schmooze the new client.

Her eyebrow raises slightly as she stands in the doorway. With a last smile and a murmured goodbye, Rachel struts out of the room, flicking her hair over her shoulder as she passes the other woman.

"We haven't met. Colin McLeary."

I rise and walk around the desk, holding my hand out to her. Her palm is warm and smooth in mine, her clasp confident and firm.

Now a similar proposition from this woman would be hard to turn down. I shift slightly to relieve the growing pressure in my pants that thought inspires. Screw professionalism. Something in my gut tells me this would be one line worth crossing.

"Brianna Chance. Welcome to C.A. Engineering. I'll be the project manager assigned to you."

Maybe this won't be as bad as I thought. The woman clearly has a spine, and if she's half as good as Stone says, this will be easy. "Pleasure. Stone told me I'll be working with his best. I'm looking forward to it."

"Thank you. I'm also your host during your visit. When you are ready to leave, just let me know. I'm sure you're eager to settle in and eat dinner."

There goes any hope of relaxing.

They have me staying with a young, beautiful woman? That Rachel woman offers to sleep with me thirty seconds after meeting? This is the strangest business trip I've ever experienced. If she sees my eyes go wide with surprise, she doesn't react.

"Leaving sounds great."

I walk back over to the computer I haven't even touched yet to buy time to gather my thoughts. I collect my luggage and gesture for her to lead the way.

We set off together at a comfortable but leg-stretching pace. I study Brianna through my peripheral vision. She doesn't look very happy. Maybe this is what she and Stone were fighting about earlier. She probably won't want to hang out much, right? Maybe I can relax without a pint.

"How did you get chosen to host me, if I may ask?"

Brianna's jaw clenches for a moment, and her nostrils flare slightly. We make it to the elevators and she seems to give great attention to the buttons as she resets her expression.

"Mr. Stone thought you would be more comfortable in a home rather than a hotel. As we'll be working closely together, it seemed a likely choice." She keeps her head straight forward and her tone even.

"That is very generous of you. You and your husband don'na mind having a stranger in yer home?" The elevator dings as I watch the side of her face. Her jaw ticks. It's barely noticeable. If I wasn't staring I would have missed it.

"I'm not married." The doors open, and Brianna starts across the lobby and out the door without checking if I'm following. "That's me on the left."

I head towards a black sedan in the direction she points, but Brianna passes it and unlocks a yellow convertible in the next spot. After stowing my bag, I lower myself into the black leather seat.

"I should pick up a rental car so you don'na have to drive me everywhere."

"It's not a problem carpooling to the office every day since I'm driving, anyway. If you have... social engagements... planned we can get you a rental tomorrow. I have dinner ready at the house, but do you need to stop for anything?"

She eyes my carry-on-sized rollaway in the back.

"Dinner sounds grand. I have what I need." I grin at her as she puts on a pair of sunglasses and checks her mirrors. I'm just happy to be leaving the office.

"Top up or down?"

"Down, please. After being stuck in that building all day, I have a need for some sun."

As Brianna navigates the streets and gets on the highway, I lean back and take my first deep breath of the day, the warm breeze tousling my hair. We drive in silence. It should be awkward, but I am strangely at ease.

The setting sun on my cheeks fills me with warmth and makes me smile. In no time at all, she is pulling off the highway and zipping down suburban roads.

"Welcome to Friendship Springs. Conveniently located to many tourist spots and a quick drive to the office. This is the residential section, but there's a nice downtown area with restaurants and shops."

The houses look nice, but all near identical copies of the last. Perfectly manicured lawns with perfectly cultivated gardens. The neighborhood screams class, money, and zero character. So very American, and I am suddenly homesick for the sprawling green hills and historic buildings of home.

She turns a curve and suddenly I see it. A house that has everything the others lack.

Yellow siding with white shutters and window boxes. A white flowered tree blooms in the front yard. The front door is painted purple and matches the lush beds of wild heather lining the front walk. It is charming, untamed, sexy as hell—and I know this is her home before she even turns into the paver driveway.

"'Tis beautiful to be sure."

"Thank you." She smiles slightly, bringing a new softness as she gazes at her home. "It was a mess when I bought it. I've worked hard to make it mine."

She falls silent, her eyes glazing over and thoughts clearly far away. After a couple moments, she gives her head a little shake and turns to me. "You must be starving. Let's go inside and get you settled in."

She unlocks the front door and barely makes it three steps before a black ball of fur comes flying around the corner. If it wasn't for the happy bark, I'm not sure I'd realize it's a dog.

Brianna's eyes widen in horror. "Crap. I forgot to warn you about Riley. He doesn't like men."

Riley stops running at the sound of her voice. His little head cocks to the side as he eyes me, the stranger in his house. With much more decorum than his initial entrance, Riley sidesteps Brianna as she reaches for him. The little dog approaches my foot and sniffs my shoe for a moment. I squat down and give him my fingers to sniff as well. Decision seemingly made, he sits down and lifts a paw to me.

"Pleasure to meet ya, Sir Riley."

I shake the offered paw and give him a scratch behind one ear. Looking back up at Brianna, her eyes are the size of dinner plates and her mouth is hanging open as her supposedly picky dog flops onto his back. Shamelessly begging for belly rubs. I chuckle and give him what he wants.

"That's amazing. He never acts like that around strangers." Brianna seems to be slowly recovering from her shock, but still very confused.

"Don't be upset with him. I've always had a way with dogs. Ma always said if she di'na know better, she'd swear I was raised by them." My grin spreads, my long day nearly forgotten after some puppy love.

Her eyebrows are still a little pinched as she watches me interact with her dog. She clears her throat a bit.

"Your room is right this way."

I rise and follow her to an open door off the spacious living room. The bedroom is large and tidy. The walls are the color of the ocean after a storm. A contemporary queen headboard, all dark wood and straight lines, is the focal point. Stepping further into the room, I find a large armoire and prim desk in the same dark wood.

"Through here is the bath. Towels are already out on the sink. There's a TV in the armoire. The Wi-Fi password is on the desk." She points out each as she speaks. Brisk and effective.

"Make yourself at home. When you're ready, go back towards the door and take a right. You can't miss the kitchen. Let me know if you need anything else."

With that said, Brianna gives a small nod and walks out, Riley right on her heels. I let out a sigh and sit on the edge of the bed.

This will certainly be interesting.

I drag a hand over my face and take a deep breath, finally noticing the intoxicating smell coming from down the hall. My mouth waters. Unpacking can wait. I'll take a quick shower and then find out what smells so delicious. If it tastes half as good as it smells, this arrangement won't be as bad as I feared.

CHAPTER THREE

Tippy Toes

BRIANNA

This is going to be worse than I thought. I take a long sip of my hard cider as I assess my situation. He's a lot younger than I expected. And Rachel is already throwing herself at him? I saw enough to get the gist of the conversation. Wonder if he would have gone with her if I hadn't shown up.

I lean back against the counter as I nurse my drink and replay our first conversation. Colin's green eyes had grown wide when I said I was his host. What exactly had Stone told him? The sooner we get this project done and get him out, the better. A man with a smile like that is trouble. If my stomach flipped after he grinned up at me—and I'm not saying it did. *If* it did, it was only because I was hungry. It had nothing to do with his piercing green eyes or that dimple that appeared when his grin reached its fullest.

Distracting myself, I stir the rice. I look down at my dog, sitting at my feet hoping for crumbs. He acts as if nothing unusual happened at the door.

"And you, mister! What was that all about? Huh?" Riley cocks his head to the side, clearly saying 'who, me?' I feel my annoyance lift and chuckle. I can never stay mad at this fuzzball. "You are so lucky you're cute." Getting a treat out of the nearby canister, I toss it to him.

Rice now done, I transfer the fluffy white side into a waiting bowl and bring it into the adjoining dining room. The table is neatly set with white, square plates, gleaming silverware, and sparkling glasses filled with ice water. The Crock-Pot insert is already on the gray wood table. Perfect, now I just need to get through this meal. Hopefully, he's too tired to talk much, and then I can escape this whole mess for the night.

Colin enters the room as I am still surveying the table. "Smells delicious," he says with a happy exhale, "even if you hadn't given me directions, I could'a found the room with my nose."

"Thank you, I hope you like chicken cacciatore. Can I get you something to drink? Water, milk, or perhaps some wine or a beer?" At the word 'beer' he visibly perks up, so I continue. "I have hard cider, Yuengling, Corona, and Guinness."

"Guinness, please." He is giving that dangerous smile again.

"I'll be right back. Sit down and help yourself." I make my escape to the kitchen and take a few calming breaths. Closing my eyes, I give my stomach a lecture to get its shit together. Butterflies are not on the menu today. Or any night, for that matter.

Returning to the dining room, I stop short. Colin is sitting at the table, eyes closed, mouth full. A look of utter satisfaction on his face. Taking advantage of his distraction, I study his face.

High cheekbones and a sharp, clean-shaven jaw. His brown hair is shorn on the sides and left just slightly longer on top. At the office, he'd combed it to the side in a fairly standard business look, but his shower has left a messy mop, giving him a boyish look. A muscle spasms as he chews, my heart beats faster. His Adam's apple bobs as he swallows the bite, drawing my eye to the strong column of his neck. His thick shoulders fill out his simple tee, proving his suit wasn't padded. My scrutiny continues to his firm chest as he heaves a content sigh, eyes still closed.

My lips tilt up into a small smile. It has been so long since I've cooked dinner for anyone like this. I forgot what it feels like to see someone enjoy my cooking. Unbidden, images of another man sitting at this same table hit me. Forget about that asshole; Riley and I are happy on our own. I have my career, my friends. My life is full enough.

Colin cocks open one eye as I place the perfectly poured Guinness in front of him. "Thanks a million. I think I've died and gone to heaven." He picks up the stout and takes a long sip before sitting back with a content sigh. "Aye, definitely."

Sitting down, I busy myself with making a plate as I try to think up polite business dinner conversation. "You must have had a tiring day. Flying halfway across the world and then sitting in meetings all day. Glad you are enjoying the meal."

"Oh, aye," Colin answers between forkfuls. "Between the travel and all the trans-Atlantic meetings over the last few weeks, can't remember the last home-cooked meal I've had. Definitely nothing this delicious since my last visit with my ma."

At his enthusiasm, heat spreads across my cheeks. I concentrate on my plate to hide the blush. I mix the rice in with the sauce from the chicken. Colin copies me and tries a bite, then promptly gets another helping of the cacciatore.

The meal continues with the typical polite topics—weather, local attractions. After we are both done, I stand and start gathering the dirty dishes. I'm surprised when Colin grabs a few more dishes and rises to follow.

"Oh, no. I can clean up. You're probably exhausted."

"No, miss. You went to the trouble to cook. Ma would tan my hide if she knew I didn't at least help clean up." Again, he shoots that devastating grin. He has to know what a weapon that single dimple is.

Together, we clear the table and head into the kitchen. I stack my plates by the sink before moving to open the dishwasher. Colin follows close behind, copying my motions. Funny, the kitchen never feels this small when it's my besties in here with me.

Pushing down that thought, I grab a handful of plates from the bottom and move to put them away.

A jingle catches my attention and I turn to see Colin holding the silverware caddy and looking at me expectantly. "Where do these go?" he asks.

The plates clink as I lift them almost above my head to the shelf. It really sucks being short sometimes. "The drawer next to the fridge." I point vaguely as I grab bowls and return to the cabinet. More clinks as I stack them next to the plates. There is a strangely companionable silence between us. Broken only by the occasional clatter of silverware or thunk of china.

Bottom empty, I move on to the top drawer and grab a pair of water glasses. I open the glass-front cabinet to the right of the sink and eye the middle shelf with a sigh. I have to tilt my head back to see it fully. These glasses are such a bitch to put away. Why haven't I moved these to a lower cabinet? I glare at the coffee and wine glasses on the lower row. Oh yea, priorities. Mouth set in a determined line, I reach as high as I can. The lip touches the wooden shelf, but the glass is still too tilted to slip into place. Normally, I'd just climb onto the counter to put them away, but that feels undignified all of a sudden.

Cursing silently, I place the other glass on the counter so I can brace my weight as I push onto my tippy toes. This time half the glass's lip gains purchase. Glaring, I strain to stretch every muscle in my body for an extra inch to my five foot five frame. Almost there! I switch to just using the tips of my fingers to balance the glass, gaining the much needed inch. The glass slips and my eyes widen as I'm powerless to do anything but watch.

Long, tan fingers catch the glass and gently push it into place.

I gasp and turn. My eyes are level with Colin's chest mere inches away. The fresh scent of pine overwhelms my senses as I take a fortifying breath. My eyes slowly rise to his face. The kitchen fades away as I'm drawn into his consuming gaze. His lips quirk into that sexy smile that's already becoming all too familiar. Colin leans in slightly and my heart pounds as my eyes meet his. Without breaking his intense gaze, Colin's other arm rises and I hear the scrape of the other glass on the shelf.

I gulp and lick my dry lips. "Th-thanks," I whisper.

His grin widens until that damn dimple winks at me. My stomach drops, the sensation finally enough to break whatever fairy spell he cast on me. I duck under his arm and I hurry to put the last few items away. It almost sounds like Colin chuckles as he loads the now empty dishwasher. My body hums as I feel his eyes follow me around the kitchen. I know it's just to learn the layout of his temporary living space, but my hormones haven't quite gotten the message. What the hell is wrong with me?

Grabbing a sponge, I take my frustration out on any surface I can reach. When the white counters sparkle, and the dishwasher quietly hums, I dry my hands on a towel and tentatively turn to the man in my kitchen. "Thank you for your help. If you'll excuse me, I need to let Riley out."

"Thank you for the meal. I think I'll be turning in, G'night Miss Brianna." His eyes are warm.

Not trusting my voice, I nod once and leave the kitchen, whistling for my dog as I go.

CHAPTER FOUR

Meeting of the Minds

COLIN

I lie in a field near the cliffs of my home, surrounded by green grass and purple heather. The ocean is a roar, canceling out any other sound. My eyes follow jean-clad legs up to an overlarge sweater that pools around a bare, pale shoulder framed by reddish-brown hair.

Brianna reclines next to me, propped up on one arm, wholly at ease. Her eyes are closed and a beautiful smile lights her face as the salty wind pulls at her hair. I reach out to tuck a lock behind her ear and she turns her smile to me. As she clasps my hand in hers, I see a traditional Claddagh ring glint on her finger, the heart and hands facing inwards. She slowly leans down to kiss my lips.

I can feel her lips on mine, cold from the wind.

Cold and wet.

My eyes snap open to find a dark, hairy face and a lolling tongue inches away. Ready to lick again.

"Good morning to ya, Mr. Riley."

Stopping the dog's impending attack, I give him a gentle pat and shake the last remnants of the dream from my head. After dressing and gathering my work bag, I exit to the living room, looking around for Brianna.

A yip to my left brings my attention towards floor-to-ceiling glass sliders leading to a stone patio. Guessing my new furry friend needs to go out, I slide open the door and take in the yard for the first time.

It is small but beautifully landscaped. A rectangular pool with a waterfall dominates the yard, serving as the main feature. The house wraps around the pool on two sides, and the other two sides have tall fencing for privacy. Flowering bushes soften the harsh effect of wood and stone.

The sounds of chirping birds and running water create a serene oasis. I love it immediately.

The sound of footsteps catches my attention. I turn as Brianna enters the living room, securing a diamond stud in one ear. Today, she's dressed in a lemon drop silk blouse and white dress slacks with another pair of killer heels. She pulled her hair back at the crown and secured it with a gold barrette. Surprise crosses her face as she sees me up and about. Then she turns towards the open patio door and her expression calms as the black fur-ball races back inside to nip at her heels.

"Thank you. I hadn't realized he had run off." Brianna gives a tentative smile that shoots through me like lightning and makes my cock twitch.

I swallow the sudden lump in my throat. Settle down, boyo, she is off limits. Be professional.

"Mornin'. It looks like a grand day. Ready to head to the office?"

"Yes, let me grab my bag and we can go."

Without another word, we make our way to the car and back to C.A. Engineering. I hold the front door for Brianna and follow her to the elevator bank. She points out her desk as she leads me back to my temporary office.

"I booked one of the conference rooms all day so we can review those project files. Just let me check my email and I'll meet you at 2A in a half hour. Sound good?"

The empty table with four chairs draws my attention in the office, as the soft glow of morning light floods in through the wall of windows. The idea of sitting in a cold conference room with no windows makes me shudder.

"No need to take up an entire conference room for two people. Why don't we just work here? Come back when you're ready to start."

Brianna follows my line of sight to the small table and seems to stiffen for a moment. "Alright," she answers slowly, "if that's what you prefer, I'll be back in about thirty minutes."

We've been poring over files for hours. Email transactions, project charters, testing results, schedules, contracts. My eyes are dry and crossing a bit. Sometime during the afternoon, I tossed my jacket over a chair and loosened my tie.

Brianna, though, is still neat as a pin. No hair out of place and not a single wrinkle to be found on her shirt or slacks. All the records are as orderly as she is. Stone may be a creep, but he's right about one thing: Brianna is a gifted project manager.

I look at the latest graph Brianna gave me, showing profits and costs. This has to be the twentieth detailed graph I've looked at. Leaning back in my chair, I sigh.

"How d'ya do it?"

"Pardon?"

"How d'ya do it?" I repeat, holding up the tablet. "There is no piece of these projects you haven'a thought through. Opportunity costs, predicted ROI, schedules, backup schedules, risk mitigation strategies." I click through the tabs of the spreadsheet as I rattle off each item.

Brianna's eyebrow cocks over her left eye, as if to say the answer is obvious. "That's my job."

I scroll down one sheet as I purse my lips. "This schedule has two hundred line items."

"It's a three-year development project being completed in three separate countries."

I lean forward again as I switch files to inspect it closer. "This budget shows a breakdown of projected costs and profits. By month... and region."

Brianna, who has been sitting on the edge of her seat with perfect posture all day, finally allows herself to lean back slightly.

"Finance likes to see details before they approve a project."

I flip files again.

"This list of contacts shows all fifty stakeholders—in both an org chart and a table with contact information. What the..." I click the screen a few times and lean closer to it. "Is that the personal phone number for a VP at Hewlett Packard?" I look up at Brianna with eyes wide and eyebrows raised. "How did you even get that?"

"We were getting pushback on a delivery date which was going to kill the entire project—so I got resourceful."

I look back down and squint as I reread a comment on the screen. "Does this comment say that he likes chocolate chip cookies?"

Her cheeks take on a rosy hue and her lips twitch into an almost smile. "I needed to know what to send as a thank you when our printers arrived on schedule."

I burst into laughter.

Never have I seen baked goods included in a project plan. Setting out on this business trip, I had been hesitant to let someone else take part in this new product. I am deeply invested in this idea. It can literally change the world—not to mention the fate of my company. The more I review her files, the more I am sure she is the right person to oversee this special project.

Lounging back in my chair, I recover from my amusement and assess the woman sitting across from me. "Well, Brianna, there's no doubt you are qualified. Let me tell you what we know so far, but first I need you to sign this nondisclosure agreement." I reach into my bag and slide the document across the table with a pen, and wait for her to review and sign.

"One of our engineers believes he has created an extremely efficient solar generator. The cooling system even doubles as a water purifier. Runs 100% off the grid. Initial prototypes look good, but it can still use some refining and testing."

"Why bring this project to us? Why not keep the profits for yourself?"

"Fair question. Innovative Solutions may have top-rate engineers, but we're still a small company. To put it bluntly, we need C.A.E.'s resources and financial backing. And you need our ideas. This project is really a test run. Our CEO and yours have been discussing a merger for a while. I'm here to protect I.S.'s interests and report back to Dublin. You'll take the lead on managing this project—it is obvious it will be safe in your hands. My job will be to ensure you have ever'ting you need from us. Does that sound alright?"

Brianna leans forward as I speak, intelligence flashing in her eyes as she takes in the situation. "Yes, sir."

"Grand." I break eye contact to check my watch. "It's six already. Let's call it a night and get some food. We'll have an early call with Dublin tomorrow to discuss the details, then we'll select the local team. Why don't you pack up and I'll meet you at your desk in... twenty minutes?"

"Ok, I'll be ready." She gathers her things and heads to the door.

"Oh, and Brianna?"

She stops and turns back to me, long fingers holding the door handle. "Yes?"

"You are now the only person besides myself and the executive boards that knows the details of this project. I trust you to keep it that way."

"Not even Mr. Stone?"

"Especially not Stone."

Without breaking eye contact, she gives a slight nod and another 'yes, sir' before promptly leaving the office.

CHAPTER FIVE

Strategic Spying

RACHEL

Many sneer at the title Personal Assistant, but I know the true importance of my position.

Richard Stone is the senior director of all research and development.

Without *him*, there are no new products, no new profits.

And without *me*, Richard Stone gets nothing done.

The saying goes, 'Behind every powerful man is a woman'—and that is my plan. Currently, Stone is concerned about this McLeary guy, so I'm going to find out exactly why the delicious Irishman is here. And what makes him tick.

I make my way to his office to invite him out for drinks—hopefully followed by breakfast in bed.

That bitch Brianna better not interrupt us again. I fluff my hair and check my cleavage and yellow miniskirt one last time. I don't care if she has the best project stats on the team, that woman has ice in her veins and I don't like her.

Raising my hand to knock on the closed office door, I pause as I hear muffled voices within. The thick door blocks most of the sound. Leaning my ear against the door, I can barely make out Colin's voice as he tells Brianna to keep the details of their project from Richard. Brianna's voice is much louder. She must be standing just on the other side.

The door handle turns. Anxiously glancing around, I dart into Richard's empty office next door—thankfully the carpeting hides the sound of my heels. I flatten myself against the wall until I hear Brianna pass by, count to a hundred, and then slip back to my office to plan out how to use this information to my advantage.

CHAPTER SIX

Office Confrontations

BRIANNA

I check my watch for the tenth time as I walk down the office hallway. 7:45 am. Perfect. Enough time for a quick stop in the ladies' room before joining the eight am call with Dublin. I've already reviewed the notes from Colin on the various engineers and executives who will be on the call. I've got this.

As I review my mental notes one more time, I think back to yesterday, working so closely with Colin. When he'd first suggested staying in his office, the idea of sitting so close all day sharing a laptop screen had made me shudder.

The day had been surprisingly comfortable, though.

It's clear I impressed him with my detailed project documents. I admit—he impressed me, too. He's been attentive but quiet, as if he's absorbing as much as possible. When he does speak, his question or comment is always insightful and never aggressive. I hadn't wanted to like him—or the warm sound of his laughter—but despite my best efforts, I find myself doing both.

I misjudged him—there I admit it. He isn't the playboy from across the pond I feared him to be. True, he is young to be a VP. But from everything I found online, Innovative Solutions is a small company, and Colin has been there since the start. He is intelligent and quick-witted; I have zero doubts he earned that title.

The simple fact Stone dislikes him enough to ask me to keep an eye on him perversely makes me like Colin even more. I chuckle to myself as I pass Stone's office.

"Chance, come here," Richard booms from behind his desk.

Speak of the devil and he shall appear. Stopping instantly, I back up the two steps I'd managed past his door and turn to face my boss.

"Yes, Mr. Stone?"

"Shut the door." He waits for me to enter and approach his desk in the now enclosed office before continuing. "How are things going with McLeary?"

"Very well, sir. He seems thrilled with the way we run projects here and is confident the new project will be very successful."

"Yes, yes, very good." Richard leans forward with his elbows on the desk and his fingertips steepled. He looks like a ridiculous cartoon villain. "Have you gotten a feel for this McLeary yet?"

Tread carefully, Brianna. "I'm not entirely sure yet, sir. After an initial call with Dublin today, I'll know more."

"What details do you have so far? What is this fancy new product supposed to do? Why is he here personally?"

I take a deep breath and plaster my most professional smile on. "Sir, Dublin hasn't shared the full specs yet, but I do know that early testing has been promising and I.S. is motivated to get to market quickly. Until I know more—and we're out of the testing phase—I won't have firm projections for you on potential profit yields. I imagine Mr. McLeary is here as a show of good faith from Innovative Solutions. A bit of team building and good business politics."

Richard's eyes narrow, and I think I see his cheek muscle spasm, as if he's clenching his jaw. Does he know I'm holding information back? He clears his throat and his eyes narrow.

"So you're telling me you spent all day with him and you learned nothing to help me? Don't make me regret choosing you for this, Chance. Next time I ask for an update, I expect some damn details!"

"Of course, Mr. Stone." Clearly dismissed, I leave his office and quickly resume my path to the restroom. My chest feels a little tight and my temples tingle. Clear signs of my temper flaring and it needs to be reined back in. This project better not cost me my job. With a deep breath, I open the door and almost bump into Rachel reapplying lipstick in the mirror. This morning just keeps getting shittier and shittier.

"Well, if it isn't Ms. Brianna Chance, the Ice Queen herself." Her gaze glitters with malice as it meets mine in the mirror.

I'd rather be an Ice Queen than a manipulative bitch. "What do you want, Rachel?"

She goes back to checking her lipstick in the mirror. "I don't want anything. I was just minding my own business until you stormed in." She tilts her head to the side. "Now that you mention it though, I want to give you a... friendly... word of advice," she says, her face full of mock sincerity.

I grit my teeth, and even though I know I'll regret it instantly, I hear myself ask, "And what would that be?"

"I'd watch myself if I were you. Mr. Stone is very much counting on this collaboration to be a success." Rachel twists her red lipstick closed and replaces the cap with a snap before meeting my eyes in the mirror. "I'd hate for you to lose your job over this. Just look at what happened to Barry Webster." With that, Rachel turns on one scarlet stiletto and swishes past me out the door.

I stand frozen for two heart-pounding minutes, fuming but trying to regain my composure. I close my eyes, my clenched fists the only outward sign of the red-hot fury raging within.

I hate that nickname. *Ice Queen*. I am proud of my ability to keep a level head and not let my emotions affect my job. It is precisely what makes me so good at my chosen profession.

There is just no winning.

I spend years proving myself to the boys' club. That I can play the politics game. That I can take the stress and the angry customers on without crying in the boardroom. The men finally accept me, and the women disown me for being a 'heartless bitch'.

Just because I don't wear my heart on my sleeve or gossip in the bathroom doesn't make me heartless.

Forcing my hands to relax, I take three deep breaths to calm down. Breath in... two... three... four. Hold... two... three... four. Out... two... three... four. Hold... two... three...four.

Most of the women here aren't bad. I just can't let Rachel get to me anymore. No matter which buttons she pushes. I'll keep my projects so profitable for the company that Stone can never fire me.

Under control and suitably pumped back up, I make my way to Colin's office just as he is dialing the conference call on his speakerphone. I shut the door and sit down, ready to get to business.

CHAPTER SEVEN

A Pint of Pity

COLIN

I let myself into Brianna's house with the spare key she gave me. We picked up a rental car earlier in the week, too, so I have the freedom to come and go. I look around as I walk through the silent house. Riley looks up from his bowl in the kitchen long enough to see it's me, then returns to eating.

"Sorry to disturb your dinner, Mr. Riley. Please carry on." I grin at the pup and give him a mock bow.

It's Friday night. We had a very productive week. The charts Brianna made projecting the potential profits from the generator are exciting. It's early days yet, but this project has massive potential. And I want to celebrate. I drove around town until I found a pub that looked decent enough, but then decided I didn't want to drink alone.

Two coworkers can go out for a pint after a productive week, right? Nothing wrong with that. So what if one of them happens to be an irresistibly sexy brunette?

Yea—I don't believe myself either.

I just want to spend more time with Brianna. She fascinates me. Something about her aloof, crisp nature makes me want to crack her shell open and see what's hiding inside.

The silence of the house is heavy as I continue past the kitchen. I can see a few lamps glowing in the living room, but no sign of Brianna. Her car is here, so where is she?

Just as I wonder what to do next, I hear a phone ringing from her bedroom. Smiling to myself, I head to the right with long, determined strides. I hear her answer as I raise my hand to knock, but the sound of her voice freezes me in place.

"Hey! What's up? Where are you?"

The efficient, brisk tone I've grown accustomed to is gone. She sounds happy. Who is she talking to?

"New York? When are you coming back? I miss you." Disappointment creeps into her voice. She pauses, listening to the person on the other end, then releases a peal of bright laughter.

"You better bring me something pretty to make it up to me! God, I really wish you weren't on this trip, Nic. I need you here now more than ever."

Another pause. A heavy sigh. "Yea, that about sums it up."

Another round of laughter. "I know, I love you too. It'll be ok."

My lungs burn and I release my breath, but my ribs still feel tight. Cautiously, I back away from her door. Retrace my steps to the front door and to my rental car as quickly but quietly as possible. Of course she has a boyfriend—not that I care.

Well—I shouldn't care, anyway. Not like anything can happen between us. It is inappropriate. Impractical. Impossible! *Shite*—why am I thinking in alliteration? Really convincing.

I find myself back at the pub. It is relatively empty for a weekend. The lighting is bright, but not harsh. Walls of dark wood paneling covered in vintage Guinness signs and black-and-white photos of Irish scenery surrounded three sides. Forest green leather booths line two walls, and a massive mahogany bar dominates the far wall.

Behind the bar stands a burly man cleaning glasses. Floor-to-ceiling mirrors behind him highlight shelves of whiskey and scotch, and large wooden beer tap handles. I can smell greasy chips and the distinctive tang of vinegar. A lively fiddle plays over the speakers. This place feels like a neighborhood pub back home.

I grab a stool near the end of the bar and order a pint. Looks like I'll have that drink alone after all. Likely followed by a whiskey. Or three.

By the bottom of my pint, I've mostly convinced myself that it is for the best Brianna isn't single. Sure. She is extraordinarily beautiful, intelligent, and unexpectedly funny. Any man would gravitate towards her. Those expressive navy eyes can make you forget your name. Groaning, I rub my eyebrows as if I can erase my thoughts.

The bartender approaches again; I notice his name tag just reads 'himself'. He appears two decades older than me, and his thick Irish brogue comforts and reminds me of home. "What else can I get ye?"

"Jameson. Neat. Make it a double."

He studies me as he pours the whiskey into a glass. "What does a lad like you have to look so down about? Must be a bonny lass."

He pushes the thick glass across the bar top. I let out a dry laugh.

"Aye. Isn't it always. I think I've met the woman of my dreams, literally. But there's nothing to be done about it." My lips twist into a grimace as I toss back the amber liquid and feel it burn down my throat before clacking the glass down heavily.

"Well then. If t'ere's not'in to be done, not'in to be done."

He wipes the bar in front of me with a towel. I hunch over my whiskey, cupping the glass between my palms.

"It's probably for the best. We are working together, and my boss is counting on me to make this a success."

Another draw of the burning alcohol. Declan O'Toole, founder and CEO of Innovative Solutions, is so much more than my boss. He is my mentor and a surrogate father figure.

I still remember when I met him at university, he gave a lecture in my engineering class. We talked after class and he gave me his contact information. For the rest of the semester, we exchanged emails. When summer came, he offered me an internship in his brand new company. When my father unexpectedly passed that spring, Declan gave me a way to support myself and my family. Devoting myself to his vision helped me keep moving forward through my grief.

This merger is important to him. It is validation of his vision and his legacy. I won't be the reason it fails. Mind set, I throw back the rest of the whiskey in one last gulp.

"We don't even live in the same country! I can't stay here. I need to get back to Ireland and my family. There's no future with her."

I hold the bartender's gaze as I deliver my speech. He gives a sage nod, as if he knows more than he lets on.

"Well then. If there is no future." He pours another two fingers of Jameson in my glass, as he returns my gaze. "But t'en again. The future is not set, t'ere is no fate but what we make for ourselves."

With that nugget of Irish proverb hanging in the air, he moves to the other end of the bar to tend to another customer.

It is for the best. Isn't it? I stare into the amber liquid as if it's a crystal ball with all the answers.

CHAPTER EIGHT

Rub a Dub Dub

BRIANNA

I've officially survived the first week of this awkward arrangement. Colin excused himself after dinner to search the city for a decent Irish pub and won't be back for hours. Finally have the house to myself and I deserve a bubble bath. What the hell, and a glass of wine!

It hasn't been easy, but we managed to find a schedule that works for both of us. In the morning, whoever dresses first lets the dog out. Then the other makes coffee before we head to the office. I check on my other projects and grab a bite at my desk while updating status reports and project plans. In the afternoon, I join Colin in his office to flesh out the details on the solar generator. After a solid ten-plus hour day, we cruise back to my little yellow house. I throw together some simple home cooked meal, and he digs into it like a man starved. We clean up dinner in companionable silence, and then move to our separate rooms for the evening. A twilight stroll with Riley for me, then a few hours alone with a good book in bed.

The initial meeting with Dublin went well. There were a few strained moments. Some tempers flared when one exec questioned if the generator would actually work. Between Colin and I, though, we smoothed the ruffled feathers and kept the meeting on track.

I was also, thankfully, spared from having to lie to Stone again. His routine is to stroll in at eight am, take a two-hour lunch with his assistant around eleven, and then disappear by three for a golf game. Since I always beat him in by at least a half hour and usually stayed until six pm, he hadn't had the chance to corner me again. I'm sure he will after Monday's staff meeting, though. I'd better come up with something good by then.

My cell interrupts my thoughts as it rings. Checking the screen, I flop onto the bed to answer with a huge smile. "Hey! What's up? Where are you?"

"New York City for a charity concert. I got some amazing shots of the skyline, though, and some local models. You'll love them."

Nicolette Kato-Atherton is my best friend, and a successful magazine photographer. We'd met at freshman orientation and quickly became inseparable. Sophomore year we'd found Anna Bennet and decided to make our duo a trio. For nearly a decade now, we've stood together through thick and thin. Bad haircuts. Worse boyfriends. Promotions. And everything in between.

My smile fades a bit. "New York? When are you coming back? I miss you."

"I'm stuck following this band for three more weeks. I promise I'll make it back for your birthday next month!"

"You better bring me something pretty to make it up to me!" I close my eyes against the anxiety building in my chest I've tried to ignore. "God, I really wish you weren't on this trip, Nic. I need you here now more than ever."

"Let me guess, Big Dick and Queen Bitch giving you grief at work?"

I let out a deep sigh. "Yea, that about sums it up."

"I really wish you'd let me slap that girl."

Nic has made it known countless times in the last year what she'd like to do to Rachel. "I know, I love you too. I'll be ok."

"You sound really stressed, love. It's got to be something bad. What happened now?"

I fill her in on the last week—from walking in on Rachel propositioning Colin all the way up to dinner tonight. "I shouldn't be so hard on the guy. It's not his fault Stone made him an uninvited guest. Colin's as much a victim here as I am, really." Another sigh escapes me. "There's just major politics in play here."

"Is he cute?"

"Nic! Is that all you think about?" I chuckle lightly. Being an artist, Nic appreciates attractive men. She is gorgeous and confident and, of us three, it is usually Nic that gets approached first when we go out.

"Hey! I stare at gorgeous men all day and can't touch a single one of them. I'm in the middle of a three-month dry spell. Cut a girl a break!" Nic's voice drops as she adds, "Does he have a sexy accent?"

I groan as I think back to that first morning after Colin arrived. I'd turned the corner and found Colin standing in my living room. The open slider had framed him perfectly as he stood in a tailored three-piece suit. Hands in pockets, just watching my dog sniff every bush in the yard. The morning sun haloed his chestnut hair, highlighting red sparks and creating tantalizing shadows on his chiseled face. My fingers had practically itched to trace those sharp planes. The only lovers I'd had for a long time had been battery operated, and it was starting to take a toll on my sanity. I'm not a teenager anymore who can't control herself. With Nic I can be honest, though, and I am dying for some good girl talk.

"Does he ever! And his smile. Oh man, Nic. You would die."

"So, are you showing him some hospitality? Seems convenient, what with him already at your house and all."

I sit up, shocked. "Of course not! One, I've known him less than a week. Two, that would be completely inappropriate—he's a client! Three, I'm not interested."

"Uh huh." Nic sounds unconvinced. I hear a sigh from the other end of the line—the kind you hear right before some tough love. "Brianna, it's been a year since Chris. I know how rough it's been, but you need to get back out there, honey. Fine, leave the hot leprechaun alone, but if you don't start easing back into dating soon, you never will."

Closing my eyes against the prickle of tears, I lay back on the soft covers with a shaky breath. "I know, Nic, I'm not against dating. It's just not a good time. I can't be distracted right now. Stone said if this goes well, he'll give me that promotion. Now more than ever, I need to keep my eye on the prize."

"Alright," Nic still doesn't sound convinced, "but if you will not take advantage of that man in your house, I will!" There is a pause, and I hear some indistinct yelling in the background. "They're calling me back in. I miss you and love you, and I'll see you in a few weeks!"

I say my goodbyes and hang up. Talking to Nic always makes me feel enormously better. I hum to myself as I get into the still-steaming bath with a giant glass of Merlot and my Kindle. Turning to my latest romantasy obsession, I push out all thoughts of work or roommates and immerse myself in the story.

As the fearless princess sneaks to the dashing knight's chambers, my breath quickens. He pulls her into the room and pins her against the door, scared someone will see her. Wantonly, she drops her robes as she stands in front of him naked. His eyes heat as they consume her and he finally gives in to the desire he's fought for so long.

My nipples harden and my skin grows sensitive beneath the cooling water. I glide my fingers over my body, leaving a trail of goosebumps. Molten heat pools in my core.

Pausing, I listen for any sounds in the house. Only Riley's occasional snore from the bathmat reaches my ears. I close my eyes as my fingers dip to my center before circling my clit. Shocks of electricity slowly spread outward as I rub myself.

My eyes fly across the screen as the hero effortlessly lifts and carries her to the giant bed. My fingers circle faster as he lavishes her body with his mouth, leaving her mewling. When he finally thrusts his impressive cock into her until they're both lost to the passion, I shift my hand to slowly slip two fingers into my slick heat. Massaging that sensitive, magic spot, I close my eyes and chase my own release. Instead of the dark and scarred knight, Colin's green eyes and dimpled smile fill my mind as I orgasm. Hard. A heavy moan leaves my lips.

The quakes subside, and I catch my breath.

Fuck.

Did I seriously just cum thinking about my client? So unprofessional, Brianna. I quickly wash and get into bed, desperate to avoid running into Colin tonight.

CHAPTER NINE

Getting Dirty

BRIANNA

The Sunday morning sunshine glows across the tile floor. Colin has headed off to explore the local beach, and I've decided to stick to my typical routine: housework and pizza. Colin has spent little time at the house this weekend, so I figure I'll have the whole day to myself.

Thanks to the pre-houseguest scrubbing on Monday, there isn't much routine cleaning left to do. It's a good day to tackle the less-common chores and get a head start on some proper spring cleaning. Dressed in an old pair of yoga shorts and tank, I crank up the radio, open all the windows, and get to work.

I scrub cabinets, dust behind the TV, wash curtains, and dig out the lonely sock stuck between the washer and dryer. Perched on a step stool, I attempt to give the entry chandelier a good scrub. Cleaning spray in one hand, dust cloth in the other, I try to reach a particularly stuck-on spot near the center of the light. I lean slightly further to get a better angle, but can't quite reach. Putting the spray down, I place both feet on the top step and reach out again.

Just as I extend my arm for the light bulb again, three things happened in near unison. The door behind me opens, catching me off guard. Riley wakes up from his nap in the afternoon sun and tears off across the entry, barking his head off. I jerk at the sound, lose my balance. Making what I'm sure is an excellent imitation of a windmill, I drop the cloth and let out an indelicate squeal. Suddenly, warm hands grip my bare thighs, and a hard chest presses against my butt.

"Careful there. Don't want ya to fall."

"Never had a problem before," I mutter. More loudly I add, "Thank you, I'm fine now." I can feel my face flaming as I look at Colin's hands on my legs. Not sure if it is purely embarrassment or the warmth from his long fingers as they slightly dig into my skin, but a warmth spreads in my belly as well. Now is so not the time to go there.

"Sure ya are. I'll spot you while you finish all the same."

Colin slowly releases my legs, but keeps close as he moves his hands to my hips. That seems safer, but does nothing for the butterflies that feel as large as elephants in my stomach. Taking a gulp of air, I hurry to finish the last bulb and then climb off the ladder and out of his hands.

"Thank you," I repeat as I turn to face him. He is standing so close, arms half outreached, ready to catch me again. He smells like summer—coconut sunscreen and salty ocean air. I quickly step back and drop my eyes to the floor, trying to rein in my thundering pulse.

He looks fantastic. The sun has left his face and arms slightly flushed. In a simple tee and board shorts, he looks just as handsome as in a three-piece suit. Which is completely unfair; I'm sure I look disgusting.

Fussing with the hem of my tank, I slowly raise my eyes to his face. I have to tilt my head back to meet his gaze. His typical grin is absent, his full lips quirk slightly in a softer smile. This close, I can see flakes of gold near the center of his emerald eyes. I swallow the sudden lump in my throat and lick my dry lips.

His eyes drop to my lips before sweeping over my face with something akin to amusement twinkling in their depths. Slowly, I watch him raise one hand towards my face. Subconsciously, I jerk back, shattering whatever spell I'd been under.

"You have a bit of dirt on your face." His smile has faded slightly. "Just here." Colin points to a spot on his own face.

I turn to the hallway mirror and let out a little groan; there is grease across my right cheek. I scrub at the spot with the heel of my palm, but it won't budge. Great, he's never going to take me seriously at work now.

"Must have been when I cleaned the oven."

Colin's reflection lifts his eyebrows as he looks around, taking stock of my progress. "My, you have been busy this morning."

"I typically clean on Sundays. Figured I'd take care of some chores I've been putting off. Like the high spots." A nervous laugh escapes. First grease on my face, now verbal diarrhea.

Nice going, Brianna. Deep breaths.

"Done now, though. I ordered a pizza," I say as I check my smartwatch. "It should be here soon if you're hungry. If you don't mind tipping the guy when he gets here, I'll just jump in the shower. Cash is by the door."

Seriously... SHUT UP, Brianna. I turn back to Colin and find his slight grin back in place as he agrees.

The doorbell rings as I scrub until I am pink and no longer smell of disinfectant. Rifling through drawers, I find a much more conservative outfit: denim capris and a navy blue V-neck tee. My hair is still damp, so up it goes into a neat bun. After a last look in the mirror, I slap on some tinted moisturizer. It has SPF 25, and this is Florida—that's my story and I'm sticking to it. It has absolutely nothing to do with my fantasies last night or nervous rambling today. I grab a pair of leather flip-flops from the closet and go in search of my pizza.

One step into the living room, I see Colin sitting out on one of the patio loungers, tossing a stick for my dog. The pizza box is on the table between the two seats, so I grab my sunglasses and go out to join them. See—the tinted moisturizer is necessary.

As I approach the loungers, I notice Colin has grabbed a mixing bowl from the kitchen and filled it with ice and a few of my favorite hard ciders. I am touched that he noticed my preference for them. He also has paper plates, napkins, and even a little speaker playing music.

Colin gives me a sheepish smile as I inspect his setup. "I figured since you've been stuck inside, a nice cold drink and pizza outside on this beautiful day was just what you needed."

A warmth spreads in my chest. That is incredibly thoughtful. Even the disposable plates, so I won't have more dishes to do. It is getting really hard to remember why I'm keeping a professional wall between us. I give him a genuine smile. "Thank you. How was the beach?"

I sit down and grab a slice. Colin opens a bottle and hands it to me before picking up a slice of his own, and starts sharing stories of the beach. I can't help laughing as he describes how two children dumped a bucket of water on their sleeping father. The dad had jumped up and chased the boys, then picked them both up and dumped them in the ocean. Thanks to Colin's gift for gab, I relax in his company as he shares one comical tale after another. It seems like no time at all before the sun sets and we both return indoors to our separate rooms.

As I get ready for bed, I realize something shifted today. I always thought that forced proximity trope was bullshit in novels, but it is really difficult staying aloof when you spend so much time under the same roof as someone. A little less professionalism wouldn't hurt.

Right?

CHAPTER TEN

Office Tongue Lashing

COLIN

The office door slams open in my haste. Ushering Brianna in, I quickly shut and latch it securely. We grin at each other, both drunk on the thrill of success. Stone tried to corner Brianna at the Monday staff meeting and I completely shut him down. On top of that, we got an email this morning that initial tests show the generator operating at 110% expected output.

We stand close, still by the door. I look down at Brianna's flushed face, my chest swells as I breathe deeply. Her cobalt eyes sparkle as she looks up at me through her dark lashes. She reaches up to adjust my tie and the tip of her tongue peeks out as she wets her lips. Lust swirls in my belly, and my cock swells.

"Brianna..."

She tilts her head back as she arches into me. Her lush breasts press against my chest. Her lips glisten as they part on an inhale. The tug she gives my tie breaks the fragile tether on my self-control.

Letting free a frustrated groan, I spear my fingers in her hair and rip her elastic out. Luscious waves of chestnut curls fall in a curtain around me.

Gripping her hips, I press my growing hard-on against her as I walk her backwards to the desk until she stumbles, perching on the very edge.

I plunder her lips in all the ways I've imagined since the first time I saw her. Rather than shying away from me, Brianna arches further, pressing fully into me and matching my passion.

My hands skim along her rounded hips. Fingers tease the outside of her thighs until I reach the hem of her tight skirt. It's one of my favorites—the material perfectly molds to her ass with a slit at the back that mocks me with every step she takes away.

Carefully, I work the skirt up her thighs as I kiss my way down her throat to the swell of her breasts. Once I've bunched the skirt to her upper thighs, I drop to my knees before her.

Leaning back slightly, she watches me with hooded eyes. Starting at her knee, I kiss my way up her creamy inner thigh. As I push her skirt further up her leg, I follow its path with open-mouth kisses. Her skirt finally bunches around her waist, I take in her thong-covered pussy in front of me. I tease her clit with my knuckle through the thin lace and urge her legs further apart.

Throwing her head back, Brianna moans sensually. I gently work my finger under the string of her underwear, pulling it aside to bare her glistening pussy. Leaning in, I give one lick up her slit. With another moan, Brianna spears her fingers in my hair, urging me back to her wet center. I enthusiastically bury my face between her thighs, teasing her clit with my nose as I work my tongue through her folds.

Using my fingers to spread her wider, I thrust my tongue into her pussy. Brianna cries out, clutching my hair and grinding against my face. I slurp as a rush of juices hit my tongue.

With a hungry growl, I move my mouth to her clit, applying slight suction to the sensitive nub. Gently, I work two fingers into her pussy as it clenches greedily around me. Slowly at first, I pump my fingers into her, turning my hand so I can stroke her G-spot better. I work her faster and harder as she clutches me and rides my face.

Looking up at her, I can see she is close. Her face flushes, her eyes glitter as she watches me eat her. I grin against her as I work a third finger into her tight passage. She moans and cries my name.

With one more pump of my fingers and a hard suck of my lips, she goes off like a rocket. There is no way the rest of the office doesn't hear her as she yells my name. A blaring alarm accompanies her cries.

With a gasp, I lurch upright and look around.

I am in my bed at Brianna's house. Another *fecking* dream.

Turning to the nightstand, I shut off my alarm before scrubbing my hands down my face. My fingers come away, wet and sticky. Grand, now I'm drooling in my sleep too.

Groaning, I fall back against the pillows. That woman can tempt a saint, and I am no saint.

When I saw her about to fall off that ladder yesterday, my stomach lurched in fear. I wasn't thinking when I moved to catch her. My hands on her bare thighs, her curvy ass inches from my face. With another groan, I palm my aching erection, seeking some relief.

Those tiny shorts and tank top had left little to the imagination. Her body had burned my hands. I'd wanted nothing more than to carry her to the shower to scrub the dirt from her. Even after she'd changed clothes, I'd spent the evening posing to hide my semi. Everything looked damn sexy on her curves.

Didn't matter though—she is off limits.

Oh well. Time to get up and ready for the day. Starting with a cold shower.

CHAPTER ELEVEN

Back to Work

BRIANNA

It's Monday morning, and I still haven't figured a way out of my dilemma with Stone and the impending eight am interrogation... I mean staff meeting. I nervously enter the conference room and take my usual seat—in the corner farthest from Stone.

Colin, who insisted on joining the meeting, sits next to me at the foot of the table. Good move. He has made a subtle—yet clear—statement that even if Stone is in charge here, Colin is equally powerful and demands respect. From the pinched eyebrows and pursed lips on Stone's face: message received.

"Alright everyone, it is 8:01. Anyone not here is late. Brianna, we'll start with you for updates."

Stone has summarily dismissed Colin's presence in the room. Proper protocol would be to introduce Colin to the staff. Throw in some warm welcome and comments about how happy we were to have him here, blah blah blah. Then again—I really shouldn't be surprised that Richard is being, well, a dick. I turn to watch Colin, to see if he's noticed the slight. His handsome features are completely calm. Noticing my attention, Colin shoots me a quick wink.

Warmth spreads in my stomach, and I take a deep breath to give my update. "Production has begun on Smart Screen. Last week, marketing held a focus group and four out of five people said they would purchase when available. Last week, we found a bug in the software for the Rover project. Fortunately, after a late-night session, the developers created a workaround. Unfortunately, the delays set us back about a week and we're trending 5% over budget because of the extra development time. The contingency budget should more than cover the labor, though, and we can gain back the time during testing next month."

"Bring in that schedule, Chance. What about your new project?"

I meet Stone's glare directly and answer firmly. "Still early days, sir. Meeting with the Dublin office last week went well, but the scope is still a bit too broad for my liking. I.S. is working up drawings for another prototype and a pitch deck this week. After that, I'll better understand what we're working with."

A muscle spasms in Stone's cheek. His ice-blue eyes shoot daggers to my right. Colin hasn't moved a muscle. He sits back in his chair, ankle casually crossed over his opposite knee and fingers laced over his stomach. Not a care in the world.

In his charcoal gray tailored suit, dove gray dress shirt, and a medium gray silk tie, Colin looks every inch the powerful executive. His green eyes sparkle with confidence and challenge. A young lion waiting to pounce.

Where had that thought come from? Dammit, Brianna, get it together.

The staring contest continues for a few tense heartbeats before Stone tears his gaze away and snaps at the next pm to begin. He can't push me for more information in front of Colin.

"Everyone needs to bring those numbers up. The end of the quarter is coming up and the executive board will review project stats. If I do not see marked improvement next quarter, there will be consequences." Stone starts to gather his tablet and coffee before adding, "Oh, and this is Mr. McLeary from Innovative Solutions. He will work in the office next to mine if you need him. How long will you be staying with us, McLeary?"

All eyes turn to Colin, who is still lounging in his chair, completely at ease. Slowly, Colin unlaces his fingers and spreads his hands palms up as he smiles at Stone. "That depends on a great many things, Stone. We'll just have to play it by ear."

Stone gives a smile that is all teeth. "I see. Everyone get back to work. You stay, Chance."

I take a deep breath and mentally stretch for the intricate verbal maneuvers I am about to perform.

To my right, Colin now stands at my elbow. "Actually, Stone, we have an urgent task for Dublin and I need Brianna. You were right about how amazing she is. Afraid I just can't spare her. Even for a minute. You understand."

Summarily dismissing my boss, Colin pulls back my chair and ushers me towards the door. His hand rests on the small of my back, the slight pressure filling me with confidence. I shoot one last look at Stone—who is turning a bit purple—and walk with Colin towards his office. I wait until we are both seated at his desk with the door shut to speak.

"What is the task for Dublin?"

Colin leans forward behind his desk and meets my eyes with that mischievous grin I am starting to enjoy. "There isn't one. I just didn't want to give Stone the chance to interrogate you. I know he's dying to know what I'm up to." His bright smile dims, and his eyes are full of sincerity. "I know I've put you in a delicate situation with Stone, and I'm ver'a sorry for that. I wish it didn't have to be this way, but I don't trust that man. Until the negotiations are complete on the merger, I need to protect my company."

I'm impressed he recognizes the uncomfortable position he's put me in. Even more so that he's actually acknowledging and apologizing for it. I haven't worked with many executives who would do either. His thoughtfulness is constantly making it difficult to keep him at arm's length. He is just too easy to get along with.

"What exactly can I say to Stone regarding your extended stay? I completely understand needing to keep the merger a secret. Stone is my boss, though, and he's already suspicious. Eventually, I need to give him updates."

"You could tell him the truth. This does not concern him and he can wind his neck in." Colin's signature grin is back in place. "Imagine that wouldn'a go over too well though."

I can't stop an answering grin of my own. "No, probably not."

"Well then. Until we come up with a better way to keep Stone's suspicions at bay, we'll just have to not let him corner you alone."

True to his word, Colin keeps me sequestered in his office for the rest of the day. Not that I really need his protection—but I appreciate the show of support.

"We need a code name for this project. I can't keep referring to it as 'that new project' when Stone asks for updates," I say, after a few hours of working independently.

"Project X? Project Clover? Who was the inventor of the first solar panel?"

"Charles Fritts in 1883, though Martin Green is the more modern father of solar panels." What can I say? I'm thorough in my research.

"Project Green. What do you think?"

"R and D already has a Project Green—and a little too on the nose with the green energy aspect." I suddenly have an idea. "Blarney!"

"Pardon? What are you calling blarney?"

I turn to Colin with a wide smile. "Call it Project Blarney. You are trying to mislead Stone with a line of pretty bullshit and your Irish charm. Call it what it is—Blarney."

Jaw slack and eyes wide, Colin is the picture of shock. I laugh at his comical expression, making his eyes open farther. Which only makes me laugh harder, holding my sides and tilting in my chair. He joins in, and we laugh together until we get our amusement under control.

"Well. I can't argue with that. Project Blarney, it is!" Colin smiles as he leans back in his chair and regards me with those sharp green eyes.

I return his smile as I maintain his gaze. My tongue darts out to lick my dry lips and his eyes darken as they follow the movement. With effort, I school my features into a more serious expression. "Seriously, though. What are we going to do about Stone? I have to tell him something. We can't just avoid him forever."

"Tell him I'm a micromanaging control freak."

"What?" My eyebrows crawl into my hairline. Seems it's my turn to be shocked.

"Hear me out. You tell him I'm just some young hot-shot engineer trying to play at being an executive. Tell him I'm still here because I can't stand letting you fully take control of this project." Colin's eyes sparkle again with wicked amusement.

I feel my lips spread into an answering grin. "Ok, we'll try that. The customer is always right. Right?"

CHAPTER TWELVE

One Month In: He Said

COLIN

The past three weeks have flown by. Brianna and I settled into a very comfortable office routine. I spend my mornings fielding calls from Dublin, reviewing reports, and generally avoiding Stone, while Brianna checks on her other projects. After grabbing lunch from the building cafe, Brianna settles in at the table in my office to review the latest on our solar generator.

We still spend our evenings in separate corners of the little yellow house, but at the office we are constantly together. Sometimes we work collaboratively, other times we work separately in companionable silence, but we always work behind the closed door of my office.

Brianna begrudgingly accepted the working arrangement. Her cube is just too open; anyone passing by can read over her shoulder. The only time we separate is when Brianna attends meetings for her other projects in the conference room.

Stone also seems to buy my cover story. At least he hasn't made a big fuss again since that first staff meeting. Though, based on the knowing smiles Stone shoots my way, I think he has a very different read of the situation. I did nothing to dissuade his assumptions. Let Stone think I am trying to seduce Brianna. It keeps the awful man out of our hair—and it doesn't take much acting skill on my part.

Brianna has gradually relaxed in my presence over the last few weeks. I love watching the woman work—she is incredible. She has an easy relationship with the engineers. She cajoles them into getting her work done first, and once she smiles at them, they are only too happy to help her. Like I'm one to talk. What wouldn't I do for one of Brianna's smiles?

If work isn't to her standards, she is firm but fair and pushes until the team resolves any issue. When they go above and beyond to please her, there is always credit given to the team. And baked goods as a reward. Her warm nature with the team and obvious devotion to her dog softens the ever efficient Ms. Chance. My admiration of her has only grown.

Brianna handpicked the engineers on the project. She then broke up the assignments into smaller parts and is selective about what information she shares. Each employee has enough information for his piece, but not enough to work out the entire Project Blarney puzzle.

The woman is bloody brilliant.

Despite my best efforts, I like her more and more. I also can't deny I'm extremely attracted to Brianna. The frequent pornographic dreams give it away.

I groan as a particularly vivid flashback of my last dream sets my cock swelling painfully against my zipper. Cool it, boyo. She's unavailable, remember. Though her fella is an eejit, obviously. If Brianna was my girl, I wouldn't be on a bloody extended trip while she has a strange man staying in her house.

Trying to shake off my unproductive thoughts, I turn back to the latest report for Dublin I am trying to finish. Before I even get three more words written, a knock at the door breaks my concentration.

The clock on my laptop screen only shows quarter after eleven. Brianna's meeting must have gotten out early. I call out for her to enter.

The door opens, but instead of Brianna, that blond assistant breezes into the room. My smile promptly fades—as does my erection.

Guess Ms. Reynolds is useful for something after all.

I've avoided the forward woman since that first day—to great effort. Sure, I pass her in the halls, but there have always been others around saving me from making excuses. I plan to keep avoiding the woman.

One of the directors recommended I let Ms. Reynolds show me around town for a 'good time'. Evidently, the executive assistant takes it upon herself to 'assist' anyone in a senior position, and some are quite grateful for her service. The whole notion disgusts me, but I've never had patience for office politics.

"Ms. Reynolds. How may I help you?" I school my features into a more professional smile, gritting my teeth.

"Oh Mr. McLeary, how sweet to think of little old me."

Her lips hold an inviting smile as she sashays towards me with a drink in her hand. Instead of stopping at one of the chairs across my desk, she continues around the surface, perching on the edge by my elbow. As she sits, the hem of her skirt rises so her bare thigh is inches from my hand. She places the drink on my work surface and leans over until her cleavage is in danger of spilling into my face.

I maintain staunch eye contact. It's not even difficult.

"I'm here to help you," she practically coos.

Does she think that nasal voice is sexy? I much prefer Brianna's lower tones.

"I know how hard you've been working, and thought you could use a treat."

She turns towards the large cup, gesturing wildly and knocking the cold contents directly into my lap. I jump up as the ice hits my crotch. Guess I won't have to be worrying about anymore trouble down there today.

"Oh my! I'm so sorry! You should dab that before it stains."

Rachel grabs a napkin and leans forward, arm outstretched as if she is going to do just that for me. Wanting the vixen nowhere near my bollocks, I quickly grab the offered napkin and move back again, using my office chair as a shield.

"N-no. That's quite alright. If you'll excuse me, I'll just clean myself up in the restroom."

I gesture for Rachel to exit ahead of me, muttering a string of Gaelic curses under my breath as I dab at the frigid wet spot on my pants.

CHAPTER THIRTEEN

Dirty Deeds

RACHEL

"You should use the air dryers in the restroom. Again, I'm so sorry, sir." I step towards Stone's office as Colin tears off for the restroom, still muttering under his breath.

As soon as the bathroom door closes behind him, I double back to Colin's office and shut the door to avoid attention. I zero in on the laptop that's still open on the desk.

Colin forgot to lock his PC. My lips twist into a satisfied smile. Exactly what I hoped would happen in the excitement.

Thinking back to how Colin's bright smile faded when he realized I was at his door dulls my good mood. My original plan was to seduce the man. Once he rolled over for some post-orgasm sleep, I'd dig through his phone for some dirt. Despite some truly head-turning outfits—and I know this to be true because Jimmy in accounting fell out of his chair as I walked by—Boy Scout McLeary here hasn't even blinked.

He must be gay. That's the only explanation.

For a month, I've tried to get him alone. Or get his computer alone and unlocked.

He is always with *her* and usually in this office doing God knows what. If I didn't know for a fact Brianna was a frigid bitch, I'd think she's screwing the client herself.

So Operation Coffee Crotch was born.

Knowing my time is limited, I quickly search his local drive for any documents referring to Project Blarney.

No hits.

I bite my nail as I look at the door. He'll be back any second. Time for the secret weapon.

I pull out the USB drive hidden in my bra. Howard in IT whipped together a little something that will record everything Colin does and report it back to my computer. Let him lead me to the files! I tap my nails on the desk as I wait for the program to run.

75.... 80.... 90.... 100% complete.

I remove the drive, hiding it in my clutched fist. Now I just need to install the sister application on my computer, and I can access everything Colin opens.

I walk back to my cube with a slight sashay. Mama always said if you got it, flaunt it. Plus, if they are staring at my ass, they won't notice anything else.

CHAPTER FOURTEEN

One Month In: She Said

BRIANNA

I lean forward and arch my back with a satisfying crack, then roll my shoulders with a stifled moan. The words on my screen blur and my ass is numb. The clock reads six pm. Where has the day gone?

The day? The past month has seemed to fly by, and it is nowhere near as painful as expected. I'm still surprised, but it is easy to work with Colin. We have very similar work habits, the same exacting expectations, and the same passion for the project. Instead of being an obstacle, or one more person to manage, Colin fits into my work life seamlessly.

He fits seamlessly into my home life too—but that is a dangerous line of thought. It is nice having someone around the house. We talked rarely, at the beginning. We eat dinner together practically every night, though.

On weekends, Colin explores the area. Similar to that first weekend, I suggest a few points of interest. He always visits them and comes back to tell me about his day on the back patio. I laugh until my eyes water at the embellished tales of his adventures.

Occasionally, he joins Riley and me on our evening walks. These are always somber strolls, fewer jokes and more quiet companionship. The silence should be awkward for near strangers, but it is strangely comfortable. Intimate, almost. Nope—strike that.

My attitude towards Colin has slowly shifted—can't deny that. The more time I spend with him, the more I respect him as a business executive and like him as a person. I'd tried to keep my distance, but when you work with someone for ten hours a day, it's easy to blur the lines.

He has an amazing mind—which is helpful in crafting carefully worded status reports for Stone. His sense of humor and warmth makes it easy to lower your shields. He is always shooting that lopsided grin in my direction—as if we have an inside joke. Maybe we do?

As an executive, Colin has a subtle leadership style. He is firm but fair and shows zero ambition for himself or ego. That is probably what I like most about him. Too many executives lose sight of the bigger picture. They're too focused on how fast they climb to care who they step on.

Colin is also loyal—that quality makes my heart ache. Every Monday, Colin stands behind me in support. Whenever Stone puts me down in front of the team, or he tries to interrogate me on Project Blarney, Colin stands with me. But not in front of me. He trusts me to handle the situation, but still shows me support. He treats me as an equal. That thought spreads warmth in my chest.

I take the last sip of the iced caramel latte from Colin. He is also thoughtful. When I got out of my afternoon meeting, he met me in the hall with my favorite coffee drink. No clue how he knows my drink.

It doesn't hurt that he seems to be the only man immune to Rachel's tits, I mean charms. I have enjoyed watching Rachel try to approach him or shake her hips right in front of him, only to be ignored. Again. And again. One time, he actively turned around and walked away! Sometimes, her mask slips and she actually glares at his back. Anyone who dislikes Rachel is trustworthy in my eyes.

I want to trust him completely, lower that last wall and share my concerns about Stone and Rachel. Let him really get to know me, but something's holding me back. My gut tells me to be more cautious. The proximity creates a familiarity—almost an intimacy between two people. I'm probably just getting caught up playing house. Be on guard, Brianna.

I look over at the man taking up most of my thoughts lately. He is sitting at his desk speaking to a lawyer from the Dublin office. At least he's easy to look at. Definitely a benefit when you have to spend all your time together. I smile slightly at my own dirty joke. Colin must feel my gaze on him; he looks up at me and gives me a panty-melting smile before returning his attention to the document in his hand.

I press my thighs together and roll my hips to relieve the ache in my core. This has been happening an awful lot lately. It's embarrassing, really. Especially since I accidentally got an eyeful last week.

I wasn't snooping! It was bedtime and I couldn't find Riley. The little shit started barking from the guest room. I heard Colin laugh, and the door was half open, so I just stepped to the threshold to call Riley out. I froze mid word—Colin was fresh from the shower. Water still dripped from his hair, glistening over tan shoulders. I followed one drop as it traveled down smooth pecs and defined abs, until it hid in the fine line of hair below his navel. He gripped a towel around his narrow hips, exposing a swimmer's V.

Unfortunately, that towel's other end was being tugged by my dog. Forcefully enough to yank the towel free just as Colin saw me. I saw it all. The shillelagh and the pots of gold. One glance was all I got before I yelled an apology and ran like hell. But it made a lasting impression.

One I have relived nightly while using my vibrator before bed.

Nic is right—I need to date again. A year and a half without sex just makes a lady horny. Don't tell me anyone wouldn't feel that way. Now is definitely not the time to fantasize about the admittedly hot exec from Dublin who just might decide the future of my career.

Shaking those errant thoughts away, I concentrate on the spreadsheets again. Something looks off on my projections. This sexual tension is evidently messing with my work now. When Nic gets home, we'll hit the nightclubs. I'll get drunk, flirt, some guy will piss me off and remind me why I hate men in the first place. Absolutely no more fantasizing about my roomie. Solid plan.

CHAPTER FIFTEEN

Before the Board

BRIANNA

I eye the twelve middle-aged men sitting at the table before me: the executive board. CEO, CIO, CFO, CTO—and every other three letter position is in attendance. It is unheard of for a project manager to present directly to the CEO at C.A. Engineering. Completely unheard of. Stone should normally be here, or even his boss. Because of the NDA, though, I'm in the hot seat.

When I first walked in, a couple of them took one look at my skirt and heels and sat back in their seats. One studied my face and gave me an indulgent smile—like you would a small child. All looks I am used to, and so sick of getting. Taking a deep breath, I count to four and switch into presentation mode.

"Gentlemen, good afternoon. First, I'll take you through the product features and design modifications. As you can see in this mock-up -, the generator is only two feet tall, four feet wide, and two feet deep. Don't let the size fool you. Tests show outputs as high as 15000 watts. You could feasibly power an entire house with one of these."

Slowly, the men who have not been paying attention, look up from their phones and turn to me. I continue to show the current status, testing results, budget overview, and profit projections.

"Based on focus groups, online polling, and market analysis, we're projecting to recoup our investment after six months. By the end of the first year, we could turn a profit of two million dollars."

The CFO jots down some numbers as he looks up at the screen. I watch him scribble out some calculations and look back up at my graph, frowning.

"Ms. Chance, are you quite confident in those numbers? That is an unheard of return on investment for a new product like this without an existing market share."

"I am, sir. While there are many generators on the market—and some even have solar capabilities—it is the built-i water purifier that sets our product apart. No other product on the market can provide this much power in such a compact footprint. Or provide filtered water for drinking and cooking. This will be a hit with campers, preppers, environmentalists—it really crosses all demographics. This chart doesn't even include the intangible positive impact we could have on remote locations with no access to power or clean water. Add in government or aid organization contracts or donations and the possibilities are endless. There really is no financial risk here."

The room falls quiet. Multiple sets of widened eyes turn to the CEO, Stefan Cullingford. He sits at the head of the table with his hands clasped on the surface. He has been attentive to the entire presentation, his laptop shut, and phone out of sight.

"What of Innovative Solutions, Ms. Chance? What are your thoughts after working with their team?"

I meet his gaze and answer honestly.

"The project's success is a testament to the joint team, sir. Neither company could have gotten here alone. Mr. McLeary is an impressive engineer and leader. This has been the most dedicated and hard-working team I've ever had the pleasure of working with."

He taps his thumb on the table twice as he studies me. "Excellent presentation, Ms. Chance. Gentlemen, I believe that's a wrap." They gather their tablets and notebooks and head to the door. A few men nod, some murmur words of encouragement as they pass me. I'm disconnecting from the projector and closing my laptop when I feel someone approach my side.

Looking up, I'm shocked to see it is the CEO.

"I've never had the chance to see you work before, but Barry used to talk about you during our poker games. He always said you were a wonder to watch, and would achieve great things for my company. Keep up the good work."

With a slight smile and a knowing nod, he leaves me alone in the conference room. Stunned. My mentor, Barry Webster, was close to Stefan Cullingford? Poker buddies close? Why did they talk about me? Our CEO knows who I am, and he's impressed with me! That promotion is as good as mine.

As long as I keep on Stone's good side. I swallow past the lump in my throat. That's easier said than done.

Replaying the conversation in my head, I amble to the elevator and back to Colin's office. When I open his door, he is pacing in front of his desk. Seeing me, he immediately pulls me in and shuts the door. Impatiently, he ushers me to the chairs in front of his desk.

"How did it go? The wait has been killing me." This may be the most serious I've seen him. There is no trace of a smile on his lips and his eyes are sharp.

"Really well, actually. The CFO seemed impressed by the projections. Honestly, they had more questions about you and I.S. I gave positive feedback on all fronts—so basically I lied." I bite my cheek to keep from smiling at my joke, but fail to keep a straight face at Colin's chuckle. "Then the CEO stopped by to say the presentation impressed him. We did it! Now we just need to get through the testing and the patent reviews and we're home free."

"Come on." Colin's grin is infectious as he tugs me back to my feet. We are almost chest to chest as he looks down at me, his breath fanning my eyelashes. He bends forward slightly and squeezes my biceps. "Let's get out of here. After pulling fifty-plus hour weeks and a killer presentation, we deserve to cut out a little early."

CHAPTER SIXTEEN

Something Pretty

BRIANNA

I let out a tired but content sigh as I pull into my driveway. We've had a very productive week and the successful board meeting today was a huge milestone. The engineers in Dublin are almost done with the final design updates for the prototype. The local team has made significant progress in machining parts and fabricating a cooling system. Legal is still working through the patent filings, but everything is on schedule.

After the solar panels arrive next month, Colin is set to fly to Nevada for a green energy expo to drum up interest and some potential contracts. He's asked me to go with him, but it seems best to stay behind and keep Stone happy. He's been a bit too restrained of late, and leaving feels like too much of a risk right now.

No matter how much a part of me wants to go.

As the top finishes closing on my convertible, Colin rounds the car and opens my door for me. I am too high on the successes of the week to maintain polite boundaries today. When he playfully holds out an arm with that sexy grin, I beam up at him and play along.

"M'lady." Colin bows his head as I stand, like some knight. Shamelessly, he eyes my stiletto pumps and bare legs with a mischievous glint.

"Good sir." Laughing as I withdraw my hand again to dig for my keys and open the door. "I feel like celebrating! How about pizza for dinner?" I look back over my shoulder to Colin as I walk further into the entryway. His eyebrows pinch as his eyes dart around the darkened room. Wait, darkened? Why is it dark? The lights are on a smart timer.

"Sounds great. I'll set up the order." His voice sounds flat, distracted. "Where's Riley?"

My stomach drops. All playfulness is gone as I frantically look around. I wrestle with my work bag as I try to set it down. Colin detangles the strap from my hand with a slight squeeze of my fingers. "He always meets me at the door. Something must be wrong." As I near the end of the hall, calling for him, I hear a muffled noise. Suddenly, the lights flip on.

"SURPRISE!"

Balloons, streamers, and people fill my living room. At the front of the group stand my two best friends—Nic and Anna—with an irritated looking Riley in their arms wearing a party hat. As soon as they let him down, Riley runs straight to me—shaking off the hat within three steps.

"Oh, shit." That's the super elegant response I give as I scoop up my dog and stare at my two favorite people in the world. They rush over and enclose me in a group hug.

"She forgot her own birthday, didn't she?" Anna, even in flats, is a head taller than me. Her chocolate brown eyes sparkle with humor—at my expense. Long blond hair hangs loose down her back and frames her oval face. Tonight, she is wearing a yellow sundress that hugs her athletic torso before flaring out into a sweet skirt.

Had I forgotten my birthday? Yes. Was it the first time? No. That's why I have these two. They never fail to pull me back up when I am drowning in the details and miss what's really important. I fight back tears as I hug them back and survey the room. A room filled almost exclusively with gorgeous men. What the fuck?

"Oh my god, Nic. What did you do?" I hope the twenty-odd guests can't hear my near frantic whisper-shout.

Nic, also towering above me, laughs as she flips her dark hair out of her almond-shaped hazel eyes. Her sleeveless jumpsuit is fantastic. The deep jewel hue perfectly accents the green in her eyes and jet-black hair. The woman is an artist and knows how to perfectly highlight her looks.

"Why, they're your birthday present, of course! You asked for something pretty. I had a photo shoot with the Olympic rowing team and I couldn't resist inviting them to your party."

Replaying our last conversation in my head, I let out an embarrassed groan. Nic knows very well what I had meant. These guys aren't here to be pretty, but to kick-start my libido so I'll date again. I really hope she doesn't expect me to hook up with all eight of them. I shouldn't have lent her that spicy RH novel last month.

"Remind me to take away your spare key."

They both laugh and hug me tighter.

"Come on, Bree. Your real present is in the bedroom," Anna says, as she breaks the hug.

I lean closer to Nic's ear. "You better not have gotten me a gigolo, too."

Laughing harder, she pulls me by the hand to my bedroom. Laid out on my bed is a beautiful designer dress in a cobalt blue that almost twinkles in the light. The thick straps and square neckline are bold and will perfectly accentuate my bust while exuding class. The material nips in at the waist and flirts across my hips and ass, framing and accentuating my hourglass figure. I never would have bought this dress for myself, but I instantly love how I feel wearing it. Like a *femme fatal*, a mafioso's wife, or Bond girl—beautiful, mature, sexy, and powerful.

With one more hug, Anna leaves to check on the food. Nic and two stylists swoop in, primed to get Cinderella ready for the ball. It definitely pays to have a professional photographer with an army of stylists for a best friend. Add a professional chef, and every gathering is an *event*.

These girls are the best.

Feeling lighter than I have in months, I let the awaiting army primp and pamper me. If this is how twenty-nine starts, thirty is going to be fantastic.

CHAPTER SEVENTEEN

Meet the Besties

COLIN

Not wanting to interrupt the reunion, I follow the disgruntled dog into the kitchen. Riley trots towards the treat jar and sits down with a harrumph. I swear the dog just sighed at me. Hear you loud and clear, little man. I pull two biscuits out of the jar for my friend, then a beer from the nearby fridge for myself.

After scoffing down the biscuits in a couple bites, Riley pads closer, stretching on his hind legs to scratch at my pants. I scoop him up and cradle him in one arm across my chest as I take a swig of my beer.

"I'd be annoyed too if I'd been stuck here with those guys."

In the month I've been here, this is the first time I feel like an outsider. First time I feel like I don't belong here. It just feels so natural being here with Brianna and Riley. Dangerously so.

It has become a secret game of mine to make Brianna laugh. It started as just a way to dispel the awkward silence between us. With two older sisters, I grew up being the comedic relief. When they were at each other's throats over who knows what as teenagers, I'd crack a joke to pop the tension and everyone would get along.

After the first time I heard Brianna really laugh, though, it became less of an innocent game. We were in my office, talking over strategies to keep Stone in the dark, and the image of her, head tilted back, throat exposed, her hand resting over her breast laughing, is burned into my memory. From that day, I craved her laughs and smiles. I hung on every word, looking for my next fix, like an alcoholic at the local pub.

I hug Riley closer and give him a soothing scratch behind the ear. Honestly, I'm not sure If I am trying to comfort him or myself.

"I feel like a right bastard. It's her birthday! You could have told me, my friend."

Riley closes his eyes and leans into my fingers. His body otherwise feels boneless in my arms. His tail thumps lazily against my elbow.

Movement in the doorway catches my attention. I look up to see Brianna's blond friend enter the kitchen. "So this is where you boys got off to. We didn't get to meet before. I'm Anna, and the other one is Nic. We're Bree's best friends."

As she speaks, she approaches me and holds her hand out to shake. Still holding Riley one-armed, I reach out to return her firm shake. Her molten chocolate eyes hold warmth and amusement. Her wide lips form an amiable smile, and the freckles across her cheeks give her an almost elfin air. I sense a kindred spirit.

"Colin McLeary. Pleasure to meet you."

Anna's eyes drop to the dog I'm still clutching like a security blanket. "Bree mentioned Riley likes you, but that pup looks positively in love."

Her gaze rises back to mine and her expression turns thoughtful. "Sorry about all this. I know you've both been keeping long hours at the office. I wanted to give you a heads-up, but couldn't figure out how without Bree getting suspicious. That woman is impossible to surprise."

"You don't have to apologize to me. This is Brianna's house. I'm glad you did this for her. She's been working too hard. Really, I should be the one apologizing for crashing. I'll just change and head to the pub and let you ladies enjoy yourselves."

"Absolutely not. Bree would be madder than a wet hen if she thought we kicked you out. It's a party—the more the merrier. It was supposed to be just the four of us for dinner and then steal her for a girls' night. Nic tends to make everything an event, and once she gets something in her mind, there's no stopping her."

Her expression is full of loving exasperation. I return her smile as a warmth spreads in my chest, but I also feel a little homesick. Anna reminds me of my sisters and how they gripe at each other. It's obvious these women are the family Brianna made for herself.

"Why don't you go change into party clothes and then give me a hand with the food? Nic and Bree are going to be a while."

I swiftly shower and shuffle through my drawers and closet. Packing *party clothes* wasn't high on my priority list a month ago. Pulling on jeans and a gray henley, I assess myself in the mirror. My hair is getting long and curling at the ends, so I grab a tweed flat cap to hide the unruly fluff.

A quick glance around the living room and patio area show no signs of Brianna or Nic. Returning to the kitchen, I find Anna half in the refrigerator with trays of food in her arms and rush to help her.

Mini portions of various snacks sit on small black plates. Savory dishes, sweet treats, salty, crunchy—something for everyone. The food is obviously gourmet—even to my ignorant eye. Although each dish is magazine ready, they are simple rather than garish. Like those fancy dishes with foams and spreads that you're too scared to eat.

I follow Anna to the dining room. Someone has moved the table against the far wall. A black cloth and acrylic boxes of varying heights cover the surface. Anna uncovers the trays I hold and arranges the dishes on the risers.

My mouth waters at each new smell. "This looks incredible."

"Thanks. I made all of Bree's favorites in snack versions. That's creamy buffalo chicken cups, cheeseburger meatballs, pizza dumplings, and salmon dip over cucumber chips. Just wait until you see the cake!"

She points out the various dishes as she names them. There has to be enough food here to feed a hundred people.

"Wait—you made *all* this?"

"Sure did. I'm the co-owner and head chef at Pop over in the town center. When y'all get sick of Brianna's cooking, you should come on down." Her focus moves to something behind my shoulder. Her eyes soften and her smile widens. "Aw, here comes the guest of honor now. Finally."

I turn as Brianna emerges from her bedroom, laughing over her shoulder at something the woman behind her says. My breath catches at the goddess before me.

Gone is the conservative professional. Her dress clings to her voluptuous form, forcing my mouth to water for a completely different reason. Shapely cream legs perch on sky-high heels.

I want those heels wrapped around my waist.

Gone is her ever-present ponytail, her russet hair falls in long waves to her elbows. Something is different with her makeup, too. Her eyes are smoky and sparkle like sapphires as she laughs at Nic. I always find her beautiful—even when she has grease on her face. She is always elegant. But tonight- tonight she is pure sex appeal.

Like more and more often recently, I find myself with a raging hard-on. Lucky for me, I'm still holding the tray and can adjust myself without notice.

Going to be another long—and unsatisfying—night.

I watch as Nic brings the rowing team over to Brianna. She is the center of attention as they fight to wish her a happy birthday, their hungry gazes fixed upon her. Someone calls for a birthday photo with the team. Brianna laughs as the men grab her and pick her up. My stomach twists at the sight of them gripping her waist and legs. I clench my jaw to keep from glowering at them.

"Hot! I'm going to post this on Insta!" someone yells.

I mutter to Anna that I'll bring the trays back to the kitchen and quickly escape to get my shit together. And grab another beer.

After a few long pulls on the bottle, I head back to the party. Groups are forming around the living room and on the patio. Looking around, I don't feel particularly drawn to any. Definitely don't want to talk to the playboy jocks. Sofa seems a safe choice—surrounded by all groups but part of none.

I can't stop myself from watching Brianna. Not that I try all that hard. She flirts with the athletes that swarm around her. Every inch a Celtic queen holding court.

They hang on her every word. Her cup never runs dry. As soon as one glass of champagne is empty, a full one magically appears in its place. I chug the rest of my beer, but it turns sour in my mouth. Why shouldn't they fawn over her? Haven't I? She deserves everything and more. She is truly exceptional.

The couch dips next to me as Riley jumps up and pads over to me. With a huff, he lays down with his head on my knee. It's as if he can sense my change in mood, or wants to show support.

The dark pit in my stomach spreads as I watch her flirt. It's not jealousy. What right do I have to be jealous? The one who should be upset is her boyfriend. Where is that bastard, anyway? Maybe he is one of the dozen eejits surrounding her. There are no pictures in the shared areas of the house, so he could be anyone and I wouldn't know.

Another dip on the couch pulls my attention. Nic dramatically plops down and turns her body to me rather than the room. Her expression is intense. She stares at me as if she can see into me.

I simply turn my head to her and raise a single eyebrow in return. "Good evening."

"So. You're the Irishman."

"Aye." I tip my head to her—not quite sure where this is going.

"What are your intentions towards our Bree?"

She is bold, blunt, and protective—I like her immediately.

My shoulders relax into the sofa and my lips curve as I reassess the situation. "Expected her boyfriend or Da to be asking me that. Not a wee lass."

Nic's eyebrows raise into her hairline and her lips purse. "Oh, you are lucky that accent and smile are so damn sexy or I'd show you just how 'wee' I am not. "She shoots me a devastating grin of her own and relaxes back into the pillows with a chuckle. "Unfortunately for you, Bree doesn't have a boyfriend and her dad's not around. So you'll have to settle for me."

My brows crease at my confusion. "I thought Brianna had a fella."

Nic lets out a peal of laughter and gives me an incredulous look.

"You've been here, what? A month now? Don't you think you'd have seen another man walking around by now? Honestly, I would have grilled you a hell of a lot sooner, but I've been in New York. Flew back last night. Now answer the damn question."

She nudges me with her pointy shoe.

Wait—New York? It was Nic on the phone, not some guy named Nick. I try to sort through the flood of emotions I feel as I realize Brianna has been single this whole time. Confusion. Relief. Hope. Guilt. Taking a gamble, I decide to answer honestly.

"It is a professional relationship only, and that is the truth of it. Look, I know how it looks with me staying here. I should have left immediately and found a hotel on my own. I thought about it. It's that wanker boss of hers. I don't trust him. And I hate the way he talks to her."

I lean closer and look Nic straight in the eyes. "I just wanna protect her, ya know?"

Nic's eyes widen and her mouth opens slightly, shocked by my words.

Deciding to break the suddenly somber air between us, I crack a joking grin. "And you have to admit, you'd take her cooking over lousy room service any day."

Tension successfully broken, Nic laughs until her eyes tear. After brushing her cheeks, she leans forward, pats my arm, and looks me in the eye. "Well, I'm satisfied, but if you hurt her or screw her on this promotion—I swear I will kick your *arse* back to Dublin."

After one last look in my eye, she nods once and gracefully stands. As she joins a group to flirt with some of the men, her demeanor transforms into one of playful charm. The woman goes from tiger to butterfly in a heartbeat. She is terrifying. And she gave me a lot to think about as the party rages on.

CHAPTER EIGHTEEN

It's My Party

BRIANNA

The party is a whirlwind of people, food, and liquor. Just the distraction I need. Very tipsy from the free-flowing champagne, I slip out to the back patio to cool off and enjoy the stars. The muffled sounds of music and laughter follow me out the open doors, mixing with the calming sound of cicadas buzzing in the trees. I love southern nights.

The patio looks like a fairy garden; someone lit candles and spread them around the pool and tables. The light shimmers on the pool surface, my personal light-show. I sit on a lounger and take a deep breath of the crisp air. Something wet touches my fingers where they hang over the edge of the chair. Turning sharply, I find Riley licking my fingers. With a chuckle, I scoop him up and settle him on my lap. My fingers trail idly over his silky head and back, and I smile to myself as I think back over the evening.

I smile up at the starry night, thankful for my friends; my found family. The food was amazing—only Anna could turn comfort food into a gourmet tapas spread. Nic was right, too. The attention of fit athletes all fighting over my attention did wonders for my mood.

Those girls always know what I need, even when I don't.

It feels good to flirt again. To be desired. At first, the sight of a dozen gorgeous men in my living room had been terrifying. I was afraid I'd be rusty or awkward at sexual banter. To be honest—I've never been that great at it to begin with. Flirtations require an overt show of emotion. Coy movements and manipulating a man's emotional response. Not exactly traits of a woman labeled efficient and professional. Especially after half a decade suppressing my femininity at work to be 'one of the boys'.

I don't miss my ex. Nothing about him personally, anyway. Hell, I found plenty of reasons I was *happy* it ended. The sting of rejection still remains, though. I haven't quite exorcised his voice from my mind, telling me I'm not woman enough for him. I'm pretty, but just not pretty enough. Affectionate enough. Sexy enough.

But tonight? It has been marvelously easy, really, to flirt and smile all night. In this dress, with my hair and makeup done professionally, I feel like a different me. Some brand new woman who is alluring, interesting, desirable.

Don't get me wrong. I know what I bring to the party. Few can match me in a battle of wits. I'm an expert strategist. Master organizer. Natural leader. I am damn good at my job and I am going to get that promotion. My plans never fail, after all.

I feel his presence more than hear him approach. This tipsy, it's hard to lie to even myself. I've become so in tune with Colin that I always know when he's nearby. I feel it in my bones. My stomach clenches and my heart beats a little faster. Turning just my head, I smile up at him as he sits in the lounger to my right. "You found me."

He chuckles and arranges himself on the seat. "I followed Riley. What are you doing out here? I believe your party is inside."

"I wanted to get some fresh air. See the stars for a bit." I roll my head back to look up at the clear night sky. "Isn't it beautiful?"

"Yes. Beautiful."

I look to my right. Colin is still facing me and not the stars. My breath catches at the yearning in his eyes. His brows are tense and his carefree grin is missing, his lips in a tight line.

"Happy birthday." His voice is low, his tone seems off, but my mind is fuzzy from the bubbles and I can't quite figure out the difference. "Why didn't you tell me it was your birthday?"

His tone implies this is not a casual question. My eyes move back to his as I answer truthfully, though it's embarrassing.

"Honestly, I forgot." I chuckle nervously. "I've been so distracted with work... and other things... that I lost track of days."

"Good thing your friends remembered, or you wouldn't have celebrated at all."

"Hey now! Pizza is always a party." I sit back in the lounger, returning my eyes to the stars, feeling utterly relaxed. "They're more like family than friends. It's awful when our jobs keep us apart. Group messaging is great and all, but not the same. I don't know what I'd do without them."

We sit in silence for a few minutes. I realize Colin is still facing me, and I shift my eyes to him again. Colin seems to turn something over in his mind—he has that calculating look he gets when he's studying an engineering drawing.

"Family isn't always blood. How did you find each other?"

"College. I met Nic at freshman orientation. She sat next to me and we instantly bonded. It was the first time far from home for both of us. Anna was our sophomore dormmate—the things that girl could do with a hot plate and toaster! Every major adult milestone we've done together. Anna and I bought Nic her lucky camera bag as a graduation present. Nic and I try every new dish before Anna serves it at the restaurant. They both helped me study and drove me to my project management certification exam. Every good time, every bad time. We've been there for each other."

I sit up and turn fully towards Colin; the champagne loosening my tongue and making me forget my plan to stay away from this man. The candlelight dances in his eyes as he searches my face. His eyes dart down to my lips and back up to my eyes. I gulp, and lick my suddenly dry lips as his hand reaches towards my face, his eyes still on mine. Gently, his fingers brush my cheek as he pushes an errant curl behind my ear.

His lips quirk up on one side. "Well, you'll have no lack of amazing parties. The food is delicious—I'll need to check out this restaurant. And Nic certainly knows how to... ah... entertain. Olympians are quite an impressive guest list."

My smile grows. The warmth in my belly spreads until I practically vibrate with it. I'm mesmerized by the shadows dancing on the sharp planes of his face. Although we are still alone, his voice has lowered and I lean forward without thought, staring at his lips as if I can read them.

"They were my birthday present. Nic thinks I need to get laid. I've been too uptight." I'm so fixated on his expressive lips, I don't even realize what I'm saying.

Colin leans towards me. My breaths turn harsh as my heart beats faster. Slowly, his lips spread into a sensual grin until his dimple shows. "Oh, really?"

I swallow, my mouth gone dry. "I just have different priorities. Can't let anything jeopardize my career. Not again." Ripping my eyes from his mouth, I look into his eyes, trying to read his thoughts. Colin draws a ragged breath as he stands.

"You should get back to your party."

He turns to leave and my heart stutters painfully. The moment stalls and nothing else matters. Not my job or my plans. I just want him to stay, to turn back time to a few moments ago.

Standing abruptly, I reach for his arm to stop him from leaving. My spiked heel slips off the edge of the patio stone, and the yard suddenly tilts around me. Strong arms catch and pull me against a firm chest.

Heart pounding, I tilt my head back to meet green eyes. His fingers lightly dig into my shoulder and hip as they band around my back, holding me in a dip like a graceful dancer. His biceps are taut under my hands. Before I can remind myself what a horrible idea this is, I skate my palms up his arms to the back of his neck.

His eyes plead with me. I don't know if he means stop or keep going—for once I don't care. Cupping my fingers around his nape, I use the leverage to bring my mouth to his. My eyes slide closed as my lips meet his and Colin stiffens. With a slight whimper at the rejection I sense coming, I retreat.

Before I fully disengage, Colin's hands tighten on me. With a groan, his lips descend on mine again. His tongue flirts with the seam of my lips and I gladly grant him entry. With a moan of my own, my fingers spear into his hair, knocking his cap off. Colin straightens and pulls me flush against him, his left arm still banded around my hips as his right hand cups the back of my head.

I press my hips into his, finding him already hard. Teasingly, I rub my core against his thickening erection. Tingles spread from my upper thighs, racing across my body. His hand fists in my hair. Colin tears his mouth away and ghosts his lips along my jaw to my thundering pulse point. Lids heavy, my eyes close as I give myself over to the sensation and more tingles radiate out from the spot where his lips caress my neck.

"Brianna." His voice is gruff, almost broken.

"Brianna!"

We both freeze as a voice calls from the doorway. Heart pounding, breathing fast, we break apart. Each searching the other's eyes for a clue of what has changed. With effort, I break his gaze and turn to find Anna waiting.

The bright lights of the party behind her, only her silhouette stands with one fist propped on her hip. "Well now, that's where y'all got off to. The candles won't blow themselves out, you know. Come on now, in with you."

Anna reaches her hand out to me, and with one look back up at Colin, I walk towards her.

"Sorry, Anna. I was getting some air."

"Mm-hmm, air." She snakes her arm around my waist as I approach and turns me back to the party. I don't miss the wink she sends at Colin over my shoulder. "Well, hurry up now before the raspberries turn my beautiful cake to mush. We'll just make Mr. McLeary do the dishes for Bogarting the birthday girl."

With a giggle, I let Anna lead me to the awaiting cake. All three tiers of it, trailing with beautiful fondant hydrangeas and filled with champagne buttercream and raspberry curd.

Chapter Nineteen

I'll Cry If I Want To

Brianna

Guests gone, I collapse onto the couch with my two besties. Besides that one balloon that has made a break for the vaulted ceiling, you cannot tell that a party has been raging for the past seven hours. Colin washed the dishes, gathered up the trash, and has now retreated to his room. He didn't let any of us help, flat out told us to sit our *arses* down and let him do it.

My head lolls on my shoulders and I stare at his closed door, trying to work out what that kiss meant. Following the line of my eyes, Anna breaks the silence.

"Ok, I can't take it anymore. What is going on there with Colin?"

From my other side, Nic laughs darkly. "You mean besides the hot accent, sexy smile, and amazing *arse*?"

I groan. "Can we stop saying *arse*?"

Anna hums lightly. "Those are all accurate statements. The man is fine. Your descriptions didn't do him justice, darlin'."

Nic's tone turns thoughtful. "I like him. Hot, funny, and he did the damn dishes! I'll say it again. If you don't go for him, I will."

I feel my cheeks flush as I think about that kiss on the patio. My core tightens as I replay the feeling of his hands and lips on me. A sigh escapes before I can hold it back. Nic and Anna both sit up straighter and exchange a weighted look before turning their attention back to me.

"Bree, babe. What is it? It's obvious he's interested in you. You should have seen his face when you walked out in that dress. You can't lie to me, sugar. I saw you two on the patio. I thought the cushions were about to light on fire. There is something there."

Instantly defensive, I shake my head, not wanting to admit the hope her statement inspires. "You're just seeing something that's not there because you're worried about me. We just have been spending a lot of time together on this project. It's not like that."

"Brianna Chance. It is like that. You just don't want to admit it," Nic states bluntly.

Anna is the caregiver of the group and will let me wallow a bit. Nic is always the tough love that makes us face our truth. She grabs both my hands as she leans forward to meet my eyes.

"You're afraid," Nic continues, "but he's nothing like Chris. My plan was to warn the guy off tonight. But, after meeting him, I couldn't. That man sincerely cares about you and wants you to succeed. If you can honestly tell me you'd have no interest in him if you didn't work together, I'll drop it."

My eyes prickle with unshed tears, and I bite my lip to keep it from wobbling. "It could ruin everything. My career, this promotion. You know I busted my ass to get here. I have a plan, dammit. If I just stick to the plan, everything is going to be fine." I sniffle and aggressively wipe at my cheek as a tear falls.

Nic lifts my chin to force my attention to her. Brows furrowed, eyes serious, she squeezes the hand she still holds.

"People can't plan their lives like one of your projects, baby girl. You're so focused on five years from now, you're missing everything around you. After Chris left, you stopped living because the idea of getting hurt again scared you, and we let you. It's time, though. Time to feel again. I can't think of anyone better to help than that honest, kind man who can't keep his eyes off you."

I lean forward and bury my face in her shoulder as I sob. She is right. I had stopped living, pushing all emotion to the back, and buried myself in my career. The truth is, I hadn't even realized I'd done it until Colin arrived. I want to be a complete person again, shatter the ice queen.

As I clutch Nic, the dam on my emotions bursts, and feelings long buried pour out. Pain. Betrayal. Rage. Loneliness. Self-doubt. I cry them all out as my friends make comforting sounds and stroke my arm and hair. When I am finally spent, I sit back on the couch with a sigh. Nic and Anna bookend me, each resting a head on my shoulder.

"You're right." My voice is barely a broken whisper.

Anna holds a tissue out to me. "Bright side. If he's a dud in bed, it'll be easy to ghost him in Ireland."

Nic groans on my other side. "Shut your mouth. If that man is a dud, I have zero hope for the rest of mankind."

After a wet chuckle, I blow my nose. The thought of Colin leaving isn't at all comforting. I rub my stomach as I feel nauseous at the thought. Maybe it's the bottles of champagne.

CHAPTER TWENTY

Breakfast of Champions

COLIN

I awake feeling distinctly unrefreshed and stumble into the shower to shock my system awake. My eyes close as I tilt my face into the hot spray of water. I rake my hair off my forehead and am reminded of the feel of Brianna's fingers in my hair and her lips on mine.

That kiss.

It was the single best kiss of my life. Lowering my forehead to the cold tiles, I let my hand drift lower to ease my aching cock. Already half hard, I think back to the feel of her curves in my hands and start stroking with purpose. Hand flat on the wall before me, I hunch over as I fantasize about what I would have done if Anna hadn't interrupted.

I would have continued to explore her swollen lips and dancing tongue. My hands would have traced those luscious curves. Who knows, I could have pulled her into my lap on that lounger. Rocked her hips against my aching length. Skirted my hand up her skirt. Her panties would have been soaked as I teased her clit, stroking her to climax. Swallowing her cries of pleasure.

Within minutes, I grit my teeth and groan Brianna's name as I orgasm. Thick spurts rope across my hand and down the drain. The quick release does nothing for the building desire I feel for Brianna.

Freshly shaven and changed, I emerge from my room to find the girls draped across the couches, still fast asleep. My lips tug into a smile at the sight.

They traded party dresses for shorts and T-shirts. Anna hugs a pillow to her chest, knees tucked under her as her head rests next to Brianna's. Nic haphazardly splays across the cushions, one leg hooked over the sofa arm and her back against Brianna's other side.

In sleep, Brianna's features soften. Her long lashes kiss her cheeks, chest slowly rising and falling in peaceful sleep. Her long hair is in a messy bun, escaped tendrils artfully frame her face. My fingers itch to smooth those tendrils. Instead, I pull the blanket off the ottoman by Brianna's feet and gently cover the three women. Brianna stirs slightly, taking a deep breath, and her lips spread into a content smile, still fast asleep.

I smile down at her and will my heart to calm as I head to the kitchen. We haven't found ourselves alone since that moment on the patio. It is frustrating, but I am so afraid to hear Brianna say it was a mistake. The delayed return to reality is most welcome.

Busying myself, I pull out ingredients and get to work on a hangover breakfast of champions. The smells of food cooking must rouse them, because the girls stumble into the dining room just as I place a plate overflowing with waffles between a pile of bacon and a bottle of aspirin. All three groan as they sit down and hurry to grab food.

Anna closes her eyes and moans around a piece of crispy bacon. "Best hangover breakfast ever!"

Nic looks up at me as I set a pitcher of Bloody Mary on the table, eyes wide and mouth stuffed with waffle. "I think I love you."

Laughing at their antics, I look over at Brianna. She is blushing a little as she spreads butter on her waffles, a slight smile on her lips.

"Enjoy your breakfast, ladies, but save room for my Ma's Guinness Pie. I'm going to run to the market for some ingredients. Need anything while I'm out?"

"Popcorn," yells Anna.

"Chocolate!" adds Nic.

Brianna looks up and smiles at me. My chest tightens at her open expression.

"Cola. Birthday movie marathon starts soon. It's tradition." Her eyes twinkle as she holds my gaze. "Everyone has to pick one, so better start thinking about yours."

I grip the back of the chair across from her, leaning towards her as I maintain her stare. My lips spread into an answering grin. "Any rules?"

She tilts her chin up and nibbles on a waffle square. My gaze dips to her lips, glistening with butter. My knuckles whiten on the chair, and I swallow back the desire to lick her lips.

"Nothing too melodramatic. Other than that, anything goes."

"Got it." I hold her gaze for another beat before turning to the others. Nic's eyes dart back and forth between us. Anna holds a strip of bacon halfway to her mouth, forgotten. "Ladies, feel free to use my shower while I'm out. I have nothing to hide."

Straightening, I walk towards the kitchen, feeling three sets of eyes on me the entire way. This is a grand morning. I get to work on the breakfast dishes.

"Hot damn. And he cooks? Think he'll marry me?" Anna lowers her voice, but I can still easily hear her Southern drawl from the quiet kitchen. I bite my cheek to keep from chuckling.

"You can already cook. I need his skills more, so I'll marry him."

That sounds like Nic.

"I saw him first."

I drop the sponge in my hand at Brianna's words. My chest swells with a deep breath, and I can't help but close my eyes, trying to contain the hope that's bubbling up. God, I hope she means it.

Chapter Twenty-One

Dinner and a Movie

Brianna

Maybe it's the post-party glow—or the caramel latte Colin picked up for me while shopping—but I am in a ridiculously good mood. A weekend with my besties is definitely the reason for my inner peace. It certainly has nothing to do with the earth-shattering kiss last night.

It really has been too long since we got together. Nic's job often keeps her away for weeks at a time, but Anna is always nearby, running the restaurant. Normally I see her there a few nights a week, but I've been off my routine since Colin arrived. I have a bad habit of hyper-focusing on a situation until I work out all the pieces—and lately, I'd been low-key obsessing about the generator in general, and the Colin situation in particular.

This promotion has been my top priority for almost a year now. If this generator is half as successful as I predict, the title of director is as good as mine. I need to survive all the secrecy and bullshit with Stone, though. Things have been so much more complicated since Colin arrived.

Not that it's Colin's fault—not really. He is actually quite pleasant to live with. Tidy, respectful, and always willing to help. Hell, half the time I go to feed Riley or empty the dishwasher, Colin has already gotten to it. He is always doing thoughtful things, filling gaps he sees around him—like that delicious breakfast this morning. Sometimes it feels like he's always been here. It is a dangerous feeling—makes me worry about what life will be like after he leaves.

"Hey, Irish, get the popcorn while you're in there!" Nic's yell breaks my inner monologue.

"Anything else, your highnesses?" I can't help but smile at Colin's flippant response. It is amazing how comfortable he's been with the girls.

"Can of cola!" I yell, smile still in place.

"Candy!" Anna adds.

We hear some good natured grumbles from the kitchen and laugh. Colin walks in carrying a tray with three bowls of popcorn, drinks, and candy. He stops just behind Anna's chair and surveys the living room, eyebrows raised slightly.

"And where is it, ladies, that you expect me to be sitting at?"

We'd all claimed our usual movie spots in the living room, while Colin was putting away his market haul and preparing something for dinner. I am on the larger couch under a giant throw with Riley laying in a blanket-nest on my feet. To my left, Nic is stretched out on the loveseat, a mountain of pillows behind her and her long legs dangling over the arm. On my other side, Anna sits in the recliner wearing an oversized sweatshirt, knees pulled up, hugging a pillow. There is not a spare cushion in sight.

Nic leans forward and pulls an extra pillow from her pile before throwing it on the floor halfway between our seats. "Newbies sit on the floor."

"Will I, yea? After slaving in the kitchen all day, this is what I get? A wee pillow?"

Anna and I laugh at their banter. Lifting Riley from his spot, I scoot back on the couch and pull my legs up to make room for Colin on the other end of the couch. "Here. You can sit on the couch, but I expect first dibs on whatever smells so good."

His eyes twinkle as I take my soda and a bowl of popcorn from him. My heart speeds up as I maintain eye contact, the moment stretching on.

"Deal." Colin's voice grumbles, lower than normal. Someone, likely Nic, clears her throat, breaking the moment.

Colin finishes passing out the bowls and drinks before settling in on the couch. "What's the first movie?"

Nic fishes the remote out and hits play. "Mine's up first."

The title screen flares to life on the latest independent film which got a dozen awards. Not my usual pick, but the message around society's reliance on technology is genuinely insightful without being overly preachy. I occasionally steal a glance at Colin, expecting him to be bored, but he watches the whole movie without even glancing at his phone.

Next up is Colin's choice—a British spoof of action movies I've never seen. Before the movie is half over, we're all holding our stomachs in laughter. Tears stream freely down our faces. As the credits roll, a timer buzzes in the kitchen. Time for dinner.

We stream into the kitchen, gathering empty bowls and glasses on the way. Colin dishes up servings, which we carry into the dining room with a bottle of wine. Rich and savory flavors tint the air. The bowl before me holds some kind of stew with beef, carrots, potatoes, and a square of flaky pastry dough nestled on top. Anna and Nic have already dug in with enthusiasm before I finish inspecting my plate.

"Oh my god. Anna, I think you have some competition." Nic spoons up some more with an earthy moan.

"Maybe now you won't be after me to feed you all the time!" Anna sticks her tongue out at Nic before turning to Colin. "This is seriously delicious, though. What did you use in the broth? Worcestershire? Apple cider vinegar?" Always the foodie, that one.

"That is a McLeary family secret. Won't be that easy to get it out of me." He winks at me.

I take up a spoonful. The broth is thick and creamy, meat tender, carrots and potatoes soft but still have a bite. Closing my eyes, I give in to a building sigh of contentment.

Feeling eyes on me, I peek to see Colin staring at me, eyes dark and jaw muscles clenched. I blush and duck my head as I smile. "It's perfect. I can see why it's a family recipe."

Colin's eyes soften, and his smile spreads at my compliment. "It has always been my favorite meal, so Ma made it fairly regularly. When I went to university, I begged her to teach me how to make it. All I needed was a Crock-Pot and a toaster."

"What did you go to school for?" The question comes from Anna.

"Mechanical engineering. I grew up in a farming community, but the machines always fascinated me more than the crops, and I wanted to build them."

"So if you wanted to build things, why are you, a VP, on extended loan to some small firm?" Leave it to Nic to go for the jugular. I shoot her a look, trying to signal for her to cool it.

"When I started working for Innovative Solutions, it was still a ver'a small company in Dublin. The owner took a shine to me and took me under his wing. I'm a hard worker. As the company expanded, he promoted me up. He's also been sharing more duties with me as he's gotten older."

"What about the extended stay here, though? Isn't your family missing you?" Now Anna takes up the inappropriate question torch from Nic. I turn my glare on her.

"When my father passed, my eldest sister and her husband took over his barley farm. They live there, in my childhood home, with their two kids, and tend to the crops. My other sister owns a shop in the city and stays pretty busy during the tourist season. Ma says she's retired but helps both my sisters when she's not spoiling the little ones. As long as I'm back for Christmas, she'll be happy."

The rest of the meal continues with enjoyable banter. Nic and Anna get into a heated debate about the independent film and the symbolism behind the ending. Colin jumps in occasionally to agree or disagree with a point made. Being long used to these debates, I just pull out my phone and look up an interview with the director. His explanation of the ending disagrees with both Anna and Nic, which gives us all a laugh.

After the plates are practically licked clean, Anna and Nic clear the table and get dessert prepped. They shoo Colin and I back into the living room. Finding Riley already curled up in one corner of the couch, I sit closer to the middle than before. Turning my head to Colin, I find him watching me with a smile.

Nervously, I tuck a couple of stray hairs behind my ear before meeting his eyes. "I haven't thanked you for being so flexible this weekend. I'm sure none of this was what you had in mind after a long week in the office."

Colin's smile widens until that single dimple peeks out. "A weekend of entertainment with three beautiful, intelligent women is definitely not what I had planned. It's better." He leans across the short distance separating us and taps my shoulder with his. "It was grand to see you relax and smile."

My breath catches at his nearness. My brain screams at me to lean back, move the damn dog, and retreat to my corner. One look in his green eyes and I'm frozen. Their depths hold warmth and affection. What have I done to earn that look? Before this weekend I had kept him at a firm distance. I gnaw at my lip as guilt gnaws at my stomach.

Leaning into him a bit more, I lower my voice to a near whisper. "I also want to apologize. I realize I may not have been as welcoming to you as I could have been."

Colin's grin relaxes and takes on a more tender feeling, his eyes softening as he keeps looking into mine. "You have shared your meals and your home with me. You've been a perfect hostess."

"Food and a bed are one thing. I haven't exactly been friendly though. The situation was awkward, and I didn't make it less so." I take a deep breath, my heart pounding in my stomach as I decide to open up. Just a little. "About a year ago, I hit a rocky patch after trusting the wrong person. Since then, I've kept things a little close to the vest. I'm sorry if I've made your time here more difficult than it needed to be."

He releases his breath on a little sigh. I close my eyes as his breath fans my cheeks. I feel his blunt finger ghost across my temple to tuck hair behind my ear again. His fingers continue their gentle path until he cups my jaw. With a sharp breath at the contact, I press into his hand as my lids gradually open to meet his again.

"Brianna, don't apologize. It was a *fecking* awkward situation. If that *gobshite* Stone had put me in a hotel like he was supposed to, would you have treated me any differently? Please don't upset yourself."

I search his eyes, not sure what I am looking for in their emerald depths. My eyes drift to his partially open lips and back up to his eyes. Colin leans the last two inches towards me, my name a caress on his lips. I tilt my head back and my eyes drift closed, waiting to feel his lips on mine again.

The sound of a pan dropping in the kitchen scares me. I jump back with a slight squeal, turning back to the blank TV screen. With a chuckle, Colin also turns ahead, but leaves his arm draped over the back of the couch behind me.

Anna and Nic return from the kitchen with a round of refreshed drinks and more popcorn. Next up is Anna's choice, a comic book action film. Lots of explosions, gory fights, and half-naked men with six packs. Every time the lead actor takes his shirt off, Nic whoops from her seat—and Anna throws popcorn at her.

During a shockingly bloody battle scene, I jerk when an opponent's head flies at the camera. Feeling a hand squeezing mine, I glance to my left. Without taking his eyes off the action, Colin has brought his arm down to grab my hand. When I fail to take my hand away, he threads his fingers through mine with a satisfied smirk on his lips.

My heart is pounding in my chest at the gesture. I am almost thirty. I shouldn't feel like a high school girl with her first crush anymore. That doesn't stop me from smiling as warmth spreads through me. We hold hands for the rest of the movie.

Anna tosses me the remote as she passes to get dessert—chocolate fondue with fruit, pound cake, and marshmallows. It is time for my movie pick.

"Let me guess." Nic's fingertips are touching her temples in an imitation of a psychic. "*Emma*, right?"

Anna launches a marshmallow at Nic that bounces off her forehead with perfect aim. "Naw, that was last time. *Wuthering Heights*?"

Nic gleefully picks the projectile off her lap and eats it. "Nope, Bronte is not birthday appropriate. I bet you a thousand dollars it's Austen."

I grin as I settle back into the cushion, still close to Colin's side. "You're both wrong."

"*Sixteen Candles*?" Anna and Nic yell in unison as the opening credits play.

CHAPTER TWENTY-TWO

Sweet Dreams

COLIN

Today has been the most fun I've had in ages. Watching Brianna with her friends reminds me of how my sisters take the piss out of each other. When she is with them, Brianna lets all of her guards down. She has mesmerized me since I arrived, but seeing Brianna completely at ease? It's downright irresistible.

I feel like a schoolboy with a first crush. Her sweet vanilla smell fills my head. When Riley unknowingly plays wingman, and Brianna scoots closer to me on the couch, I thank all the Irish saints. When she lets me hold her hand during the action scenes, I pray she can't hear my heart pound.

Halfway through the final movie, I feel Brianna's arm press more firmly into mine. I absently rub my thumb over her knuckles under the blanket. Her head gently falls onto my shoulder, and I chance a quick peek at her. My lips quirk in a slight smile as I take in her long lashes as they caress her cheeks.

Brianna is completely asleep and curling into me. Careful not to wake her, I reach across both of us to tug the blanket higher over her shoulder. As the final credits roll, Brianna is still fast asleep. I lift my eyes from her peaceful face to find Anna eying me thoughtfully.

Nic stands and stretches. "Damn, it's already one am? We better get going."

"Guess we better wake sleeping beauty." Anna steps closer to the couch.

"Let the lass sleep. She could use the rest. I'll just carry her to bed."

With effort, I detangle my fingers from hers before slowly tugging the blanket off of Brianna. Sliding my arms around her back and under her knees, I easily lift her petite frame. She stirs slightly, but only buries her head further into my neck. Her fingers flutter against my chest before they grip my T-shirt.

"I'll help you get her settled, Nic get the plates into the sink." Anna still has a speculative gleam in her eyes as she observes me.

I silently follow her down the hall to Brianna's room. Never having been in here myself, I seize the opportunity to glance around. A king-sized bed dominates one wall, crowned by a floor-to-ceiling tufted headboard. Neat stacks of books sit on the nightstands and dresser. Anna rushes forward to pull back the white, fluffy comforter so I can lower Brianna to the bed.

Brianna stirs again as her head hits the pillow. Her eyelashes flutter once before she rolls towards me, still gripping tight. Careful not to wake her, I uncurl her fingers before pulling the covers up to her shoulders. She smiles dreamily and snuggles under the blankets.

"Sweet dreams, *a ghrá,*" I whisper. *My love.*

I smooth her hair behind her ear and watch her turn her head, as if seeking my touch. My lips twitch in a gentle smile.

Anna is waiting in the doorway still. She flips the light switch and closes the door as I pass, but doesn't let me get far before pouncing. "What are you hoping for from Brianna?"

"Whatever she wants to give. I will not insult you and say I'm not interested in her. She's the boss here. I'll happily dance to any tune she plays. You don't need to worry about me."

My lungs burn with the breath I hold, as Anna's eyes narrow. After an unending moment, she finally nods, and the air rushes out of my chest.

"Don't make me regret trusting you. I have four brothers. I know how to hit where it hurts." Anna lifts her eyebrows, the message quite clear.

I gulp.

"Yea, and I have a trust fund so big they won't find your body when I'm through." Nic slinks up and throws her arm around Anna, her careless tone at odds with the threatening words.

I raise my palms in complete surrender. "I wouldn't expect any less."

I see the girls out the front door and lock up behind them. Riley keeps me company in the kitchen as I clean the last of the movie marathon dishes. It is past the time to go to sleep, but the repetitive task helps me focus my thoughts.

Something shifted today. I can feel it in my bones. We never got a chance to talk about that kiss. The girls' presence prevented any discussion, and I don't know where we stand. Without her friends here, Brianna's walls might go right back up tomorrow. Where does that leave us?

What do I want from Brianna? Anna's question circles in my mind on a loop as I let Riley out one last time. My heart flutters. I want it all, if I'm being honest.

No woman has ever captured me the way Brianna has. I can see my future with this woman, and I'm desperate to explore the possibility. That may sound crazy after only a month of knowing each other, but I believe in epic love stories. My parents loved each other fiercely, and weren't shy about showing it in front of their children. Growing up, I always believed I'd find a love as deep and true.

I told Anna the truth, though. Brianna would lead this dance.

That doesn't mean I can't drop some hints. Like when I linked our hands. I can flirt more openly when we're alone.

She isn't immune to me. I just need to be patient and wait for her to decide what she wants.

Feeling confident, I head to my room to turn in. I hope I dream of her again. As I drowse, I feel a weight settle at my side. Surprised, I open my eyes and find Riley curled up by my hip. My fingers find his soft fur, and I aimlessly trail my fingers over his back as I drift off.

The next day is full of long looks and heated silence. I stay at the house and help Brianna with the cleaning.

We never discuss the kiss. I'm determined not to mention it first. Doesn't stop me from thinking about it.

A number of times, we find ourselves close together. Switching over the laundry. Folding blankets. As our eyes meet, mere inches apart, the air hangs heavy. I watch her swallow, her eyes on my lips.

If she leaned forward, just halfway, I'd lean the rest and kiss her again. Each time, I'm disappointed when she turns away. The flush on her cheeks and the way she bites her lip each time keep me hopeful. I'm not the only one feeling this.

Chores complete, we spend the afternoon in quiet reflection in the living room. This marks another notable change. Before the party, we would have each slipped into our separate rooms. Today, we sit on the couch together, reading separately.

Brianna shivers slightly, so I tuck her toes under my warm thigh and cover both of us with the nearby throw. She sends me a grateful smile and doesn't pull away. I could happily spend every Sunday like this.

And that thought doesn't scare me at all.

CHAPTER TWENTY-THREE

Blast from the Past

BRIANNA

Another Monday, another long to-do list in the office. I am ready to face the day ahead. The weekend had been exactly what I needed to recharge my batteries and get back into Badass Brianna mode.

Colin and I have already gotten through a progress review with the Dublin executives that went as well as my solo presentation on Friday. Since Colin opened up about his personal relationship with his boss last week, it proved entertaining watching the two interact. Mr. O'Toole smiled at Colin through the conference screen like a proud papa and congratulated him on the generator's success. Colin reddened adorably and grinned back at his mentor.

We've spent all afternoon poring over documents, helping Colin prepare for the upcoming conference. He wants to have a preliminary white paper ready just in case.

"Damn, where's that..." Colin looks around the stacked pages on the table.

I lift the sales projections graph off a pile in the middle and hand it to him. "Graph's right here."

His lips quirk. "Thanks. How about the...?"

"Budget versus spending to date?" I smile smugly as I hold up a second page.

Somewhere over the weekend, any remaining awkwardness vanished. I am entirely at ease in Colin's presence. We work in comfortable unison—a well-oiled machine. Not that we haven't always worked well together, but today is next level. It's like we know what the other is thinking without a word.

He laughs, winking that dimple at me. As he turns back to his screen, his smile fades. A wrinkle forms on his brow as his eyes dart from the screen to the page in his hand. "That doesn't make sense. These don't line up."

"Let me see." Walking around the table, I rest my hand on his shoulder as I lean in to view the screen. I don't even realize I'm touching him until I straighten back up and look down at him. The warmth of his shoulder seeps into my palm and spreads up my arm.

I am standing so close, the smell of his cologne tickles my nose, and my core clenches. I watch his Adam's apple bob as I remove my hand and step back.

Colin turns his head to meet my eyes over his shoulder. I lick my parched lips and catch my breath as his eyes swiftly darken. I can't look away from the emotions spiraling in his gaze. Lust. Hope. Frustration. Need.

"Colin… I…" My voice is barely a whisper. I'm trapped, captured by his warm eyes.

"Brianna." My name sounds like warm honey on his lips. Liquid heat pools in my center. How can just my name be so damn hot?

I feel myself lean forward towards him. Our kiss from Friday night replays in my mind. We haven't talked about it—I took the easy way out and let Colin suspect I didn't remember. But man do I ever. That kiss has been playing on repeat all weekend. Every time we sat on the couch together. When we ate together. And yes—even when I was alone in my room.

A loud laugh from the hallway makes me jump and breaks the connection. I swallow and shake the last fragments of lust from my head.

You're at work, Brianna. Get it together!

"Uh… I'm going to grab some coffee. You want anything from the kitchen?" I grab my cup from the table and head towards the office door. Not waiting for a reply.

"No, thanks."

I hear Colin sigh loudly as I close the door behind me and lean back against it. Closing my eyes, I take three deep calming breaths before heading off to the nearest kitchenette.

My heart is still pounding as I place my cup on the bland Formica counter. Deciding that more caffeine is definitely the last thing I need with my nerves already frayed, I stand on my toes to search the upper cabinet for the box of tea, usually forgotten up there. The box slips just out of my reach with each attempt. Cursing my short stature, I use the counter for leverage as I try to stretch a little higher.

A well-tailored arm, covered in expensive navy cloth, comes into my view just as I realize there is someone standing close behind me.

Alarmingly close behind me.

With a gasp, I step to my left and turn, simultaneously extracting myself and facing the man behind me. My eyes snap to brown ones filled with amusement. His dark blond hair is parted on the side and slicked over with gel. A light beard has been artfully trimmed to frame his face. Thin lips curve in a cocky grin—no, it's more of a sneer. Only after a month of Colin's good-humor grin do I realize what that smile actually means.

Christian Accardo—my ex fiancé.

"Nice to see you, Ree. How have you been?" He leans forward into my space. My mouth is dry, and my throat has relocated to somewhere in my stomach. I lean back again, trying to get some air—he's so close I can practically taste his heavy cologne.

What is he doing here? I haven't seen him since I threw his ring in his face almost a year ago. Not long after everything went to hell, he'd gotten a promotion and transferred to another office.

"G-good" I clear my throat and curse myself for stuttering. Chris's eyes sharpen, the look of a predator who smells prey.

Seeing Chris after so long throws me off, and my balance is already shaken by the raging hormones lit by Colin. My life is about precision and planning. I don't take surprises well. There's no problem I can't fix professionally, but I need a couple minutes to recenter first. "Busy, but no complaints. Why are you here?"

"Always the good worker bee. I hear you are in deep on this super secret new project. The whole Tampa office is talking about it."

"Shouldn't you be at the Tampa office?" I wipe my sweaty hands on my skirt and try to take a step back.

Chris steps with me, caging me back in. His grin spreads, all teeth. "I'm here to see the CFO, but I'm happy to run into you. This project sounds promising. There's even a pool going on what the product really is. Come on, you can tell me."

I narrow my eyes as I look at the man in front of me. The tailored clothes, expensive watch, grooming. Everything is artificial. Every part of his image is carefully chosen to send a message. I am important, handsome, charming. You should want to make me happy. It's all bullshit. Why had it taken me so long to see the truth?

With a deep breath, I square my shoulders and meet Chris's smirking gaze. Mentally, I count to five and force my standard professional expression onto my face. "I really can't talk about it, I'm afraid. Nondisclosure and all, a businessman like you understands. Now if you'll excuse me."

I take a step to the right. Chris reaches out and grabs my left arm in his meaty fist, squeezing hard enough that I wince. His smile strains as he clenches his jaw before the charming mask returns. My arm burns where he grabs it, and my stomach twists in disgust. And a little fear. "Let go of me."

"God, why are you being so difficult, Brianna? Do you know how embarrassed I was after your stunt last year?" The words are low and clipped, raising my hair on end. "You owe me, so just tell me what the product is. As an old friend."

"Christian, one thing we've never been is friends." With one hard jerk of my arm, he releases me. I step back, just as the fresh smell of trees and citrus envelopes me and a warm hand settles on my shoulder.

Blindly, I lean into Colin's muscular arm across my back. I am only mildly embarrassed at how grateful I am for his support at this moment.

In our three-year relationship, Chris had never been violent, but that grab on my arm scared me. It is the inherent fear all women are trained to feel, from the first buds of puberty. Always watch your surroundings. Don't walk at night alone, but if you have to, make sure your keys are between your fingers. It's a fear that's cemented as we grow, when they give the girls rape whistles in college, but not the boys.

"Is there a problem, Ms. Chance?" Colin's voice rumbles at my shoulder. It sounds calm, but lower than normal. His hand tugs, firmly bringing me closer to his side, and further from Chris.

Chris has to tilt his head back slightly to meet Colin's chilling gaze. After a quick assessment, he turns to face Colin fully. "No problem, just catching up with a... close friend." Chris's smile spreads with innuendo as he looks at me. Colin's arm turns to steel around me.

"Chris Accardo, Director of Finance in the government division. You must be the famous Colin McLeary." Chris holds his hand out to Colin as he introduces himself.

The moment drags on awkwardly as Colin just looks at the offered hand like it's a piece of trash, one eyebrow raised. Colin lets the tension rise to the breaking point, before turning his head to me. "Dublin just called a meeting. I need you to run me through the numbers again."

Without a look back, I let Colin lead me from the kitchenette back to his office. Colin's hand never leaves my arm as he guides me to the chair in front of his desk. His hands glide down my arms as he squats down in front of me to look me in the eye.

I can feel my thoughts spiraling. All the things I wish I said to Chris. Snippets of past conversations coming back to me. How many times has he put me down like that? Made me look like a joke? Made me feel like I was in the wrong, when he was actually to blame? That gaslighting son of a bitch.

Colin's brow knots in concern as his eyes dart back and forth between my own. I keep to my box breathing to calm my racing heart. In two... three... four. Hold two... three... four. Out two... three... four...

Launching to his feet, Colin rakes his hands through his hair and mutters something that sounds like 'king maggot'—which makes no sense—before telling me to stay put as he storms back out of the office.

CHAPTER TWENTY-FOUR

Spill the Tea

COLIN

That *fecking* maggot. In the weeks I've lived with Brianna, she's never looked so lost. Her sapphire eyes are missing their fire, and it scares the fucking hell out of me.

First things first—I need to calm down. The last thing Brianna needs right now is a raging Irishman on top of that *gobshite*. With long strides, I head down the hall towards the men's room, hoping some cold water will help.

I grip the edge of the counter until I feel the granite bite into my palms. The pain a welcome ground for the building rage. I stare into the sink unseeing, the scene between Chris and Brianna running repeat in my mind.

When Brianna first left, I'd taken a minute to adjust the raging hard-on Brianna's nearness always inspires. She smells so goddamn good—slightly sweet, with hints of amber and spice. I've been in an almost constant state of arousal since our kiss on Friday night. I had looked down at my half-filled coffee cup and decided the last thing I needed was to be hyper and horny. Thinking a cuppa tea was exactly what I needed, I'd set out after Brianna.

From down the hall, I saw Brianna on her toes. She was trying to reach something on an upper shelf, and I couldn't stop smiling at the reminder of our first dinner together. I was so distracted by the view of her skirt stretching over her curves as she reached up, that I hadn't seen the man approaching until he was already caging her in.

Frozen in place, my stomach had twisted with jealousy as he stood so close to her and smiled down at her... intimately. He was attractive enough, very clean-cut and oozing confidence and entitlement. A real, what do the Americans call it—bro?

"Afternoon, McLeary."

I had torn my gaze from the couple to find one of the other project managers standing next to me. "Johnson. How are ya?"

About my age, a bit of a pretty boy, but an overall decent fella. I'd taken a liking to Johnson fairly early on. He was friendly, but not a kiss-up, which I appreciated. He was actually the one who'd suggested the Irish pub I'd been frequenting.

"Well, that's surprising." Johnson had jerked his chin in Brianna's direction, a slight curl to his lip.

"Oh?" I'd turned slightly, to give Johnson and Brianna equal attention.

"Yea—I shouldn't gossip..." He looked up and down the hall quickly to see if anyone was coming, before leaning in a little closer. "But—those two used to be together. Engaged, if the diamond ring she used to wear was any indication. About a year ago there was a big shake down. Not sure what happened exactly, but suddenly our boss retired, Chris transferred to another office, and the shiny ring disappeared. All within days."

Johnson checked his watch, completely unaware that his words had left me reeling. Engaged? "Shit, man, I'm late for a call. See ya."

Nodding at him absently, my eyes narrowed as I inspected Brianna. At first glance, Brianna looked relaxed. But I could tell her shoulders were tense, and she seemed to be leaning away rather than towards him. I watched her try to step away, and the man followed. Like a dance.

As Chris grabbed her, the jealousy in my stomach churned. She had turned her head slightly, and I could finally catch a glimpse of her face. Her eyes were wide and her lips tight. I was already approaching when she yanked her arm away. As she collided with me, I could feel her trembling.

What the fuck was going on? How could I instantly see that she was upset, and this man she was supposedly going to marry could not? This was no lover's quarrel.

Jealousy fully doused, rage filled me as I looked at this smarmy asshole. The need to protect Brianna pulsed—not unlike my temples. I'd made up an excuse and got her the hell out of there, barely acknowledging the guy.

Brianna hadn't said a word. She'd just let me drag her away and seat her in a chair. The woman had a sassy comeback for everything. At least for me. Even if she didn't say it out loud, I always saw the fire sparkle in her eyes. Seeing her just sitting there, wringing her fingers with dull eyes, twists me up inside.

If I ever see that twat again, I'll fucking kill him. I have half a mind to chase the bastard down. With one more squeeze of the counter, I force myself to take a deep breath and calm down.

None of this is helping Brianna right now. I left her in my office alone and shook up. She is the priority. I can plot the ex's murder later.

Hell, Nic will probably help me!

With a cruel smile on my face, I leave the men's room. Passing the kitchenette, I notice Brianna's favorite mug still sitting there. Quickly, I clean it out and brew a cuppa to bring back to my office.

Brianna is still sitting in the chair I'd left her in. Her color is still too gray for my liking, but she's stopped wringing her hands at least. I hook the other chair with my foot to turn to face her as I press the warm mug into her hands.

Mechanically, she lifts the mug to her lips and takes a sip. Her eyes widen with surprise. She looks down at the mug for a moment, before taking another sip and looking up at me.

"Tea?"

"Yea, I know you said you were going for coffee, but you usually go for tea when you're stressed." I swallow around a sudden lump in my throat.

She silently studies my face and it makes me nervous enough to keep babbling. "I grabbed the herbal bag you like, squeezed the honey for fifteen seconds, and then added one ice cube so it isn't too hot."

Her lips part slightly as she continues to stare at me like a puzzle she can't quite figure out. By now, I am very familiar with Brianna's thinking look. That particular look she gets when she's turning a problem in her head and looking for the solution. I can't begin to guess why she is looking at me that way, though.

"It's not poisoned or anything."

Her eyes widen more before she starts laughing. The sudden noise startles me, but seeing her react with emotion quickly relieves the tension in my shoulders. Soon I am smiling and chuckling with her. She is still smiling after she calms enough for another long sip of her tea.

"Thank you. This is perfect. Now, what were you saying about budget numbers?"

"The budget's fine. There's no meeting. I... uh..." I can't really tell her I just didn't want her talking to the maggot.

"You just read the room?" Her eyes are downcast, staring into her tea.

"Yea, I guess. Didn't look like a pleasant conversation." I'm trying not to pry. Truly, I am. All I want to do is ask her what the hell she ever saw in that guy. Nic's grilling over the weekend makes a lot more sense, now. This Chris guy had fucked up.

The question was, how does Brianna feel about him now?

"It wasn't." Brianna nibbles on her bottom lip as she darts a little look up at me.

I can tell she's mulling over what to say. How to explain that interaction. How much to trust me. God, I want her to trust me. I also want to pull that full lip from between her teeth with my thumb.

Decision made, Brianna looks back up at me. "He just surprised me while my back was turned. Gave me a bit of a shock, and no, I'd rather not talk to him. So the interruption was welcome."

She gives me a half smile; the color is slowly coming back to her cheeks and eyes. My stomach twists with disappointment that she didn't share the whole story with me. I force a small smile, desperate not to add my emotions to her burden.

CHAPTER TWENTY-FIVE

What the Foxtrot

BRIANNA

Still feeling unsteady, and cheeks burning with embarrassment, I silently sip the rest of my tea. I can tell that Colin wanted to ask more, but I don't want to discuss Chris with Colin.

It's not that I still have feelings for Chris. Far from it. Frankly, I can't even remember a single reason I agreed to marry him, besides it fitting into my five-year plan. No, I am embarrassed that I didn't see through Chris's bullshit, and I don't want Colin to judge me for it.

If I am being honest, my thoughts are more stuck on Colin than Chris right now. He has this uncanny way of knowing what I need and just doing it. Like the tea. He's right. I prefer tea when I'm feeling stressed. Caffeine and nerves don't exactly mix. More than that—he memorized precisely how I take my tea. He'd *noticed*. A warmth that is both comforting and terrifying fills my chest.

My pocket vibrates, pulling me from my self-reflection. I am mildly relieved to see a text from the production manager asking me to call him right away. Production issues are never a good thing, but in this case, I will happily take the distraction from my blast from the past encounter. I stand to leave and cut a quick exit.

"I really need to take this. There is a problem with one of my other projects."

"Brianna... Are you sure? Can I do anything?" Concerned creases still mar his brow.

He's already done so much for me, I can't stop myself from offering him some comfort, too. With only half a thought, I lay my hand on his firm bicep and give a slight squeeze. "You've already helped. The tea was perfect, thank you."

Colin's green eyes search mine. His hand covers mine and squeezes.

Excusing myself, I walk towards the door, my phone already up to my ear before I cross the threshold. On the second ring, Stan Meyrick picks up, and I smile at the gruff hello from the production manager.

"Hey Stan, how can I help?" I weave through a few people milling the halls as I walk to my cubicle.

"About time you called me. What does a man need to do to get your attention?"

My smile widens. I love working with Stan. We bonded when he was my fabrication engineer on a project years ago, and we have stayed close. Stan managed to retain his sense of humor as he earned promotions. He lacks an inflated ego or any patience for office politics. Yet he gossips like an old biddy and always knows what is going on.

"You know, Stan, most of the managers are happy when they don't hear from me. Means things are going well. I called you as soon as I finished my tea break."

"You actually took a break? That's progress."

"Har har. My workaholic tendencies aside, what exactly is the problem?" I sit in my chair and lean back, lazily tapping my pump.

"The plastic pellets came in for your smart screen project today."

"Still waiting to hear the problem, Stan."

"They're pink."

I freeze, trying to process what he just said. "Excuse me?"

"The pellets that arrived are pink. Barbie Dreamhouse, bubblegum pink."

With a groan, I reach into my bag for my tablet, already searching through my email. "Hold on, let me check the purchase request I submitted. This definitely says gray. Do you have the SKU number off the box? It should be Alpha Bravo Tango 8843 Golf."

"Nope, this is Alpha Bravo Tango 8843 Foxtrot."

I groan. "What the foxtrot?"

Stan chuckles at my misery. "Want to bet they let the intern process the purchases again?"

"Probably. Thanks, Stan, let me call the vendor and see what I can do."

"Thank me with more of those raspberry bars you made for my birthday."

"Finish my screens on time and I will," I tease him back. Stan is the only one at work I let my professional mask slip for.

Disconnecting the call, I shoot a quick text off to Colin, letting him know I need to take care of something from my desk. First, I reach out to purchasing to check the SKU on the request sent to the vendor. They have the correct color there. Next, I call the vendor to trace the issue. It takes three hours, but I finally work my way up to the senior account manager on the phone.

"Ma'am, standard process is for no exchanges to be processed until the original order is returned." His voice is flat, annoyance clear in his tone.

"I understand, but can't you make an exception since your company did not process the original order correctly?"

"So you say, however, your company accepted the shipment."

I take a deep breath and pinch the bridge of my nose, trying to dispel a brewing migraine and keep the frustration out of my voice.

"Honestly, sir, at this point I don't care how the mix-up happened. Not trying to point fingers; I just want the material I ordered so production can move forward. I'm sure you understand why I can't go to my customer with a pink product when they are expecting gray. That might be a bit of a shock."

The manager chuckles faintly. Encouraged, I plow on with my monologue.

"Normally, I would be happy to overlook who did what, however I just don't have the time to wait. It's already six here, all shipments have already been picked up and I won't be able to overnight these pellets back to you until tomorrow. You'll get them Wednesday. Take another two days to process the return and the new shipment. Add another two days for shipping back to us. By the time I have the right materials for my team, I've lost a week of production time and can't make my deadlines. All because somewhere along the way, someone hit an F instead of a G on a keyboard. Doesn't that seem a little silly?"

"Well, when you put it that way, based on our long-standing history with C.A.E., we can bypass the standard process. I'll mark this order top priority and overnight you a new package first thing in the morning."

"Excellent. I'll collect the unopened bags from engineering tonight and send them out on the first truck in the morning. Thank you very much for your help, and have a lovely evening."

Hanging up the phone, I give myself a little victory fist bump. I am a fixer. This is what I excel at. With one more sigh, I crack my neck before shooting a text to Stan, asking him to pack up the pellets and leave them on his desk for me. That complete, I set a reminder for the morning to get the box to shipping before the first FedEx pickup. My phone vibrates with Stan's reply, a thumb up emoji followed by a cookie emoji.

A shadow falls over my desk as I shake my head at Stan's antics. Colin sits on my desk at my elbow and smiles down at me. "Pack up, bird, it's time to go."

I lean back in my chair and stretch my legs out in front of me, raising a single eyebrow. "Go where?"

"Anywhere that's not here." He nudges my heel with his foot. "Come on, I'll take you to dinner and you can tell me all about whatever it is that kept ye busy all afternoon."

Muscles stiff from sitting too long, I groan as I reach for my laptop bag, throwing my items in haphazardly. Rolling my neck on my shoulders, I turn to Colin as we fall into step heading to the elevators.

"I need a tall glass of wine if I'm going to get through one more discussion on the apparent complexities of shipping and receiving."

Colin tosses his head back with a hearty laugh as he ushers me into the elevator. "That I can arrange."

CHAPTER TWENTY-SIX

Dinner for Two

COLIN

As we wait in the silent elevator, I reach over and transfer the laptop bag off of Brianna's shoulder and onto mine. She relinquishes the bag with little resistance and even smiles her appreciation up at me. I'm not sure if she is more comfortable being casual with me or if she is just distracted from the emotional day. I really hope it is the first option.

The doors open with a bing. I rest my hand on the small of her back to guide her to my rental car. Quickly moving around the car, I stow the laptops in the boot and settle myself behind the driver's seat.

Sneaking periodic glances at Brianna, I navigate to the trendy downtown area. Sitting silently in the passenger seat, she watches the world pass by through the window, her mind seemingly elsewhere. While Brianna is often quiet, this silence hangs heavy in the air between us. Although she seems more herself, something still weighs on her mind.

Brianna lets out a soft, sad sigh and my knuckles whiten on the steering wheel. What did that bastard say to her? Who is he to be able to shake her confidence?

I am burning with questions, but don't want to push her. She just started opening up and I want to keep it that way. I can't quite silence the voice that says she's already withdrawing from the connection formed this past weekend.

We still haven't discussed that kiss Friday night. Does she regret it? Hell, does she even remember it? She flirted with me, and was more soft and open the rest of the weekend, as well. That must mean she shares at least some of the same feelings I do. Right?

Pulling into the lot, I am out of the car and at her door before she moves. Taking my offered hand to climb out of the low sedan, she gives me a brief, sad smile. I squeeze her hand and keep it in mine as I lead us to the front doors of Pop. I only let go of her hand to open the giant double door, then move my hand to the curve of her spine.

Hopefully, a nice dinner at her friend's restaurant will cheer her up. Her friends help her relax, and after a stressful day, some of Anna's amazing cooking will be just the thing.

I pull Brianna closer to me, my hand sliding to her hip as I guide her through the crowded entry to the hostess stand.

The young hostess notices me first, as we approach. Her eyes scan over my suit and her eyes sparkle as she gives me a sensual smile before welcoming me to the restaurant.

"Reservation for two. Should be under McLeary."

At the mention of two, her eyes dart to Brianna, who is still tucked to my side. The sensuality drains from her face, and possibly some of her color, as her eyes widen in recognition and some other emotion. Of course, the hostess knows her. Brianna said she eats here regularly.

The hostess rushes around the podium and approaches Brianna, looking in distress as she tugs at her tight black dress. Seems a bit of an overreaction, but ok.

"Ms. Chance. I'm so sorry, but your usual table isn't available. We weren't expecting you this evening and there's a large party tonight."

Brianna gives the poor girl a warm smile and places a reassuring hand on her arm. Ok, this is getting downright weird.

"That's alright, Chrissy. I wasn't expecting to come in myself. Really, any table will be fine."

Despite the reassurance, the hostess looks unsure as she picks up the tablet again.

She chews on her lip as she reviews the available tables. "Ah, yes, McLeary." She clicks a few times on the tablet, grabs two menus, and then looks back to Brianna. "Follow me, please."

As we follow the hostess, I stay a step behind Brianna, taking in the surroundings as I walk.

Almost every table is full, and I can see why. This place looks amazing. Large color photographs grace silver walls in simple black frames. Small papers next to the photos give the name, artist, and advertise a selling price.

Sleek lines and modern flair dominate the space. Simple tables and chairs featuring polished chrome legs and covered in black linens sit throughout the venue. The vibrant art and plates of food pop against the austere surroundings.

On the far side of the restaurant sits a bar and sunken lounge. The lighting is dimmer in that area, the majority of the glow coming from LEDs around the bar shelves, which slowly change color and provide ambiance. A neon sign behind the bar boasts the restaurant's logo—a champagne bottle, cork flying out with bubbles and sparkles near the bottle mouth, and the word 'POP' in all caps.

Chrissy sits us at a small, round booth at the rear corner of the restaurant. It is an intimate table, but provides an excellent view of the rest of the restaurant. The hostess wishes us a good dinner before scurrying back to the podium as a large party walks in.

I've barely read through the appetizers before a waitress appears at Brianna's elbow to take drink orders and read today's specials. Again, the waitress's sole focus is on Brianna. Deferring to her for an appetizer and wine selection, then fumbling our menus before practically sprinting off to the bar to grab the wine.

Well and truly confused, I turn to Brianna for an explanation, but she is scanning the specials menu as if running waitresses tripping over themselves is a normal occurrence. I can't hold back my curiosity anymore. "Brianna, what the *feck* was that about?"

"Vicky? She's just shy. She's still new."

My eyes widen at her flippant answer. Like that is a legitimate explanation? I am still staring at Brianna when Vicky returns with our bottle of wine and takes our dinner order. At least she doesn't trip, as she rushes off to put in our selections.

"That doesn't explain the hostess. You have a usual table? I knew you probably came a lot to see Anna, but that girl looked almost scared."

Brianna scrunches her nose as she finishes a sip of wine and lowers her glass. "Oh... that... I don't usually come in on Mondays. I have a standing Friday night reservation at my favorite table. Chrissy is great at her job, but a surprise visit from the boss is enough to throw anyone."

I choke on the sip of wine I've just taken. "Boss?" I sputter and cough into my napkin.

Brianna relaxes back into the booth, smiling at me over the rim of her wineglass. Mischief dances in her cobalt eyes. "Anna told you she was part owner. Nic and I are the other owners. Anna is a culinary genius, but isn't so talented at payroll, business plans, or tax filings. That's where I come in—I handle the business side. We couldn't leave Nic out, though. She's our resident art curator and angel investor. All of those photographs are hers, or an artist handpicked by her."

Speechless, I stare at her, jaw open. She laughs at my expression and some more of the recent tension leaves her shoulders. That's fine; she can laugh at me all she wants if it cheers her up.

I reach across the small table, clasping Brianna's hand in my own and giving it a gentle squeeze. Shaking my head slightly, my smile grows as I lean in. "You, Ms. Chance, are amazing. Is there anything you can't do?"

Brianna smiles at me, her eyes warm, clearly pleased by my praise. We sit there smiling at each other, me still holding her hand, until the waitress returns with our appetizers. Breaking the eye contact, Brianna thanks the waitress and I reluctantly withdraw my hand and busy myself with my silverware.

The appetizer is delicious—calamari tossed in a buffalo sauce. I had been skeptical at the combination, but should have trusted Anna's palette. As we nibble on our starters, I ask Brianna about the call she'd gotten. She groans around a bite of spicy squid and, after another sip of wine, explains the pellet mix-up.

I laugh at the image of pink executive smart screens and toast her success with the vendor, refilling both our glasses of wine. By the time the entrees arrive, we are taking turns telling stories of purchasing disasters. Trying to one up each other.

I dig into the stuffed tenderloin—thin slices artfully arranged down the center of a plate, highlighting a perfect pinwheel of pork rolled with spinach, goat cheese, and red pepper chutney layers. Brianna opts for the sea bass special and lets me steal a bite. The black truffle risotto is amazing. As impressed as I'd been with the party food, my respect for Anna's cooking increases tenfold.

Anna comes out to check on our dinner, slipping into the booth on Brianna's side so she scoots closer to me. The girls share a side hug and Anna studies me over her friend's head. "You stalking me, Irish?"

"What can I say? One bite and I'm hooked."

Anna turns to Brianna again, a frown marring her brow. "You ok, Bree?"

Heads bent close together, I barely hear Brianna's response. "Chris was at the office today."

Anna's lips pinch together and her eyes narrow. She furtively glances at me and back at Brianna. Whatever she wants to say, she doesn't want to say it in front of me. What did that maggot do to deserve even sweet Anna's ill will? Maybe I should have introduced his face to my fist.

With one more squeeze, Anna dips her head to whisper in Brianna's ear. "I'm closing tonight, but call me later if you need to talk." She leans her temple against Brianna's, her care and concern for her friend clear on her face. More loudly, she says, "I should get back to the kitchen. I'll send out some dessert."

Rising in one fluid motion, Anna takes a step toward the kitchen, pausing next to me. She rests her hand on my shoulder. Her eyes are serious as they stare into mine, trying to convey a message. I nod, trying to assure her I have this handled. With one more look back at Brianna and a squeeze to my shoulder, she leaves.

We finish our dinners in silence, the absence of the earlier banter sorely felt. Brianna retracts back into herself at the reminder of the confrontation at the office. As I'm still trying to think of a way to break the silence, our waitress arrives with dessert.

A plate of delicate, colorful, round sandwich cookies appears in front of Brianna. The waitress points to each, stating they are raspberry, espresso, and lemon macrons. Before me, she places a shiny dark chocolate dome with colorful disks down one side. Vicky declares it a dark chocolate and Bailey's mousse dome.

A little light returns to Brianna's eyes as she smiles down at her dessert. She takes a delicate bite of the burgundy cookie and sighs. Seeing me smiling at her, she holds the cookie out for me to try. It tastes delicious; a slight crunch to the shell with a soft chewy center and tart raspberry buttercream filling. I slice my spoon through the dome in front of me, finding it filled with a light brown mousse.

I hold the spoon out for her. She maintains eye contact as her lips close around the spoon still in my hand, and my breath catches. Feeding her is erotic, and after a month of blue balls, it doesn't take much to get my cock's attention. She licks those sinfully lush lips, missing a spot of chocolate at the corner of her lip. Before I can stop myself, I reach out and clean the chocolate off her mouth with my thumb. Brianna's eyes darken with hunger as she watches me lick the chocolate off my finger. I swell painfully behind the zipper of my pants.

Adjusting myself, I signal for the check.

After some bickering over who should pay, I convince the waitress to take my corporate card. Bill settled, I step to Brianna's side of the booth to help her stand. Hand firmly settled in my new favorite spot, I lean into Brianna's ear.

"Let's go home."

CHAPTER TWENTY-SEVEN

Taking Charge

BRIANNA

The drive home is quiet. I can't speak for Colin, but I keep replaying dessert over and over again in my head. I'm still pressing my thighs together at the memory of Colin licking the chocolate off his thumb. After weeks of sexual tension, my panties are uncomfortably wet. I am going to need a long bath and a session with my vibrator.

Colin meets me at the front of the car and casually rests his hand on the small of my back as he guides me to the front door. What is it about that small action that is so unbelievably sexy? A happy Riley waits for us in the entryway. First, he jumps at my leg with a joyful bark and then scratches at Colin's leg for a pet.

"Well," I finally break the silence. "I should probably let him out and turn in. Thank you for dinner." My stomach flutters and I cast my eyes down, not quite able to maintain eye contact.

"Brianna." Colin reaches out and catches my wrist gently, stopping my escape. He tugs lightly until I turn back to face him, then shifts to hold my hands. "I think you are the most incredible woman I've ever met. You are smart, beautiful, and caring. Any man who doesn't realize how special you are is a *fecking eejit*. Don't let him take your spark."

He leans forward and gives me a kiss on the cheek near the edge of my mouth before straightening again. His eyes burn with emotion. I am caught in his gaze. Speechless and helpless to move.

With one last gentle squeeze of my hands, he lets go. "Sweet dreams, Brianna girl."

I watch as he strolls to his room and gently shuts his door. In a daze, I go about my nighttime routine. As I sit on my bed in my favorite nightgown and robe, a novel forgotten on my lap, I try to make order of the swirling mess in my head.

Chris has scarcely been a blip in my mind the last year. At least not actively. Anna and Nic tried to talk to me about it many times, but I just wanted to move on with my life. Throw myself into work and the restaurant.

While I can't deny the pull I feel towards Colin, I've done everything in my power to bury the attraction. From the beginning, I used my past with Chris as evidence that starting something with a coworker again is a terrible idea. After seeing the two men side by side, though, the excuse is wearing thin.

They are nothing alike. That is abundantly clear now. Chris is a user; he pushes and exploits individuals to meet his own needs. While Colin is undeniably charming, he is also genuine. A caring leader who supports and celebrates his team.

I fuss at the lace hem of my nightgown. Sure, mixing a professional and personal relationship can get messy. Haven't we already blurred those lines though? The man lives in my house for God's sake. Plus, he's definitely spent more time with my best friends in the last few days than Chris had over a three-year relationship.

Why am I really fighting this pull to Colin? I rub my thighs together to relieve some pressure in my core as I replay his goodnight kiss. It wasn't even on my lips, but the brief contact left me more aroused than any goodnight kiss I've ever had before.

Am I hesitating because I know he is leaving soon? Isn't a guaranteed expiration date better? At least my eyes are wide open, knowing the end before we start. My head says I am going to get hurt. My ovaries say this is a brilliant idea. My heart—well, I don't want to open that door, but my gut is strangely calm and silent on the matter.

I like the way I feel when he looks at me. How perfect his hand feels on my back. How comfortable I feel around him... safe. I want Colin McLeary, and for once I am going to do what I want instead of sticking to the safe choice.

Resolve firm, I stand and make my way across the house to his door. Before I can lose my nerve, I knock once. Not waiting for Colin's response, I open the door.

He is sitting up in bed in gray sweatpants, chest bare. Reading glasses perch on his nose and he holds a tablet in one hand. I freeze at the sight of him, swallowing my instantly dry mouth. He is truly gorgeous and looks every bit like the cover of a romance novel.

As he looks up at me, his eyebrows pinch with worry. "What is it, *a ghrá*?"

I rush into motion, walking straight towards him with long strides. In a fluid motion, he deposits the tablet and glasses on the nightstand and swings his legs off the side of the bed. I step between his knees before he can stand. His eyes turn molten as they rake up my bare legs and slinky robe.

Cupping his sharp jaw in my hands, I tilt his head back sharply and lower my lips to his. He freezes for only a moment before I feel his hands grip my hips. For a moment, I'm afraid he's pushing me away. With a guttural groan, Colin stands, slanting his mouth to deepen the kiss.

His tongue passionately traces the seam of my lips, begging entry, which I eagerly give. Our tongues dance an intricate give and take. His hands lower, cupping my ass and squeezing a moment before he lifts my feet off the ground. With a gasp of surprise, I wrap my legs around his hips; the world falls away as I lose myself to his kiss.

Still holding me against him, Colin sits back on the bed so I straddle him. His cock is already hard beneath me. Desperate for some friction, I rub my aching center against him.

With a strained groan, Colin tears his mouth from mine. I whimper at the loss, but the sound rapidly becomes a moan as he traces kisses down my jaw and throat. Arching my throat back to give him more access, I spear my fingers into his thick hair and continue to work my hips against his. He keeps one arm banded around my ass as the other snakes up to support my neck. Tingles radiate from every contact spot and down my spine.

My name is both a curse and a prayer against my skin as he continues to leave open-mouthed kisses on my tender pulse point. My core clenches and my back arches at the waves of desire spreading through me.

"I want you." My voice is a sultry plea.

I whimper as his hands still, and he removes his lips. Slowly, I open my eyes and look down to meet his gaze. I tremble at the heat I find in his eyes.

His pupils are so dilated they appear more black than green. His gaze intense, he fervently searches my eyes, trying to make sense of my sudden change. "Are you sure?"

"Yes. I'm tired of fighting this."

He looks conflicted. "Brianna, I'm not gonna lie and say I haven't pictured this dozens of times, but I'm not sure after the day you've had..."

I cover his lips with my hand to stop his words. "I'm sure. He's nothing. You're not him."

With that, I watch his reservations vanish. He nips my fingertips where they still rest on his lips. Shrugging my shoulders, I let my silk robe slip down my arms to pool at my elbows. His eyes follow the path of the fabric. They drink in my bare shoulders, the plunge of the neckline, and the outline of my hard nipples. I brush my fingers down his chest, exploring the dips of muscles I've admired through his shirts for weeks.

His fingers grip my thighs as his lips return to mine. Our breaths turn harsh, our fingers more desperate. Leaning back, I let the robe drop to the floor. His reactions fill me with confidence. I provocatively lift my nightgown over my head before dropping it to the floor. Straddling his lap in nothing but a pair of lacy panties, I feel his cock twitch underneath me.

"You're perfect." Colin's voice is rough with desire, the slight lilt of his accent intoxicating.

I cry out as Colin captures one dusky nipple with his lips. The roll of my hips becomes more urgent as I chase my pleasure. His hands grip my hips and he pulls me harder against his erection. "Please," I beg.

He snakes a hand between our bodies and cups my core. Colin's fingers tease my folds through my sopping underwear, and his palm applies pressure against my throbbing clit. I shudder at the sensation and dig my nails into his shoulders with a moan.

His hand leaves me, and I immediately feel the loss. Almost instantly, I feel one blunt finger push the lace of my panties aside and firmly press at my opening. With a groan, I push down against the digit, desperate for more.

"So wet, for me, *a ghrá,*" he groans against my breast. Unhurriedly, he works a second finger into my greedy pussy. His fingers curve and find that perfect spot, causing me to clench down around his hand, head thrown back in ecstasy.

I ride his fingers, chasing my release. My legs start to shake against his thighs. A coil of heat unfurls from my belly as I lean forward to grind my clit against his palm again.

"That's it, *a ghrá,* let go for me." Colin's ardent kisses trail back up my throat and jaw. With one last curl of his fingers and press of his palm, I shatter in the best orgasm of my life. I open my eyes as I feel the aftershocks of my release, finding his eyes on my face. Hot with hunger. My pussy clenches around his fingers again at the sight.

Gingerly removing his fingers from my tender core, he brings them to his mouth without breaking my gaze. He licks my juices off of his fingers with a satisfied groan. With his other hand, he catches the back of my head. Eagerly, but tenderly, he pulls me in for a searing kiss.

I feel desired. Powerful. I push firmly on his shoulders as he clutches my hips tighter. "My turn," I whisper against his lips, my voice husky.

I push harder on his shoulders until he lays flat. Leaving a trail of kisses down his muscular torso, I carefully slide down his body and sink to the carpeted floor between his feet. Dipping my fingers into his waistband, I tug until his cock springs free. As my fingers close around his hard shaft, the tips barely touch. He watches me with hooded eyes as I slowly work one hand up and down, getting a feel for him. A bead of pre-cum appears at his tip, which I capture with my thumb. When the next bead appears, I watch his face as I dip my head to lick his crown.

"No, love, you don't need to."

"Shut up, Colin."

"Yes, ma'am." His throaty laugh makes my toes curl.

I swirl my tongue over the head of his cock and tease the slit as I work one hand up and down his shaft. Colin's groan is all the encouragement I need. I take him deeper, bobbing my head.

Colin's thighs stiffen beside me. He fists the covers with one hand and tangles his other in my hair with a hearty groan. His fingers aren't forceful, but they give a slight tug to my scalp that sends flashes of pleasure to my core. Encouraged, I take him deeper until his cock bumps the back of my throat, then gently cup his balls with my hand.

Colin shoots up to a half-sitting position, like he was struck by lightning, his abs rippling at the motion. "Brianna, please, I'm not going to last like that."

The power goes to my head. Chuckling, I hollow my cheeks and suck him harder.

Colin's head falls back with a satisfied moan, his fingers tightening in my hair briefly. With a growl, he bolts up, tugging me by the armpits. I release his cock from my mouth with a pop and wipe my swollen lips with the back of my hand.

He's released something within me. I've never felt this powerful before.

His glassy eyes flash with an emotion I can't place, and his eyes widen. He pulls me forward by the hips before lowering his forehead to the valley between my breasts with a groan. "Shit. Brianna, I wasn't expecting... I don't have a condom."

Relief floods me that he isn't regretting this already, and I release my breath in a rush. "That's ok. I'm on the pill and I'm clean." His beautiful emerald eyes looked up at me. "I trust you," I whisper. His nostrils flare on an inhale and his eyes heat.

Colin slowly works my panties down my hips with light touches that send shivers through me. I step on his pants so he can discard them completely. With one last kiss under my left breast, he pushes himself back onto the bed until he sits against the headboard again. He holds out his hand and I crawl over him until I once again straddle him.

Leaning forward, I capture his lips with mine. Languid kisses full of promise and discovery. I tease his cock with my dripping pussy, butting it up against my entrance without actually allowing him entry. He growls in mock frustration as he nips my lower lip.

With a sultry smile, I lean back as he chases my lips. Reaching down, I take him in my hand again and guide him to my aching core. I feel that initial delicious stretch as his crown slowly spreads my folds. I pause, getting used to his size slightly before lowering myself another inch.

Sweat breaks out on his brow and he groans at the torturous pace I set. His fingers clutch at my hips like he wants to take over, but he stills, giving me full control. I lift myself again, almost completely dismounting, before slowly seating myself until I've taken him fully. With a satisfied groan, I pause again, desperate to memorize this initial union.

We stare into each other's eyes. His cock jerks and I clench down on him with a groan. He lifts his lips to take mine in a searing kiss. I roll my hips so he presses into my G-spot. Slow strokes build the pleasure for both of us. No idea how long this will last, not wanting this to end.

As I feel another orgasm building, I roll my head to the side. Needing no further encouragement, Colin traces a burning trail of kisses down my throat again. I groan in pleasure and quicken the pace of my movements. My nails dig into the muscles of his back, clutching him to me.

Suddenly, Colin's teeth close down where my throat meets my shoulder. The sharp pain causes me to cry out his name as a white hot orgasm bursts through me. As I come down, Colin takes over, grabbing my hips and thrusting to prolong the orgasm.

"Mmm," I moan, "harder."

He complies, and I meet each thrust with a roll of my own, taking him as deep as possible. The only sounds in the room are our harsh breaths and the slap of skin.

"Colin," I gasp, "I'm going to come again."

"Yes, *a rún.*"

Colin reaches down between us and gives my clit a slight pinch, sending me over the edge. My entire body tenses as wave after wave of pleasure bursts through me. My pussy quivers and clenches around his shaft, setting off his orgasm. His cock pulses within me for a moment before he shouts and his hot cum releases into my waiting womb.

We sit entwined as the last tremors of our releases dissipate. My head rests on his shoulder and my arms hug his chest. He strokes my side and buries his lips in my hair.

After we've both caught our breaths, he gently lifts me off of him and rolls me to my back. With a kiss on my forehead, he tells me to stay put and heads into the adjoining bathroom. I hear the water run before he returns with a wet facecloth. He tenderly cleans me, placing a kiss on my hipbone before returning to the bathroom with the rag.

Too blissed out to be embarrassed, I lay boneless on the disheveled bed.

Still gorgeously naked, Colin pauses in the doorway, raking his eyes over me. "So beautiful." He climbs back into bed, slips his arm under my shoulders and pulls me tight to his side. I sigh as I rest my cheek on his pec and lay my palm on his stomach. His heart still thunders under my ear.

Colin turns his head, burying his nose in my hair as he traces lazy designs on my bare back. I shiver slightly. His muscles tense and he pulls the blankets over us, engulfing me in his heat. As my breaths calm, doubts creep in. He must feel me tense up, because Colin places a comforting kiss on my forehead and keeps rubbing my back. "Shh, Brianna, just sleep, love."

He is so warm, and with his arms around me I feel safe. My eyelids drift closed. A thump on the other side of the bed draws my attention moments before a warm weight presses against my legs.

A chuckle rumbles in Colin's chest. "Good night to you too, Riley," Colin says, as I drift off to sleep.

Chapter Twenty-Eight

Setting Terms

Colin

The first thing I notice is the warm pressure along my side and over my stomach. The second is another, smaller warm pressure against my thigh and bollocks. I open my eyes, squinting against the morning sun, and turn to find Brianna tucked against me. Her cheek rests on my chest, her hair pools over my arm where I cradle her. One bare leg drapes over mine and her arm circles around my waist in a possessive embrace.

One mystery solved. I snake my free hand under the covers to poke the other warm lump in the bed. I carefully prod a furry head and am rewarded with a canine huff.

When the *feck* did Riley crawl under the covers? Better question, how the *feck* did he crawl under the covers? I quietly chuckle at the dog's strange behavior before turning back to the gorgeous brunette of my dreams.

I half expected to wake up and find it had all been a dream. Last night was incredible. Not just the sex—though that was hands down the hottest sex I'd ever had. It's the connection that's stayed with me.

I felt more in tune with Brianna than anyone before. Including my own family. First times are usually a little awkward, a guessing game of what the other person likes and dislikes in bed. With Brianna it's like I know immediately what she likes and give it to her—like magic.

She came to me.

That thought fills me with a satisfied warmth. Brianna chose me. Hell, she seduced me. On the day her ex reminded her why she put up those walls, she still let me in. She had a terrible day and instead of calling Anna like she'd offered, Brianna had turned to me for comfort.

For comfort.

The warmth in my belly turns to ice. What if she was only looking for a onetime thing to forget the maggot?

Brianna stirs at my side, nuzzling my chest with her nose a bit and moaning slightly. I was still hoping to buy a little more time before she wakes up.

Bollocks. Is she going to regret this when she wakes up? *Feck* me, will she think I took advantage? I really don't want this to be a onetime thing.

Her soft fingers whisper up my abs and chest as she rubs her nose. Her eyelashes tickle my chest as they flutter, and her nose wrinkles. Brianna's head tilts back slightly. I hold my breath as her beautiful blue eyes slowly open. As her lips curve in a dreamy smile, I finally relax and my breath escapes in a rush.

"Morning," she says. Her voice is still heavy with sleep and sexy as hell. I shoot her a grin as I tuck a piece of hair behind her ear.

"Morning."

"So... that happened..." She drops her eyes and traces invisible shapes idly on my chest.

I chuckle. I've never seen a shy Brianna—she is *fecking* adorable. Gently, I place my hand over hers on my chest. "Yea, that it did. I, for one, would be quite amenable to it happening again."

Leaning down, I kiss her head. When Brianna looks back up at me, her lips quirk into a shy smirk. I can't resist and capture them in a brief kiss. Just a peck, but making it clear I am down with whatever leads to more kissing.

"I would be open to that idea. With boundaries." Her eyebrows pinch slightly, turning serious.

My heart clenches, then races under her fingers. "Brianna, love, as far as I'm concerned, you set the pace and the boundaries."

"Number one: Separation of church and state—what happens here, stays here. When we walk through those doors, it's purely professional."

"Sounds fair. What else?"

"Number two: No strings. When this project is over, you're going back to Ireland. My life is here. Let's set clear expectations so no one gets hurt later."

My chest already hurts at the thought of saying goodbye. Truth is, I can't imagine a future without this woman. I am a red-blooded Irishman who's fallen fast and hard. How to word this right? "No long-distance relationships, agreed."

After a tense beat, Brianna gives a slight nod. "Number three: Exclusivity. As long as we are sleeping together, there will be no other partners. Cheating is an automatic end to this. No questions, explanations, or discussion. Just done." Her eyes harden and lips pinch. It's clear that this is her hard limit, and it is one I absolutely endorse.

"Absolutely." I look her in the eye with as much sincerity as I can convey and cup the side of her face with my palm. Her smile widens as she leans into my hand. I capture her lips in a languid kiss. There will never be another Brianna, not for me. I'll do anything to not fuck this up.

Reluctantly, I pull away. "Come on, unfortunately, we still need to go to work."

CHAPTER TWENTY-NINE

Here There Be Spies

BRIANNA

I feel amazing today. Nic was right about how badly I needed to get laid. After the months of buildup, I half expected the real thing to be a letdown. Nope, Colin surpasses even my wildest fantasies. Shivers tingle down my spine as I recall last night. My hand tentatively raises to rub my neck, where a high collar hides a rather sizable hickey.

Strong arms pull me against a firm chest as I stand at the kitchen counter. I smirk—the smile of an utterly satisfied woman. His jaw nudges my temple until my neck is exposed. His lips tickle my pulse with the barest of kisses and my core clenches at the sensation.

I feign a serious expression as I try to push down the rising arousal. "Is that your favorite spot? You left quite the mark behind. Are there Irish vampires?"

His laugh rumbles through my back, and he kisses my temple. "Well, there are tales about gingers and the sun."

I turn and smile up at him. He somehow always finds a way to make me laugh. His smile is tender as he brushes a thumb across my cheek. I tilt my head back, wordlessly asking for a kiss. The side of Colin's eyes wrinkle as he leans down to kiss me. What starts as a tender kiss quickly grows passionate.

His tongue glides over mine in an intricate dance. I nip his bottom lip as I pull back. My breath comes fast as I look at him through my lashes. With a growl, Colin cages me against the cabinets. I spear my fingers into his thick hair and arch my hips into his. His hands slide to my ass, each cupping a cheek and massaging the muscle. As his lips slip to my jaw, I moan with need.

The smell of coffee breaks into my concentration just seconds before the alarm on the coffee pot goes off. With a sigh, I pull away from Colin while leaving my hands on his shoulders. "We need to get into the office before the status call with Dublin."

Colin pouts like an adorable little boy. I chuckle as I wipe my peach lipstick off his lips with my thumb. "Just think how much better it will be tonight after all that tension." I duck under his arm, leaving him with a shocked look behind me. "Oh, grab the coffees, please. I'll be in the car." Tossing a smirk over my shoulder, I walk away.

Hours later, I am still smiling as I walk through the production floor. Stan texted me earlier he'd taken care of the pellets already, but I want to thank him in person and check on a few of my projects. Plus, I brought him some of Anna's cookies. I am incredibly happy and I want to pay it forward.

As I approach Stan's office, my smile grows. He is leaning over some blueprints spread across his desk. "Look at you, hard at work."

When Stan looks up, his eyebrows draw low over his eyes and his lips twist. At his expression, my pulse races, and I regret my extra large coffee this morning. Exhaling in a rush, I enter his office, closing the door behind me. "Stan, I'm in a really good mood. Finally, got one of those lives you've been talking about. Please don't ruin today for me."

He breathes heavily and rubs the back of his neck with one hand. Cocking his head, he sighs at me. "Well, now I feel terrible about this. How good of a mood are we talking about? Pumpkin spice latte is back happy or just binge watched *Bridgerton* happy?"

"Stan..." I plead.

"Nope," he holds his hands out in front of his chest, "I need to know how long to hide from you after this." His lips spread into a rueful grin. "Plus, I'm thrilled for you and really want to know."

I fold my arms, cock my hip, and raise my eyebrow—my best boss bitch expression. "Day at Disney World happy."

"Whoop! Good on you, girl. Now I'm really... really... sorry to say this, but something really suspicious is going on with your project."

"Smart screens? You don't think the pellets were part of some elaborate plot, do you?" I laugh at that ridiculous thought.

Stan straightens, his arms falling to his sides, and the drawings roll back up. His eyes fill with concern and a little pity. "No, Brianna. Your top secret project, and why the new prototype exploded this morning."

"What?" My bagel is threatening to make a reappearance. I stumble up to Stan's desk and hope like hell I misheard him.

"You'd better sit down. Are those cookies for me, by the way?"

He has the decency to blush, at least. Wordlessly, I hand him the bag and sit in the chair across from his desk. I lean forward, hands clasped between my knees, waiting for him to continue.

"Junior on the third shift was trying to get a jump on putting the generator together and the thing damn near took his arm off when it blew up. Kid's lucky the battery was out of charge or the blast would have been bigger."

"Is he ok?"

"Yea," Stan runs his fingers through his unruly hair, "sent him to the ER to get checked out and some minor burns seen to, but the kid is fine."

I nod absently, staring at my hands. Suddenly something Stan said clicks and I jerk my gaze up to his. "Did you say generator?"

"Yea." I gulp before he continues. "Don't worry, Brianna, you did a great job breaking all the pieces apart. I'm the only one who connected the dots. You know the boys all notice how you appreciate their work. They all come to me to make sure it's perfect for you. I saw enough pieces to get the picture. I didn't tell anyone."

I crumble in the chair, feeling lost. "Ok... I'm still confused. You said something suspicious is going on?"

Stan sits down and leans forward, lowering his voice despite us being alone in his office. "I got a good look at the parts Junior was working with this morning. There is no way the casing would fit together with sufficient vibration dampening. That battery would shake to unsafe levels."

He looks at me like he expects me to draw some obvious conclusion, but I'm not following. "Ok, so that would be how it exploded. Couldn't it just be a design error? They were trying to cut down on weight for this version."

"No way." Stan's tone is firm and confident. "As head of production, all engineering drawings need to be approved by me before fabrication begins. That's *every* version of every engineering drawing. I would have noticed a mistake like that and sent it back to engineering!"

I waver. "Stan, I know you're the best, but is it possible you missed it? Just this once?"

He vigorously shakes his head and rolls the plans back out. "I remember, those plans came on one of the kids' half days at school. My VPN doesn't work at home and I didn't want to hold your project up, so I printed out the plans and took them with me to review while the kids played on the swing set. They've been locked in my desk ever since. Look."

He points at the top document. It shows a case with two inches of space between the inner and outer layers. Stan flips to the second nearly identical drawing, except the clearance shrinks to one inch. The top copy has a CRM scrawled at the bottom corner in red pencil, the other is blank.

"The top copy is from two weeks ago when I approved it. The bottom is a fresh copy off the server yesterday. They don't match and there should be no way to replace the file without me and the head of quality control notified of the change." He leans back and rakes a hand through his hair, then turns to me with wide eyes. "Something weird is going on, Brianna."

I clench my teeth against sudden nausea. My fingers are ice as I grip my hands into fists to stop them from shaking. "Have you told anyone about this?" My voice is surprisingly calm to my ears.

"No, wasn't sure who to trust besides you."

I nod absently as I try to come up with a plan. "I'm going to go audit a few of the project files I have printed upstairs. You start working with engineering identifying the right designs. In case someone is messing with the server copies, save everything locally on an encrypted USB drive. Hopefully, there is a simple explanation, but better safe than sorry."

Stan reaches out and clasps my arm. He gives it a supportive squeeze before releasing me with a tired sigh.

"Hey, Brianna," he calls out as I reach for the doorknob. I turn back over my shoulder to meet his gaze questioningly. "Happy looks good on you, kid. I never liked how that turd dimmed your shine. We'll fix this and you keep that happy going."

I smile affectionately at him before heading back to start my investigation. He is quickly becoming a real friend, not just a 'work friend''. I'm learning that when you let people in, sometimes they surprise you in a good way.

Settling back in at the desk in Colin's office, I pull up the last board presentation off the server. These sales projections look way off. I feel my forehead pinch as I dig through my bag for the printout I used during the meeting. Comparing the two documents, I find notable changes. The copy on the server makes the project look like a risky investment rather than the golden egg it is.

Quickly flipping through files, I find five more with glaring discrepancies that could have sizable impacts on the project. Wiring diagrams, budgets, donation projections. Someone changed all of them—just enough to cause issues without raising suspicions. I stare down at the documents spread out and chew on my thumbnail.

Who has the access to do this? Who benefits from us failing?

Warm hands cup my arms, and his distinct smell pulls my focus. Colin leans over my shoulder and follows my gaze to the table. "What are you working on?"

I'm not ready to share this news yet. Not until I know more. "Just checking on something Stan mentioned. How was the call with legal?"

He hums, pausing before answering. "More delays on the provisional patent filing. Can't quite get a straight answer out of them on why it's taking so long to hear." Colin strokes my biceps with his thumbs, sending shivers down my spine. "Ready to get going?"

I stare down at the papers still spread in front of me. "I have one more call to make here; gotta clean up a couple of things." Turning my head towards him, I look up at his handsome face. "Did you hear about the prototype exploding this morning?"

His hands still. "No, everybody alright? They find the cause?"

I turn to face him fully. "Yes, and yes. There was a wrong dimension on the drawing. They're refabricating the pieces now. We lost a bit of time, though."

"Well, that's *fecking grand*. I'll go check it out while you make your call. Leave for dinner in, say… twenty minutes?" Despite the stress in his tone, his eyes turn molten as they meet mine.

Another deep breath of his comforting smell and I relax my shoulders. Since he walked in, my tension has lessened a bit. I don't feel as alone or in my head as I had five minutes ago. Returning his smile, I allow myself a moment to imagine. What if this was my life? To go home with him like this after every long day. Wouldn't it be nice to have someone to lighten the load, like he did yesterday? Already thinking about another night in Colin's arms, I nod to him. "Twenty minutes."

With a last squeeze of my arms and a wink, Colin heads out to the production floor and I pull out my cell, already scrolling through my contacts.

The call picks up after the third ring. "What's up, Queen B?"

"Hey Gabe, I need a favor…"

CHAPTER THIRTY

Himself

COLIN

When I get to the production floor, I can still see ugly black marks on the workbench and back wall where our prototype had sat yesterday. Anything salvageable seems to be laying out on top. Frowning, I pick up a hunk of melted, twisted plastic from the bin of broken pieces under the workbench to inspect.

What the hell happened here?

Feeling a presence beside me, I turn to find a man at my side, also staring at the piece in my hand. He is maybe in his mid-to late-forties, dirty blond hair and intelligent brown eyes. Trim, not overly bulky in a polo shirt and jeans.

"Hell of a mess." His tone is neutral, maybe a little cagey.

"Aye. I don't think we've met. Colin McLeary—engineering lead on this mess." I turn fully and hold out my hand to the man.

He pauses briefly before giving a single firm pump. "Stan Meyrick, production manager."

I give him a nod and grin as I recall dinner with Brianna last night. "Stan, the production manager of the pink smart screens?"

Stan chuckles and his whole demeanor changes. His shoulders relax and his expression becomes more friendly. "Brianna told you about that, huh?" I give him another smile and nod. "Wish shipping fuckups were all I had to worry about today."

That's a sobering thought. "Thank goodness everyone is ok. What happened? Brianna mentioned a dampening issue?" I ask.

He studies my face for a beat with a curious gleam in his eyes. "Yea. The dimension on the server copy was wrong. One of the guys turned it on and the vibrations set the battery off."

"I'll get the Dublin engineering team on a call in the morning. They'll have to remodel all the designs. This shouldn't have happened. If you need anything at all from my guys, just let me know. C.A.E. has been working on this for months, but we've been pouring sweat into this for years." I look Stan in the eye to make it clear how serious I am.

"Ok, happy to sit down with the engineering team after you run those models."

"Grand, I'll set it up."

Tossing the scrap back in the bin, I brush my hands off on my pants and check my watch. "Well, I better go get Brianna. I promised her I'd be ready to get dinner about now. Good to meet you though, happy to put a face to the name."

Stan's eyes narrow as he squints slightly. "You and Brianna seem pretty close." He shoves his hands in his jean pockets and rocks back on his heels. The casual stance belies the intensity of his gaze.

Taking a moment to collect my thoughts, I can't help but feel a tinge of discomfort under the weight of the man's penetrating stare. "Aye, we've been joined at the hip on this project for over a month. She's one hell of a woman. Who wouldn't want to get to know her?"

Stan's eyes relax, and a smirk appears on his lips. He looks like a man who's just figured out a puzzle. "That she is, indeed. One hell of a special woman. Better get going before she gets hangry. See ya around, Mr. Disney World." Chuckling to himself, Stan strides back to his office before I can ask what he meant by that.

No time to ask now, anyway. I rush back to my office to find Brianna done with her call and ready to go.

Since we went to Pop last night, I decide to take Brianna to my favorite local pub for some Irish comfort food and a drink. She still looks distracted as we pull into the lot. The pub is a bit more crowded with the dinner rush, so we opt to sit at the bar.

I wrap my arm around Brianna's waist as we move towards the stools. We pass a table of men who haven't stopped staring at her ass. I glare at them as I move my hand to the small of her back in a clearly possessive move.

Brianna seems oblivious to the attention she's receiving as she looks around the pub. "Is this where you disappear to sometimes?"

I relax as I slide onto the stool next to her. Does she realize how *beautiful* she is? "Not as posh as Pop, t'a be sure, but the food is good, and it reminds me of home."

The owner, the same burly bartender I'd met on my first visit, steps over with a couple of menus to plop down in front of us. "What's it t'a be?"

"Evening. I'll have a pint of Guinness. Brianna, dear, they have Magners Cider on tap. The fish and chips are fantastic here." I turn to her as she scans the brief menu, lips pursed.

"That sounds good. Pint of Magners and the fish and chips, please—," she looks up and squints briefly at his name tag, "—Himself?"

I quirk a smile at her confusion. A surprised Brianna doesn't happen often, as far as I can tell, but she is almost as adorable as Shy Brianna. "I'll have the shepherd's pie, Brendan." I gather the menus up and hand them to the man, who only grunts and heads back to the computer.

Turning back to Brianna, I smile as her wide eyes continue to take in the pub. With her slim dress, high heels, and sleek ponytail sitting ramrod straight at the bar, she seems out of place. She is a sapphire surrounded by gold- both precious, but one just sparkles more.

"I like the aesthetic here. Sophisticated man cave crossed with a rustic cabin thing. How did you find this place?" Brianna turns towards me, the momentum sets her stool swinging. She tries to catch herself on the rail, but her heel slips. Moving quick, I snake my arm out to catch her and drop a quick kiss on her surprised lips. She smiles and blushes as she turns her seat back forward.

The entire table of men now glares back at me over Brianna's shoulder, which only makes my smile widen. Call me a jealous son of a bitch, but I'm *fecking* proud to be the man with Brianna. "Johnson suggested it, actually."

"Johnson? As in the pm I work with, Johnson?" Her eyebrow quirks up in disbelief.

Brendan returns with our pints, allowing me to extend my amusement at her expression.

"Aye, Johnson the pm. By the way, is that a first name or last name?"

Brianna's drink pauses halfway to her mouth and her lips purse in a comical expression. "You know what? I have no idea. He's always been just *Johnson*."

"He's a decent lad when you get to know him. Also, the only non *kiss-arse* in the place." Her eyebrow hitches higher over the rim of her drink. I chuckle and hold my hands up in mock surrender. "Present company excluded, of course."

Brianna gives a content sigh as she places her cider down in front of her. The tension leaves her shoulders bit by bit.

"So you've never told me. How did you end up in this career?" I take a sip of my Guinness and wait for her response.

"Oh, I've always been a bit of a control freak. Figured I should find a way to monetize it." She gives me a self-deprecating smile, and I chuckle.

"No, seriously."

She looks thoughtful as she takes another sip of her cider. "I got a business degree in college, but wasn't sure what to do with it. When I was an intern, I worked in the finance department. I'm good with numbers, but found it kind of boring. There was this one project manager I worked with, though, who was amazing. I watched him get involved with every department on the project. It was magical." Lost in a memory, her smile spreads across her face and her eyes take on a distant gaze. After another fortifying sip of cider, she continues her story.

"I cornered him in the cafeteria one day and just started asking him questions. He indulged me. I spent the rest of that summer following him like a puppy. When I graduated, he hired me as a project coordinator, working under him at C.A.E. Taught me everything I know." Her smile turns bittersweet. "He... left C.A.E. last year, and I still miss him."

Brendan arrives with our food and a second round of drinks. I watch Brianna as she takes her first bite of the flaky fish.

Her eyes close, and she moans slightly before raising her napkin to her lips and turning to me. "This is amazing. You were so right. The batter is crispy without being heavy, and the fish is so buttery." She eagerly dives back into her meal.

We chat as dinner continues. Her walls are down and I'm able to ask questions about her childhood and family. This is the traditional first date we would have had if we'd met the conventional way.

As Brianna scrapes the ketchup off her plate with her last fry, her cell rings and she excuses herself to take it somewhere quieter. I follow her with my eyes as she weaves through tables to the back by the bathrooms.

Brendan puts the check down next to me, an assessing look on his face. "That be your dream lass, I assume. I t'ought it were impossible?"

I lift one hip as I fish my wallet out, a happy grin splitting my face. "I guess I made my own fate."

"Fair play, you. Now don't fuck it up." He taps my card on the bar top once before running it.

"I don't aim to."

Brianna's eyes cloud in thought as she returns, but they clear, and she smiles as she reaches me. "Ready to go home?"

Home.

My heart swells at the sound of that. With a last nod at Brendan as I take my card, I lead Brianna to the car, my hand firmly anchored to the small of her back. She surprises me by pushing up on her toes to kiss me as I hold the car door open for her. Her fingers trail down my chest and her eyes hold promise as she lowers herself into the vehicle.

I keep my hand on her thigh during the drive. She twines our fingers together as we walk to the front door. Riley happily barks as he bounces at our feet. As I watch him sniff around the backyard, Brianna twines her arms around my waist from behind. I turn in her embrace and drop a kiss to her forehead. She tilts her head back and I indulge in a sensual exploration of lips and tongue.

This is heaven.

A bump at my calf draws my attention. Riley is back and making his presence known. Reluctantly, I end the kiss and lock up behind me. As Brianna takes my hand again, her eyes darken with desire. She bites her lip as she walks backwards towards her bedroom, guiding me with her.

I need no encouragement. We come together in a hungry rush of hands and lips. Clothes drop abandoned along the way. Brianna climaxes twice before I find my own release and we fall asleep in each other's arms. Utterly content.

CHAPTER THIRTY-ONE

Make it a Double

BRIANNA

"Do you want a drink?" Anna asks from the depths of her refrigerator.

I slick back my already smooth ponytail and look up from the piles of documents spread across her kitchen island. "Got any Jameson?"

"Not unless I run down to the bar. I got Fireball!"

I consider for a beat. "Got any hard cider?"

Anna disappears deeper into the fridge until only her denim-clad Georgia peach is visible. Glass clinks as she digs through the various supplies. "Yes! Found two bottles—you want the cider or the whiskey?" She stands and looks at me.

"Girl, do you need to ask?" I level her with a weighted look.

"ANGRY BALLS!" we cry in unison, laughing.

Anna pours the amber cider into fresh glasses and then digs out a shot glass.

"Better make it a double," I say, as the first shot of cinnamon whiskey joins the cider. With a shrug, she pours more directly from the bottle without measuring.

I take a sip—like apple pie in a glass.

Anna takes her own drink and comes around to sit on the stool next to me. She waves her hand at the stacks. "So what's the verdict?"

"Business is good. Still might be a little too early to talk expansion, but we're heading in the right direction." I push my latest calculations towards her on the counter.

"Shoot, I've been itchin' for a challenge. Anythin' we can do in the meantime?"

"Well, ladies' night is always a hit! The bar is packed down there. We can do more events or theme nights. If that goes well, we could expand the back section a bit and add doors. Make it more event friendly?"

Anna lets out a whoop of excitement. We brainstorm ideas as we finish our drinks—80s night, five course prix fixe menu. She jots them down on her phone and promises to come up with some more. "So," Anna says as she lowers her empty glass to the counter with a thunk. "How is it going with the gorgeous Mr. McLeary?" She must be tipsy because she waggles her eyebrows at me, looking ridiculous.

I blush and chug the rest of my drink as I think about how to respond. It's been a few weeks since we started sleeping together, and it's felt like a dream. Our days have changed little, but they are more light-hearted. Our nights are spent together—it's not always mussed sheets and seeking hands. Some nights, we just sit and read on the couch together. Others, we talk about nothing and everything. By some unspoken agreement, Colin always ends up in my room with me. I've gotten some of the best sleep of my life. "Good. Just keeping it casual—roommates with benefits." I keep my eyes on the papers as I gather them up, avoiding eye contact.

"Sure, casual." Anna draws out the word to twice its length, sounding about as sarcastic as a Southern girl can. She lifts her phone and starts typing out something.

"Oh, no—what are you up to?" I eye her uneasily.

"Calling in reinforcements." Moments pass as she sends another message and waits for a response. Her phone buzzes once and she puts it down with a satisfied smile.

"Nic?" Really don't think I'm up to an inquisition from both of them.

There's a knock on her door, and Anna jumps up to answer. Asher Ramstead—our lead bartender from Pop—strides in with six hard ciders held between his fingers. "You rang, ladies?"

I laugh. "Well, I guess that's one benefit to living over a bar!"

"The commute to work is fantastic too!" Anna shuts the door and settles back into her seat.

Asher places the bottles on the counter and scrutinizes the Fireball skeptically. "What the hell are you girls drinking?"

Anna and I exchange a glance, then shout "ANGRY BALLS!" again in unison before crumbling into laughter on the counter.

Ok, maybe I'm tipsy too.

Anna walks Asher through the recipe, and soon we have fresh drinks in our hands.

"So what are we angry about?" Asher stands with his hands braced on the counter, muscular forearms on full display. A blond eyebrow arches over an icy blue eye as he eyes the drinks dubiously.

I laugh again. "You don't have to be angry to drink angry balls. You just need to like apple pie. Here, try it." I push my drink across the counter to him.

Normally, I keep a professional distance from the staff. As Pop's business manager, I often end up being the bad guy, and it's just easier when you are not friendly. Asher's different, though. He was our first hire, he helped us grow the business. As head bartender, we often include him in discussions and decisions. Also, did I mention I'm tipsy?

"Ok, yes, that is delicious; I will start recommending that. So, how is that new boyfriend of yours?"

Dropping my head into my hands, I grunt indelicately. "He's not my boyfriend! He is a client," Anna gives a snort of disbelief, "whom I am casually seeing." I glare at Anna. Traitor.

Asher is shaking his head. "Bullshit. There is nothing casual about how that man looks at you."

"That's what I'm saying!" Anna flails her arm wide at Asher as she takes another sip of her drink.

"We agreed—exclusivity but no strings. When he goes home, it's over." I nod with confidence I'm not feeling, and drown my doubts in liquor.

"But darlin', if you have actual feelings for the man, why not give it a real shot? You've been so happy lately. Why end it?" Anna's eyes are full of sympathy. And cartoon hearts.

"For what it's worth, I think he's a stand-up guy. We've chatted a few times when you've come for dinner or stopped in for paperwork." Asher shrugs.

"It doesn't matter. He lives in Ireland. His family is in Ireland. Hell, his job is in Ireland. When this project is over, he will be returning to..."

"Ireland," they say in unison.

"Exactly. There's no point getting attached." My heart twists. Colin is heading to that environmental conference this week and being here alone is going to feel so weird. If I'm this affected by the thought of a week apart, how am I going to take it when he leaves for good?

"Well, ladies, I better head back downstairs. Thanks for the break from the hordes of horny women." He shudders as he heads to the door.

"Hey!" I yell after him. "Those horny women pay all our bills. Better get that smile back in place."

Asher turns back, his signature toothpaste smile in place. "How's that, boss?"

Laughing, we send him off and finish our second round. I fish my cell from the back pocket of my jeans. "I better get a ride home. Wasn't planning on drinking this much."

Me

Hey - can you pick me up at Pop?

I take another slug of my drink while I wait for a response. The three dots appear almost immediately.

Colin

You Ok? What happened?

His response makes me smile. His first reaction is so protective and caring. My heart flutters.

Me

Yea - ended up having a couple drinks with Anna and shouldn't drive.

Colin

haha you girls have fun?

Me

always! :)

Colin

good. Let me get changed and I'll head over. Want any greasy drive-thru?

My brows knot in confusion. Why would I want fast food? I'm literally sitting next to a genius chef.

Me

… you do remember I'm at a restaurant, right?

Colin

yea, but would Anna ever serve greasy nuggets and fries that soak up the alcohol?

My cheeks ache from smiling. I look up to find Anna watching me with a smile ghosting her lips. Ducking my head to hide my warming cheeks, I drain my glass.

"Colin coming to get you?" Her voice is even.

"Yea—in a bit." I reach over and grab a few items off the charcuterie plate Anna set out earlier. I chance a glance back up at Anna—she's still watching me. "What?"

Anna shakes her head slightly, the corners of her mouth tilting up more. "It's just great to see you happy again. You're so relaxed. I don't think y'all were this centered even in college." I open my mouth to reply, but she holds her hand up to stop me and continues. "Ya don't need to tell me this has nothing to do with your roommate with benefits situation. Don't care what got ya here, darlin'. Just keep making room for joy." Anna reaches across the distance between us and clasps my hand.

A warmth spreads in my chest. Growing up, I didn't get much support or affection. It was Anna and Nic that taught me what love feels like. Even after a decade, I sometimes forget how good it feels to have someone in your corner. "As long as you do the same, Anna. Your food is best when you're happy. Just keep wowing those critics and we'll be able to expand just like you want."

Her eyes glitter with unshed tears, and I feel an answering burn in my own. Slipping out of my seat, I reach out to her, and we clasp each other tightly. We both sniffle as we fight back tears. We've both fought so hard over the last decade to get where we want to be. Just a little more. One more hard push and we'll be there.

Emotions spent, we lean away from each other, sharing a wet chuckle. We wipe our cheeks and point out where mascara has run. One more shot of whiskey each seems like a brilliant idea—which Anna insists on pouring pineapple juice into.

"To us—chasing our dreams." I cry as I lift my shot glass, scrutinizing the contents.

"To us—choosing joy." We clink glasses before throwing back the shots. Surprisingly, not terrible!

My cell vibrates on the table.

My heart thumps at the endearment. He probably meant it funny, but it turns my insides liquid all the same.

Anna pushes off her stool and heads for the door. "Come on, let's head down before your hormones light my stool on fire."

I chuckle and follow her out. "We'll come grab my car tomorrow."

Anna shrugs as she shuts and locks her apartment door behind us. "No rush. Come for dinner and grab it then. I have a new recipe I want to try."

We head down the back stairs and through the kitchen of Pop. A chorus of "Hello, chef" follows Anna. She nods to each person in return. As we exit the swinging doors, I see Colin, and my chest flutters as his grin spreads.

"There's my girl!" Colin reaches an arm out to me and I let him tuck me by his side.

I can't help but grin as he kisses my forehead. We've kept clear boundaries outside of the house—even at Pop. This is the most PDA I've experienced, but I'm too tipsy to care. A warm feeling of safety and contentment washes over me. I'm not ready to let that feeling go.

We say our goodbyes, and Colin leads me to his rental car. Once in the car, he checks my seatbelt and drops a surprise kiss on my lips. True to his word, he takes me through the nearest drive-through and I giggle as I dig into a packet of nuggets and fries.

Once home and settled into my king-sized bed, I curl against his side, seeking his warmth. Colin wraps his arm around me and absently strokes my back with one hand as he holds his tablet in the other to read. I drift off with a smile on my face and my fingers resting over his heart, the steady beat comforting me.

Chapter Thirty-Two

Ladies' Night

Rachel

My finger trails around the stem of my martini glass as I watch the bartender through my lashes. When his attention turns towards me, I let a sensual smile spread across my scarlet lips and lean forward slightly, squeezing my arms to better frame my cleavage. The man next to me drones on, and I spare him a glance.

His suit is expensive, as is his watch, and the Tesla fob he casually swings on his finger. Not bad looking, late thirties, maybe, with one of those dad bods and the early signs of thinning hair. The faded line on his left hand tells me he's probably married. I don't care, as long as he keeps paying for my drinks.

It's Ladies' Night at Pop, and I haven't paid for a single drink all night. Normally, I stick to the higher end lounges. It's a better hunting ground for rich men. The other assistants won't shut up about this place though, so why the hell not give it a try? The drinks are definitely yummy.

As is the hunky bartender. I watch as he makes his way across the bar, back towards the kitchen doors. He props his palms on the surface as he leans towards a customer, his biceps and pecs pop under his tight T-shirt.

Yum.

For the next hour, I compete for the bartender's attention. If I can't land a potential sugar daddy tonight, might as well go home with the hottest man in the bar. Eventually

Mr. Dad-bod leaves and another man takes his place. My martini never runs dry, but the bartender never stays long.

My new suitor is closer to my age, handsome in that all-American jock kind of way. Nice dress shirt and jeans, fancy watch and haircut. He works at his daddy's company and his whole demeanor screams 'trust fund baby'.

The bartender looks towards the door. A slow grin spreads across his face and he walks towards the server station, wiping his hands on a rag. "Hey, man." He reaches out and shakes the hand of a man I can't quite see through the crowd.

"Asher, how's it going?" the newcomer says. His voice is familiar, so I continue watching the scene. The man leans forward into one of those weird one-armed man hugs through the opening.

Holy shit, it's Colin McLeary. What is he doing here? How is he on a first-name basis with the hot bartender?

Fuck, are they both gay?

I lose the trail of their conversation over the noise of the crowd. Enough with this. I'll just walk over and talk to Colin directly. I take a few steps closer, tugging my neckline further down. The kitchen doors open beside him and two women walk out—a taller blond and a shorter brunette.

"There's my girl." Colin smiles and wraps his arm around the brunette, tucking her close to his side and kissing her forehead. She turns to speak to Asher, giving me a clear view of her profile.

Brianna!?

Darting back to my seat before they see me, I stare daggers at them. Drinking in every detail I can from this distance. Brianna hugs the blond girl, then waves at Asher as Colin escorts her to the exit. My vision tinges red as I notice his hand resting on her ass.

He's ignored me for months, but the Ice Queen has him wrapped around her finger? We'll just see about that. I'll burn her to the ground.

CHAPTER THIRTY-THREE

Unhealthy Competition

COLIN

My cell vibrates on my desk, pulling my attention from the latest test report I am reviewing. Shocked to see my sister's name on the screen, I quickly answer the call. "Hey, Aisling, is everything ok? Ma? Sinéad? The kids?"

She chuckles, but it sounds off. I'm instantly on alert. "Hey baby bro. How do you always know? Ma, Sin, and the kids are fine. It's Bryan… he's cheating on me."

"What? I'll kill the bastard. *Feck* the convention, I'm coming home." I turn to my laptop, pulling up a travel site, intent on getting home to my family.

My stomach drops as guilt hits me. I'm here obsessing over a woman and my family is imploding.

"Hold it right there, mister. There will be no *fecking* of conventions." She laughs, but I don't think it's funny. "It's probably best you aren't here. Don't need to be explaining to the kids why their favorite uncle is in jail for murdering their Da."

"I'm their only uncle," I mutter—more out of habit than anything else.

"Look, I know you are busy changing the world, and we're all immensely proud of you. I didn't call so you'd feel guilty and come home. Figured if you found out from Ma or Sin you'd blow a gasket and jump on the first plane. Admit it, you already looked at flights." Silently I close my browser window with the flights search still up. "I think I also just wanted to hear my favorite little brother's voice."

My chest heaves with a heavy sigh, and I pinch my nose. "Again...only brother." The heat is gone from my voice. "I wish I was there to help. What do you need?"

"Nothing. I kicked Bryan out—it's our family farm and I'm staying. Mammy is going to move in with us to help with the kids."

"What about the farm? Don't you need another set of hands?"

"We'll be ok. Liam is old enough to help with more of the chores. If Ma is watching Emily, that frees me up more. I'll just hire another hand this season. So don't rush back. I know you."

I drop my head into my hands, feeling powerless. "I'm so sorry, Ash. You deserve so much better."

She sniffles slightly. "I know. So what's new with you? How's it going with Brianna? I want all the details. Make me believe love still exists."

"She's amazing. You would love her. You should see her with these engineers. She's this tiny fireball who just makes things magically happen. We had a hiccup on the project, but she's somehow gotten everything back on schedule and budget."

Things are actually going well. The only real holdup is legal and the provisional patent filings. With a sigh, I refresh my email again, willing some new information to appear.

"That's awesome. I *will* love her when I meet her. What's this about a conference? Are you going together?" Aisling's tone is even. She seems happy to be talking about something other than her marriage.

I should focus on the conference right now, anyway. Since the engine is still at an extremely confidential point, we didn't book a booth or presentation slot. My primary goal is to network with other companies interested in expanding their green energy presence. If I come back with connections and future pitch dates, that's all we really need.

"It's a green energy conference in Las Vegas. Unfortunately, Brianna has to stay here and keep the project running smoothly." Leaning back in my chair, I spear my fingers through my hair. The conference is an important opportunity, but I can't help the disappointment I feel at leaving Brianna behind.

"You sound happy when you talk about her, Col. It's good to hear you happy. You must really love her." Her voice sounds wistful, but also full of pride.

My mind drifts to visions of a future with Brianna. I do *fecking* love her and I am going to find a way to make this work long term. "I do. I really do love her—is that crazy? It's only been a couple of months."

"Sometimes it just takes a moment. Look at Ma and Da."

We'd grown up hearing stories of how our father saw our mother at a crowded festival. He instantly fell in love with her and they were married within a month. My eldest sister, Aisling, was born barely nine months later. Our father was never afraid to show his devotion to our mother. He raised me to respect my feelings rather than bury them. It may be too soon for most people, but I need to tell her how I feel.

A commotion on the other end of the line breaks my train of thought. I hear Ash sigh. "I gotta go, baby brother. Emily had a nightmare and needs me. I love you, Col. Don't rush back, but maybe... call a bit more often? We miss you."

I say my goodbyes, promising to call more often, then disconnect the call. Groaning in frustration, I bend, head in hands and elbows on the desk. Between Richard breathing down her throat, and that sudden reappearance of her ex, I really don't want to leave Brianna here alone.

Her argument makes perfect sense—someone needs to stay behind to keep an eye on Dick—I mean, Richard. Doesn't mean I have to like it, though.

She'd be *fecking* pissed if she heard what I was thinking. I know she can handle herself. Hell, she's probably the most capable woman I've ever met. Doesn't stop me from feeling protective of her. If it's within my power, I want to make her load lighter. Support her in all ways.

Another buzzing to my right pulls me back to business. Clearing my throat, I answer the phone.

"Hey, this is Joe Fuentes from legal," the voice on the other end says. "Do you have a minute?"

I sit straighter in my chair, fully at attention. "Heya, Joe. Go ahead, assuming this is about the patent?"

There is an awkward clearing of his throat. "Yea. Turns out there's an almost identical application under review. They submitted papers the day before us. Everything's being held up while the patent office compares both designs," he takes an audible breath, "but it's not looking good."

My stomach twists in knots and my temples tingle as the blood drains from my face. "How is that possible?"

"Sometimes these things happen. Like when two movies come out the same summer with similar plots. It's possible two different people had the same idea around the same time." His tone doesn't sound confident. That's one hell of a coincidence.

"You don't sound so sure, man."

"Well, there are other, less pleasant, explanations. As a lawyer, I try not to throw accusations around until I'm sure. But, as a lawyer, I'm also highly suspicious. Especially of a tiny startup out of California coming up with the exact design in a couple months that took your team two years."

I turn that over in my head as I swivel to face the window. "What do you need me to do?"

"You keep doing the engineering. Let me do the lawyering. I got a guy looking into this company. I'll let you know when I find something concrete."

I'm not sure how long I sit there, blindly staring at the skyline after the call disconnects.

What the fuck is going on here? This project can't fail now. I've spent two years trying to make this dream a reality. Duncan has been hinting at wanting to retire, spend more time in the country with his grandkids. This engine was going to be Duncan's legacy. I have to protect it at all costs.

Vaguely, I register my office door opening and closing. The warm smell of vanilla hits me just before her delicate fingers gently land on my shoulders. Silently, she rubs the knots out of my muscles. With a contented grunt, I reach out and squeeze her hand, bringing her palm to my lips for a kiss before turning to face her.

Brianna tilts her head and scrunches her nose as she studies my face. "What's wrong?"

"Legal called—more delays. Another company submitted a very similar design before us."

Eyes widening, Brianna gasps in surprise and drops her hand. Craving her comforting touch again, I catch her hand and twine my fingers with hers, tugging her between my spread knees.

She looks shocked, but at least she doesn't pull away. "What is legal going to do?"

"Joe said they'd handle it. We're supposed to just keep moving forward with development in the meantime." I sigh and look up into her wide, cobalt eyes. "So, I guess I should still go to the conference tomorrow." My voice sounds whiny, even to my own ears.

"Right, the conference. I'd almost forgotten." She sounds disappointed. Is that a slight pout on her full lips? Adorable.

"That's not like you, Ms. Chance." I use our entwined fingers to pull her even closer until her thighs touch my chest and my chin rests on her soft belly. "You know you can come with me." I shoot her the grin that usually makes her melt.

She rewards me with the barest twitch of her lips in amusement. "Oh, no. We already settled this. If things are going off track, I need to stay here even more now."

Standing, I tease her by gliding my body up hers. Ok, maybe I'm teasing myself more than her.

I place a tender kiss on her temple before stepping away. "Let's grab an early dinner and head home so I can pack."

CHAPTER THIRTY-FOUR

Splish Splash

BRIANNA

Colin excuses himself after dinner to pack a bag for the conference and call his sister. I've wandered to my favorite thinking spot out by the pool. Usually, the sound of the waterfall soothes me, but today it just isn't cutting it. As I nibble a bit of dry skin on my lip and play with my fingers in my lap, my thoughts are anything but peaceful.

I'm not sure what to do about the discrepancies in the project files. Something is still not adding up, but I can't figure out what exactly is wrong. Someone is changing the server copies. But why? And who? And what about the patent?

"Hey, love. What are you doing out here?" I turn my head to see Colin standing beside me. I didn't even hear him come out here. He straddles the lounger and sits behind me, kissing my neck before rubbing my shoulders. "Why so tense?"

It's time to share my suspicions with Colin. "I think someone has been messing with our project files." I hold my breath, waiting for his response.

His fingers pause as he speaks, and his voice is cautious. "What makes you think that?"

"First, I noticed the numbers were incorrect in one of my spreadsheets weeks ago. Then, after that explosion, Stan noticed someone had altered the blueprints. To be safe, I made an offline backup. When I started comparing more files against the server copies, I found more anomalies."

"Ok," his voice is slow and measured, "shared files get messed up all the time. The offline backup is a good idea. Maybe an engineer overwrote the file? Are you sure you have the right version? Maybe you made a mistake."

My stomach drops and my chest feels tight as I jump up from the lounger and pace towards the pool. He doesn't believe me. This is why I said nothing before. Breathe, Brianna. Two deep breaths. I grip my hands into fists and whirl to face Colin.

"You're not listening. My files don't get 'messed up'. You've seen how careful I am with project records. I've been twice as vigilant on this project! Something weird is going on, Colin. I think it might have to do with the patent interference." I let out another shaky breath, begging him with my eyes to hear me. "This is an inside job. I feel it in my gut."

Colin's face is carefully blank, but his eyes pinch with concern. He stands from the lounger and slowly approaches me. His hands gently stroke my tense arms reassuringly and he wears a sincere expression as he places a tender kiss on my forehead. "You've been under a lot of stress. Just take a few breaths and calm down."

My breath rushes out. Bands of anxiety tighten around my chest. My heart pounds. Each breath is harder and faster than the last. It feels like someone has replaced the oxygen with acid. Every muscle in my body tenses painfully. My eyes sting with mounting tears and I feel like I'm going to throw up. My skin is hot and tight, like I'm about to explode.

"No," I practically yell as I shrug out of his hands and step closer to the pool and further out of reach. "Don't patronize me. My job is to worry. All the time. Keep everything organized and remove every obstacle before you engineers realize they're there. You have no idea what it's like as a woman in a male-dominated industry. I have to work twice as hard to be taken seriously, just to make 20% less money than my male coworkers. And most of them are half as qualified, too."

I aggressively swipe at the angry tears escaping down my cheeks. "And God forbid I show any sort of emotion at work. If I were a man, I'd be called focused, but as a woman, I'm *the Ice Queen*. If I step up to drive results, I'm a bitch whereas a man is called assertive. So I smile and bury all the shit deep and don't let them see my cracks. Society has a million expectations for me—and most of them conflict! I play the game, I keep my head up. Every minute of every day. It's fucking exhausting."

By the end of my speech, I'm trembling and my voice is shaking. I turn towards the waterfall, willing the sounds to soothe me.

Colin steps in front of me, his eyes wide with surprise. One hand reaches out to touch my arm. "You're right, I don't know what it's like. If you just calm down..."

Before another word can leave his lips, I lose my tenuous hold on the anxiety attack that's been spiraling through me. I let out a scream and shake my hands in front of me to stop his reach.

Colin takes a step back to avoid my flailing. I close my eyes and let out another screech. A shout hardly even registers in my mind, but the splash of cold water on my feet shocks me from my chaotic thoughts.

I open my eyes to find myself alone. My lungs are still heaving with great breaths, hungry for oxygen. I look around just as Colin clears the surface of the pool with a gasp. I cover my open mouth with my hand as I stare at a very wet Colin.

The shock snaps the last tendrils of anxiety holding my thoughts hostage. "Oh my God, did I push you in? I'm so sorry." I rush over to the towel bin and then to the pool stairs to meet him.

Colin slowly wades to the stairs, the weight of his sodden clothes an obvious hindrance. His face unreadable, water drips out of his curls and traces the harsh planes of his nose and cheekbones. His white dress shirt is now sheer, and it clings to every dip and curve of his muscled chest.

My own Mr. Darcy emerging from the lake. A warmth spreads in my belly at the sight of him. So not the time.

His eyes smolder. He keeps walking towards me. Slowly, more of his drenched frame emerges. Like the shirt, his dress slacks mold to his body, leaving absolutely nothing to the imagination.

I step closer to the edge to hand him the towel. I bite my trembling lip to stop myself from laughing as the absurdity hits me. An indelicate snort escapes. Colin raises an eyebrow at me. The tension snaps, and I burst out laughing. Great gusts of laughter that leave me bent over, clutching my stomach.

"That's it." Colin darts forward and grabs me around the thighs to haul me backwards into the pool.

"NO! Colin, stop it. I said I was sorry! It was an accident!"

The cold water is already up to my knees. I balance myself on his strong shoulders and toss the towel back to the patio to save it from the soaking I'm about to get. With two hands now free, I weave my arms around his neck so he can't throw me.

Taking a deep breath, Colin flops back under the water and brings me down with him. As we resurface, I cling to his neck with one arm as I push the sodden hair out of my face with the other hand.

Colin can stand this deep in the water, but I'm struggling. His arm snakes around my back to hold me up. Automatically, I wrap my legs around his waist and hug him tighter with my arms.

He tries to give me a stern look, but the growing bulge pressing against my throbbing center is undeniable proof he's not mad. I give him my best innocent look and am rewarded with his slow grin and a chuckle. He cups my cheek with his free hand and gives me a tender kiss on the lips.

With a content sigh, I lay my head on his shoulder and cuddle him. I can feel his pulse against my forehead. I breathe deeply in time with the steady rhythm as my racing heart calms. He locks his arm around my hips, keeping me close. The other hand rubs my back in a soothing, slow pattern.

As I count my breaths, I stroke my fingers through the hair at the nape of his neck until I can feel the last traces of the panic attack dissipate. "You should never say 'just calm down' to a woman having a panic attack. Or really anyone."

He clutches me closer. "I'm sorry—that came out wrong. The rest of the sentence was going to be 'we can sit down and talk it through'. Maybe I should have started with that part."

I give him another indelicate snort and pull his hair slightly, which makes him chuckle.

"I never meant I didn't believe you. I'm an engineer, *a ghrá*, I tend to try to fix things. Starting with ruling out the most logical explanations first. I'm sorry my words were careless. You are exceptional at what you do. I've met no man, or woman, as clever. Or anyone with such a talent for keeping engineers on time! You are a force of nature, my Brianna girl. Joe from legal also said he thought this was suspicious, so you are not alone at all."

I snuggle deeper into his neck, letting his words soothe my insecurities. I know what I bring to the table, but sometimes it's overwhelming fighting for the least I deserve. Sometimes, my inner voice is a real bitch. She tells me I'm not enough. If I was prettier, or smarter, or softer, I'd get what I want. The guy wouldn't cheat. The promotion would be mine. My father wouldn't have left. I know it's all bullshit. But knowing something and truly believing it in your heart are two different things.

"I'm sorry I pushed you into the pool," I mumble.

His chest rumbles with a chuckle under my cheek. "You didn't. I stepped back to give you space and my foot landed on nothing but air." Colin kisses my forehead again. His hand still traces lazy lines on my back. I feel calmer. My chest is still a little tight, my breaths still shaky, but I don't feel alone.

The warmth of Colin's body around me in the cool pool seeps into my bones. His arms are tight, but supportive rather than constrictive. He isn't judging me. Colin listened to my concerns and trusted me enough—no, respected me enough—to believe me and want to help.

Like a partner.

My breath catches. Colin's always acted like my partner—even when I tried to keep him at arm's length. Sure, he is passionate and easygoing where I prefer structure and discipline, but that is why we work so well. We balance each other. Compensate for the other's weaknesses, but wholeheartedly celebrate each other's strengths.

Over the past few months, I've felt lighter than I have in years. All the best moments have been with him. My comments to Colin are true—I do constantly have to compromise myself to make life easier. I haven't done that once with Colin, though. With him, I can completely let go and be my genuine self.

I lift my head off his chest slowly to look into his eyes. His brows pinch slightly with concern, but those clear green depths hold warmth and care. De-tangling the fingers still clutching his shirt, I cup the sides of his sharp jaw. He leans into my palm briefly before turning his head to kiss my palm. My heart swells in my chest, feeling like it might burst. The realization hits me.

I am in love with Colin McLeary.

With slight pressure from my palm, I straighten his face and lean down to meet his lips with my own. I pour all the emotion I feel but am still too scared to say into the kiss.

After a moment of surprise, Colin kisses me back with the same tender urgency. His fingers spear the hair at the back of my neck, holding me close.

I rub my core against the growing bulge of his erection.

He moves both hands to my ass and grips me closer against him as he wades to the pool stairs again. I lock my ankles behind his back and grip his shoulders tighter. With purposeful steps, Colin climbs the stairs and heads towards the patio doors.

"My room," I mumble against his lips between kisses, "there's tile."

Without missing a step, Colin changes direction and heads towards where my bathroom opens to the courtyard. At the doors, I frantically unhook my feet and slide down his body, eagerly feeling for the handle behind my back. After a couple of tries, I finally get the door open. I back into the room, dragging Colin by the shirt with me.

He fumbles as he tries to kick off his shoes. One hand cups my jaw gently as his other fingers tuck into the back of my waistband. I skate my hands up his rapidly cooling shirt and my fingers get to work at his buttons. Our mouths barely leave each other, too busy weaving in an intricate pattern for words. Or breath.

Shivers race across my skin as his fingers inch up my shirt, his hand settling on the curve of my lower back. Urging me closer. Pulling back for air, I hold his heated gaze as I pull my shirt over my head. His eyes consume every inch of exposed skin like a man starved. Reaching behind me, I unsnap my bra, letting the straps fall off my shoulders in a striptease before dropping it completely on the floor.

With a groan, Colin steps forward. His lips are cold, but his touch leaves a hot trail from my lips to my throat. His hands skim the sides of my breasts slowly as he strokes down to my waist. My nipples, already peaked from the cold water, harden further. Hungry for his attention. As if reading my mind, his lips trail further to capture a pink nipple. Crying out at the sensation, I arch my back, pressing my breast further towards him. My hands clasp his shoulders for support, the wet fabric meets my touch. I attempt to work the fabric down his biceps, but it clings like a second skin.

Colin lifts his mouth, his eyes smoldering as he looks at me. He jerks at his shirt and it finally falls free to the tile. Before the wet plop even reaches my ears, he is already lavishing my other nipple with his tongue. I spear my fingers through his hair and hold him there. Seemingly satisfied that I won't move, Colin lets go of my waist and starts working on the button of my pants. His fingers whisper against my chilled skin as he rolls the slacks and underwear down my legs. As the material reaches my knees, he gracefully kneels down before me. I balance against his shoulders as he gets first one leg free and then the other.

"Colin, please. I need you." My voice is breathless and needy.

He stands immediately, the need in his eyes matching my own.

He cups my face with both of his hands and leans in for a drugging kiss. I drop my hands to his pants and try to undo them, but my numb fingers fumble at the button. I arch into the kiss, flattening my breasts against his chest. The sensation of his bare skin gliding over my nipples couples with the frustration of him still being partially dressed. I whimper as I continue tugging at his pants, then again at the loss of his hands. With a hurried jerk, he removes his pants and underwear. The motion completely at odds with the tender undressing I received.

Once we are both naked, we simply stare at each other as deep breaths rack our bodies. At some unspoken sign, we move in unison. A tangle of limbs and tongues. I cannot get enough of this man. His touch. His very presence.

He walks me backwards until the backs of my legs bump into the mattress. Lips still fused together, I wrap my arms around his neck and pull him with me as I sit on the edge of the mattress. Colin moves with me, one arm wrapped around my back while the other supports his weight. As we move further up the bed, I wrap one leg around his back, clinging to him.

Colin eases my head onto the pillow. He shifts his weight to the arm underneath me. His free hand trails along my arm until it finds and entwines our fingers. Reaching between us, I find his cock already hard and ready. After two languid pumps, I impatiently guide him to the entrance of my already wet core. He flexes his hips and nudges me a couple of times, teasing my clit. As I wrap my other leg around his hips, I tilt my hips to better meet his slow entry.

Panting, Colin lowers his forehead to mine as he finally buries himself to the hilt. We both lay there, unmoving, basking in the feeling of being connected. Colin begins to move in unhurried strokes. Almost fully leaving me before pushing back in.

A growing tingle at the base of my spine spreads as my orgasm builds. My breath comes in desperate gasps, and my free hand digs into the muscles of his ass to keep him near. Colin whispers heated words to my jaw and throat. I can't understand the Gaelic words, but his tone conveys passion and emotion.

My legs shake around his sides as my core clenches. "Colin, please." I have no idea what I'm asking for, but I know only he can give it to me.

His strokes are still slow and sensual, but he uses his arm to lift my hips higher, shifting the angle. With every thrust, his pelvis bumps my clit. And with every withdrawal he strokes my G-spot. The shaking of my legs increases and my fingers knead his muscles.

I open my eyes to find his expressive green gaze staring down at me. I see desire, affection, and determination. The look in his eyes is my undoing, and I shatter. Still staring into his eyes, I cry out as wave after wave of pleasure takes me.

My orgasm still raging, Colin gives in to his own. He drops his forehead to mine as wracking shudders take his body. I feel his cock pulse as he empties himself into me. As the shudders slow, Colin tightens his arm around me, holding me against him as he rolls onto his back. We lay like that for some time. Neither of us in a hurry to move and ruin the moment. Each of us trying to extend the connection as long as possible.

Eventually, I feel him soften inside me. With a sigh, Colin captures my lips in one more emotional kiss. Reluctantly, I roll off him and pad into the bathroom to clean myself up. As I wash my hands, Colin, in his naked glory, struts into the bathroom.

The picture of a man completely satisfied.

I hold his gaze in the mirror as he walks up behind me. He plants his hands on my hips for a quick squeeze and a passing kiss on my neck before he turns to lock the outside door and drape the soaked clothes over the side of the tub. I crawl back into bed with a happy sigh and stretch. I don't wait long before Colin is crawling in behind me and pulling me against him.

I smile as his comforting scent surrounds me and wiggle closer into his embrace. His warning moan makes me chuckle as I settle in. Tonight was different. This wasn't fucking. This felt like making love. That is my last thought before I drift off to sleep in his arms.

CHAPTER THIRTY-FIVE

I'm Done

BRIANNA

The sound of tinkling bells infiltrates my sleep and slowly wakes me. As I stretch my slightly aching muscles, I smile, remembering the mind-blowing night before. Eyes still closed, I reach out looking for Colin, but find only a warm pillow. Blinking back the last remains of sleep, I push myself up on my elbow and look around the room.

I am alone. Not even Riley is in his usual spot at the end of the bed. Where is everyone?

I am still debating if I should get up when Colin walks back into the bedroom, fully dressed and carrying a steaming cup of coffee. Seeing me awake, his lips spread into a tender smile as he approaches the bed, placing the mug on my nightstand. The bed dips as he sits, and I slide closer to him.

Colin tucks my tousled hair behind my ear before dropping a kiss to my forehead. "Morning, beautiful. How'd you sleep?"

"Fine, you?" The sheets fall to my waist as I sit up to take the steaming coffee. Colin licks his lips, eyes darkening with desire as he stares at my half-naked body.

A half-strangled moan escapes his lips. "God, I wish I had time to give you a proper good morning, but I have a flight to catch." He leans forward and nips at my lips and shoulder before standing back up. "I already let Riley out, but I have to finish packing. Get ready for work—if I stay here with you like that, I'm going to miss my flight." With one last heated look over his shoulder, he leaves the room.

After another long draw of coffee and a contented sigh, I go through my morning routine. Twenty minutes later, I'm walking into the living room, showered, hair in a French braid, dressed in a navy sheath dress and yellow heels. Colin is waiting by the door, giving Riley an affectionate scratch and whispering to him. They make an unlikely but adorable pair. The sight of them together never fails to make me smile.

He straightens as I approach and I tug on his button-down shirt to bring him down for a kiss. "Have I told you this is my favorite shirt?" The fabric is dark maroon, highlighting the red tones in his dark hair and making his green eyes pop. The collar points sport his initials embroidered in matching thread, giving it a bespoke look.

"In that case, I'll be sure to wear it more often, eh." He deepens the kiss, gripping my still damp braid to keep me close.

Reluctantly, I break the kiss and lean back, straightening the wrinkles out of his shirt. "You're going to miss your flight."

His dimple winks as he smiles down at me. He cups my jaw and strokes my cheek with his thumb. "I wish you were coming with me. This conference is going to be so boring."

Leaning into his hand, I smil back. "Someone has to stay behind and keep things going. Rounding up potential buyers is important too. You'll be back before you know it."

Suddenly looking serious, Colin lifts his hand to cup the other side of my face too. He leans down and his lips meet mine in a kiss that is all soft lips and tender emotion. Pulling back slightly, he searches my eyes. "I love you, Brianna. I'll hurry back."

Frozen, I'm still standing in shock as he drops one last kiss to my forehead before grabbing his bag and heading out the door.

Did he just say he loved me? I can't have heard that right. On autopilot, I find my purse and head to the office. What just happened?

Once I get to the office, there's no time to obsess over Colin's parting words. Everyone is buzzing about the news of the competing generator. The hours speed by as I field one call after another. I've taken over Colin's office and declared it a war room. Stan and some engineers have been in and out all day, helping with the investigation and gathering evidence that we invented the technology first.

As I respond to an email from the legal team, Richard Stone bursts into Colin's office. "Everybody out."

Those still in the room get up to comply. Stan shoots me an unmistakable look, asking if he should stay. I wave him off with a minute shake of my head. He doesn't look happy, but with a last pointed look he leaves, shutting the door behind him. I stay in my seat and look up at a fuming Richard.

The man is a mess; his hair is sticking up and his normally impeccable suit looks wrinkled. "Brianna, do you understand how bad this is? The board is out for blood and breathing down my neck. How did you let this happen?"

Anger flares at his words. Before I say something I regret, I bite my cheek and count to five. "I didn't let anything happen, sir. All project files were encrypted, and I followed all company policies. You can't blame me for this. I've been working with the team and legal all day to gather proof our designs are original so we can stop this competing patent."

Richard paces and pulls on his silvering hair. That explains the hairstyle. "IT found emails from our servers to the other company. They haven't found the sender yet, but someone is going down for this and it won't be me." He stops his path and turns to me sharply, his blue eyes crazy with stress. "We should turn it on Innovative Solutions, so C.A.E. doesn't go down. Yes! You can say it was all that McLeary guy. If you say he did it, the promotion is yours."

I sit in stunned silence. Richard is offering me everything I want. What I've pulled fifty-plus hour weeks at the office on top of the nights and weekends at Pop to accomplish. The job is mine. I just need to betray a man who has been nothing but supportive of me. The culmination of my five-year plan, and it just feels hollow. Taking Colin out of the equation, I still don't feel right taking the job if it means stepping on someone else to get there.

My heartbeat is surprisingly steady as I eye the man in front of me. For the past year, I've let him push me around. Insult me, belittle me, and disenfranchise me. He's played the pied piper, and I, the fool, danced to his tune. Again and again, I've made myself less and sucked up my pride to appease this man. I feel some slight delight at holding his fate in my hands, but I am done selling myself short. I deserve better.

"No."

The single word sounds like a gunshot in the empty office. Richard flinches as if shot, his face turns an unhealthy red and his breaths come in angry pants. He leans over the table where I sit, trying to intimidate me with his size. That won't work anymore.

"No? You have the nerve to tell me no?" He is practically screaming. Spit flies from his mouth.

I stand from the desk and look him straight in the eye, letting my professional mask slip enough to show the hatred I feel. "Fuck this, and fuck you. I'm not lying to save your ass. You're crazy if you think I'd actually agree to this. I quit, effective immediately. Good luck, Dick."

Richard collapses into a chair, sputtering. I snatch my few items and storm off, slamming the door behind me.

Barely three steps from the door, Stan is by my side, his long legs keeping up with my furious pace. "Brianna, what the hell happened? Also, how the fuck do you walk so fast in heels?"

Not slowing, I dump my stuff on my desk and look through my drawers for a bag. "I quit."

"You did what?" Stan steps into my path and puts his hands on my arms, forcing me to stop and look at him. His eyes shine with concern as he searches my face. "Why did you do that? What did that asshole say to you?" His voice is so husky it's nearly an angry growl. The fact he cares about me is evident.

Sighing, a little of my anger fades. Placing my hand on Stan's arm reassuringly, I look up at my friend. "He offered me the promotion if I said Colin is the mole. I refused." Stan's eyes widen, and he lowers himself to my desk, swearing under his breath. "It's fine, Stan. I can't sell my soul for this place. I have the restaurant and I'll find another project management job. Really, I'll be ok."

He looks crestfallen as he gazes up at me. I'm really going to miss him. Stan stands and pulls me into a hug. "This sucks, kid. Promise you'll call me."

I sniff back sudden tears. "Yea, I'll reach out when I settle somewhere."

With one last squeeze and a sniffle of his own, Stan heads back to his office, head hung low. I watch him walk off and fish out my cell, clicking Colin's name. The call goes straight to voicemail. Dammit, he must still be flying. "Colin, it's Brianna. Call me back as soon as you get this." I toss my phone in my purse and get back to packing. The first drawer isn't even empty yet when a shadow crosses my desk. Looking up, I find my favorite IT specialist, Gabe Diaz, standing over me. One of his eyebrows cocks as he surveys my packing.

"Hey, Gabe. Glad you're here. I just quit and I don't trust anyone else with these." I hand him my work laptop and tablet.

"Uh, if you quit I guess you won't be wanting this." He holds up a USB drive.

Don't do it, Brianna. Not your job anymore. In the end, my curiosity wins out. "What's that?"

"You were right. The trail to McLeary was a red herring. I found a bit of malware installed on his PC. The trail went cold until a few days ago when there was an unusual log-in late at night. I traced the IP addresses and discovered someone accessed the files and emailed them from a secondary PC assigned to the temp pool. The executive admin temp pool." He pauses, letting that sink in. "If you quit, though, I'll just turn this in to legal."

"Wait." I grab a pad of paper and a pen and write off two quick notes. "Please, make a second copy and send them to these people with these letters. I'll buy you dinner at Pop as a thank you."

Gabe takes the papers from my hand and purses his lips in thought. "For you, Queen B, anything. Take care of yourself." With a nod, he leaves me to my packing.

Fifteen minutes later, I've cleared all personal items from my desk. It's surprising security hasn't come to throw me out yet. Maybe Richard is still having a meltdown in Colin's office.

I juggle my purse on one shoulder, a canvas tote on the other, balance a box on one hip, and hug a potted palm to my stomach. Damn fronds keep hitting me in the face. It is slow going, but I manage to only stumble twice on the way to the elevator. How the fuck am I going to hit the button? Didn't think this one through, did you, Brianna? Just as I am blowing the frond out of my face for the hundredth time, and contemplating balancing on one high heel to shift the items, a voice calls out behind me.

"Here, let me help." Masculine hands take the box and plant from my hands. I'm surprised to find Johnson standing next to me. I hit the elevator button with a quiet thank you as I try to think of what to say. At the bing, he jerks his chin to indicate I should go first. We descend in silence, which continues as he follows me to my car. After I've belted the plant into the passenger seat, I turn back to Johnson.

He stands with his hands in his pockets, looking down at his feet awkwardly. "Brianna, this isn't right. You're the best project manager they have. I've learned so much from watching you work. I may not know you well, but I know there's no way you had anything to do with the leak." His words ring with certainty as his face pinches with unhappiness.

His sincerity surprises me. True, we've worked in the same department for almost four years, but we've never interacted outside of staff meetings. In fact, this is probably the longest conversation we've ever had. Impassioned outrage I can see from Stan and

Gabe—we've spent countless hours together on different projects. This unwavering trust from Johnson is touching.

My lips quirk into a smile, and I rest my hand lightly on his shoulder until he looks up at me. "Thank you, Johnson. It's for the best. I should have quit a long time ago."

Still looking conflicted, he pulls a card out of his pocket and gives it to me. "When you land somewhere running a project office of your own, give me a call if they're looking for more project managers. I would be honored to work for you."

Eyes widening, I take the card and read it: Leslie Johnson, Project Manager.

Leslie?

I look back up but Johnson is already walking back into the building. I give the doors of C.A.E one last look and get in my car, pull out of the parking lot, and don't look back.

CHAPTER THIRTY-SIX

What Happens in Vegas

BRIANNA

I stumble into the house and drop all of my work items in the home office. That shit can wait. Riley yips happily at my feet as I try to call Colin again. He should have landed by now. Why is it still going straight to voicemail?

In my bedroom, I wrestle out of my work clothes and throw them on the bed. I freeze, my sleeve still half-stuck on my arm, as an idea hits me.

Colin asked me to go with him to Vegas at least a dozen times, but I said no because of work. Well, work isn't a problem anymore, now is it? A slow smile spreads across my lips as the thought takes hold. I can fly to Vegas and surprise him. His confession this morning left me speechless, but I am ready to give him my answer. I can just fly out there and tell him I feel the same way.

The more I think about it, the better the idea sounds. I can help him at the conference during the day. Even if I don't work at C.A.E. anymore, this project is very important to Colin. And Colin is important to me.

Bright laughter bubbles up at the realization. Who knew quitting my job would be so freeing?

Now, I'm open to all sorts of spontaneous adventures. In a rush, I swiftly type out a group message as I head into my closet to pack.

> **Hey - can someone dog sit for the week last minute?**

LettyGo

> **I have a shoot in Bermuda. What's up?**

Annabanana

> **I can if you drop him off - dinner rush is crazy tonight. Everything OK?**

Breehive

> **Yea. I quit my job and decided to surprise Colin at the conference in Vegas.**

Annabanana

> **Is this a joke?**

LettyGo

> **WTF?**

> **Why did you quit?**

Annabanana

> **What do you mean surprise him?**

LettyGo

> **I'm calling you… pick up…**

Laughing, I accept the call and switch it to speaker as I sort through my clothes. "Hey. How many pairs of lingerie are too many to pack?"

There is stunned silence on the other end—but it only takes Nic a moment to get unstuck. "What the fuck happened, Brianna? We've been telling you to quit that job for a year and you refused. Why today? Are you ok?"

I wince as her voice pitches louder and higher with every word. Damn, she's going to blow my speaker. "Yea, I should have listened to you ages ago. Stone pushed me one step too far. He asked me to throw Colin under the bus for something he didn't do. I just realized life is too short for this bullshit."

"Ok," Nic makes the word sound ten times as long. "So what is this about Vegas then?"

"Colin's there at a green energy conference. He asked me to go a bunch of times, but I didn't want to leave Stone unsupervised. Since I don't work there anymore, there's no reason I can't take off for a week with my... boyfriend? Lover? I don't know, we haven't put a label on it."

A heavy breath comes through the line, as if Nic is searching for patience. I can picture her rubbing her eyebrows like she does when stressed. "Bree, I don't want to discourage this newfound spontaneity... God knows we've both been trying to get you to let loose since college... but are you sure this is a good idea?"

I take the phone off speaker and hold it up to my ear. "He told me he loved me this morning, Nic. Right before he left for the airport. I know it sounds crazy and too soon, but I've spent every day with this man for almost three months. He is supportive, and caring, and nothing like Chris or really any man I've met. I love him, Nic."

Silence prevails as she processes my revelation. "Ok, you finish packing. I'll book you a flight and come pick you and Riley up. I'll take you to the airport and then drop him off with Anna so you don't lose time."

I squeal. Nic is the tough one, and her support fills me with confidence. "Thank you, Nic. You're the best."

"Yea, I know. Oh, and Bree?"

"Yea?" I hold my breath, waiting for a warning or dose of reality.

"There's no such thing as too much lingerie. I'll be there in twenty minutes and I'll fill Anna in on the way. Love you."

The last six hours were a whirlwind of travel. I finally arrive at the conference center at ten pm local time. Thankfully, I still have my work ID on me and sweet-talked the front desk into confirming Colin's room number.

As the elevator ascends to the twentieth floor, I rehearse the speech I prepared on the flight. Butterflies dance in my stomach. For once, it feels like excitement and not fear. I bounce on my toes, practically vibrating the last five floors. I'm eager to see Colin and tell him how I feel.

When the doors finally open, I dart down the hallway to room 2013. Smoothing my off-the-shoulder sweater and leggings one last time, I knock on the door. My face splits into a grin as I see a flash of familiar maroon in the opening. A second later, my face falls as the door opens further.

In the doorway stands a woman wearing a maroon button-down shirt and nothing else. My eyes widen as I take in her bare feet, shapely legs, and the impressive cleavage where she clutches the shirt closed. When I get to the satisfied smirk on Rachel's swollen lips, I stumble back as if slapped.

A jolt of pain shoots through my stomach as it clutches. Desperate, I glance at the room number again, double-checking this is the right room. The number 2013 laughs at me.

"Well, isn't this a surprise? Moonlighting as room service, Brianna?" Her eyes burn with triumph. Without breaking eye contact, she adjusts the shirt, bringing my attention to the bite mark on her neck right next to the embroidered collar. C.A.M.

I gulp back bile as I try to make sense of this nightmare. The door widens, revealing a rumpled bed behind her and a trail of discarded clothes. My nose is assaulted with the musty smell of sex and the sounds of a shower and masculine humming filter through the silence.

"Aw, sweetie, you feeling ok?" Her lips tilt down in mock concern, but her eyes remain cruel. "You should know by now, you're just a tool to them. A walking spreadsheet and a bottom line. They don't see you as a woman. You emasculate them with your intelligence. In the end... Chris, Colin, anyone... I'm what they really want. They'll always turn to me when they want to feel like a man."

Say something, Brianna!

My mind is blank—just a swirling void of chaos. I always suspected Rachel, but I never had the proof Chris's affair was with her. In the end, there was no dramatic showdown. I just handed him my engagement ring and told him I was done. Blinking my stinging eyes, the words just won't come.

The sound of the shower shutting off shocks me into action. There's no way I'm giving them the satisfaction of seeing me fall apart. I turn on my heel and sprint back to the elevator. My shaking hand mashes the down arrow as I try to slow my stuttering breaths. Fisting my sleeve, I wipe harshly at my nose, willing the elevator to move faster.

Ding. The doors open and I stumble into the back of the car to brace myself against the railing. My breaths come in gasping spurts. The mirrored walls show red-rimmed eyes and nose. Two trails of black tears smear down my pallid cheeks. If I close my eyes, the image of Rachel in Colin's shirt haunts me.

My stomach lurches as the elevator reaches the lobby. I stumble to the nearby ladies' room, falling to my knees in a stall moments before losing what little I'd eaten on the flight. I can hear a group of women laughing by the sinks. Let them assume I'm some drunken tourist. What do I care anymore?

Minutes pass. When I'm sure my stomach is done, I hobble to the sinks to clean my hands and mouth. I splash cold water on my face and dry it on a towel, spreading another trail of black mascara. I'm sure I looked like a raccoon. Who the fuck cares?

Numb, I trudge to the entrance, hailing a taxi back to the airport. The trip is a complete blur of light and sound. As I approach the ticket counter, the teller's eyes widen at my bedraggled appearance.

"You ok, honey?" She has a friendly face, her eyes concerned.

"No."

As I admit it out loud, my tenuous hold on my emotions snaps. My breath catches on the sob I've been holding in. Eyes widening, she reaches out with a tissue box. Thanking her, I take one and blow my running nose. "I flew out to surprise my boyfriend and found his secretary in his room instead. Naked. I need to change my return ticket to the first available flight back to Orlando. Can you help me," I check her name tag, "Mary? Please." I sniffle again as I look into her eyes, holding out my ID.

Mary gasps and snatches my ID; her fingers fly as she types it into the computer. "Oh my, men can be fucking pigs. Ugh, don't they know what happens in Vegas doesn't really stay in Vegas? Honestly." A few more violent clicks on the keyboard, and a new boarding ticket prints beside her. She grabs my hand as she hands me my ticket and ID, squeezing it slightly so I meet her eyes. "I upgraded you to first class, honey. Be sure to drink all the champagne they offer. You're on the next flight—just go on through security and it'll be boarding in less than an hour. You give him hell when he gets back, alright?"

Despite still feeling like the ground is crumbling beneath me, my lips twitch in a slight smile. This woman is a guardian angel. Thanking her, I rush off to catch my flight.

CHAPTER THIRTY-SEVEN

Ice Queen Shatters

RACHEL

I finally made the *Ice Queen* shatter. She tried to hide it, but the mask was slipping. Her eyes shone with pending tears as her lip quivered. It only could have been better if she'd actually cried.

What a fantastic turn of events. I'd been expecting room service with dessert, but watching the bitch crumble was even more satisfying. Though I still fucking want those chocolate-covered strawberries and champagne.

Guess the Tin Man has a heart after all. And I just broke it.

That alone makes the months of rejections worth it. Well, almost. I still don't see what the hell he saw in Brianna. She's short and chubby with the passion of a toaster. What man would possibly choose *that* when they could have *this*? Secretary fantasies are basically a part of the American dream, dammit! This complete bullshit was seriously messing with my head. After a performance worthy of a porn star, all is right in the world again, though.

Brianna may have won the battle up to now, but I just won the fucking war.

I study my reflection in the hotel mirror. Colin's shirt looks good on me. Maybe I should wear maroon more often. Eyes bright, blond hair a sexy cloud around my head, the woman looking back at me is full of confidence and sex appeal. I'm not even as pissed about the hickey on my neck, not after Brianna turned white looking at it. She shouldn't have taken what I wanted. Now she has nothing.

No man. No job either, since I heard the bitch quit! Not so high and mighty, now, is she? And no way she can fuck with my plans.

"Ray," a masculine voice calls from the bathroom, "where did you go? This dick isn't going to suck itself."

"Coming." My cheeks ache from smiling as I toss the maroon shirt on the floor.

"Well, I better be soon. You owe me." My eyes roll at the commentary. He's not the best lay, but he's going places.

Plus, round two will be infinitely sweeter after crushing Brianna.

CHAPTER THIRTY-EIGHT

The Calvary Arrives

BRIANNA

Hours later, I bang on another door. Nic answers her apartment door in yoga pants and a hoodie. It's barely eight am in Florida. "Brianna? What in the world?"

She only gets out my name before I collapse at her feet, great racking sobs shaking my body. I'd regained a tight rein on my emotions on the way here, but as soon as I see Nic, the dam bursts free.

Arms surround me, and I realize Nic has knelt on the floor with me. She murmurs nonsense, trying to calm me down. I have no idea how long we sit there. Gently, Nic pushes me upright so she can see my face. "Bree, honey, you're scaring me. What happened? I sent you off on a plane barely twelve hours ago. Why are you here?"

"Rachel... hotel... naked." Another round of racking sobs takes me. I've never cried like this. I might never stop.

Nic gasps, and her hands tighten on my arms. "Come on, let's get you inside. Have you slept at all?"

I let her lead me through her spacious penthouse, completely in a fog. Like a rag doll, she sits me on the bed, pushes water into my hands, and takes off my boots. Once she's satisfied with the amount of water I sip, she eases me down onto the bed and covers me with a blanket. The door bounces open a bit behind her, leaving a line of light in the otherwise dark room.

My body feels heavy. Amazingly, the tears stop. My face is tight and gritty where it rests on the pillow. Every time I close my eyes, Rachel opening the door plays over again in my mind. So I just stare at the door and let the numbness spread.

Eventually muffled voices catch my attention from the main room. The door crack brightens and the sounds intensify. The bed dips lightly and then Riley's warm, furry body rubs against my chest. He whines softly before working to lick the tears off my face. I wave him away and he lays down next to me, head tucked on his paws, eyes watchful.

"I'm telling you, Anna. I've never seen her like this. I'm really worried." Nic's words are clipped and slightly breathy. She's no doubt pacing.

"She was so excited to go out there." The slight clang of a pan can be heard. When there's a crisis, Anna cooks. "Nic, is this seriously all the food you have in the house? Sweet Jesus, this fridge is empty!"

"I'm leaving for a week-long shoot tomorrow, remember? Seriously, not the point right now, Anna."

"I'll tell you what, you have a point, but we will be circling back to your eating habits. Did she say what happened?"

"All I got was something about Rachel being naked in a hotel. You don't think..."

The indelicate snort sounds like Anna. "Wouldn't be the first time with that jezebel."

"Yea, but she wasn't this upset when she broke up with Chris. Remember? I'm not even sure she cried after Chris. Anna, you weren't there. She literally collapsed at my feet and I had to put her to bed like a child. Brianna doesn't get upset, she just makes a new plan and keeps going."

Glass clatters on a hard surface, drawers open and slam closed. "Ok, ok, let's go see if she'll eat some noodles. We're also going to have a chat about how much processed food you eat."

Increasingly loud footsteps pad across the floor. I don't move. The room brightens as one of the girls opens the door. Riley whines and butts my arm with his nose. I still don't move.

"Brianna, honey? I got some food for you. Care to sit up and tell me what happened?" The smell of butter hits my nose first, then a bowl enters my eyeline as Anna sets it on the nightstand. The bed dips, first on one side and then the other, as both Anna and Nic sit next to me. I take a shuddering breath, releasing it as a broken sigh. Anna's eyes widen as she looks past me.

A hand grips my arm and pulls me to a sitting position. I shake Nic's hand off before she can dislocate my shoulder and grudgingly push myself to a seated position against the headboard. Numb, I stare straight ahead.

"Come on, just tell us what's wrong and we'll make a plan together." Anna's smile is slight but encouraging as she presses the warm bowl into my hands.

I stare down into the bowl. Egg noodles, butter, and a sprinkle of grated parmesan cheese. My stomach rumbles slightly, a reminder I've barely eaten in the last fifteen hours. Normally, anything Anna makes is delicious, but the food turns to ash as I force one bite after the other into my mouth. As I swallow the last bite, Anna swaps the bowl for a cup of tea. Clutching the teacup to my chest, I haltingly tell my friends what happened at the hotel.

Cried out again, I sit with my head on Anna's shoulder, Riley in my lap, and Nic on my other side slowly stroking circles on my hand with her thumb. The hole in my heart starts to heal a little, surrounded by the love of my friends.

"Why aren't I enough?" My voice breaks on the final word. A hot tear rolls down my cheek. Funny, I thought I was out of tears.

"Brianna Sadie Chance! Don't you say that." Nic's tone is sharp and her hand pauses its motion.

"Why don't they stay? Colin... Chris... Even my father left when I was a kid. What do I have to do to be good enough?" I lift my head and look Anna in the eye.

"Sugar, that's about them, not about you. You are perfect the way you are." Anna's eyes fill with pain and she strokes her hand down my hair.

I shake my head and turn away from her. Dropping my head back against the headboard, I stare ahead, unseeing, my mind stuck in the past. "Don't you get it? There's a clear pattern and I'm the only common denominator here! After my father left, I never wanted to be abandoned again. If I was just good enough. Smart enough. Pretty enough. Maybe my father would have stayed. Maybe my mother would be proud of me for once."

My chin trembles, and I squeeze my stinging eyes as more tears fall. "So I pushed myself at school. I thought if I planned everything, I wouldn't be surprised again. That way I couldn't get hurt. Then Chris used me and cheated on me. Sleeping with your secretary is so cliche, but I didn't care. He used his access to me to make insider deals, then covered it up by implicating my mentor. And I saw none of it coming!"

The girls gasp and share a look. I never told them what really happened, but the words flow out now.

Laughing bitterly, I shake my head and wipe my nose on my sleeve. "Me! Whose whole job is to foresee issues and work around them, I didn't even notice my own fiancé was committing a fucking felony. And better yet! Couldn't gather the proof to accuse him. Didn't stop him from getting my boss fired when I called it off. Did I fall apart then? Hell no, because I never really loved Chris. He just fit my plan. I went on like nothing bothered me. I pushed myself at work. It got me dubbed the Ice Queen, but I had the last laugh when my billables doubled theirs. I adapted. Until Colin."

I choke on a fresh sob. "With Colin, I felt more myself than I ever have." I shrug with a teary smile. "No longer the uptight robot so many people see. I trusted him. Completely. I relaxed for maybe the first time in my life. Stopped planning." Turning to Anna with blurry eyes, I continue, "I got surprised."

Anna's eyes glisten. "You got hurt, sugar." I nod, my breath hitching.

Nic puts her arm around me and tugs me closer. "You really loved him, didn't you?"

"I think I really did."

We sit like that for a bit. When my breathing steadies, Anna straightens and claps her hands. "Ok, this is what we're going to do. Bree is going to get some sleep—medicated if need be. Nic and I will head to your place. I'll pack up all Colin's things while Nic gets your locks changed. Then you, my dear, are going to Bermuda for some R and R." She jumps off the bed.

"Wait! I can't just crash Nic's trip!" I look at Nic for support.

"Sure you can. I'll say you're my agent. It's a week on a yacht. You can hang with models and forget all about dipshit leprechauns." She nods. The matter settled, I scrunch back down onto the pillows, settling in for my ordered sleep. Who am I to turn down a free Bermuda cruise? With no job and no boyfriend, what else do I have to do?

CHAPTER THIRTY-NINE

Homecoming

COLIN

I am *fecking* exhausted. The flight back—hell, pretty much the whole trip—was terrible. It's late and I am hungry, but that can all wait until after a reunion with Brianna.

The last three days apart were torturous. My life just doesn't work without her anymore. Or that nutty dog of hers.

I'm also a bit worried. I haven't heard from Brianna since I left. Maybe texting just isn't her thing? She works two jobs; she's probably just busy.

Racing over the empty roads, traffic lights flash by as I think back over the last few days. The trip had started so positively. I'd still been smiling when I reached the airport. Completely ecstatic that I'd told Brianna I love her. It didn't even matter that she hadn't said it back. Long lines at security, weather delays, screaming children, none of it had put a damper on my mood. Not even when I pulled out my phone and found it dead did my grin crack. Wanting to give Brianna an update, I'd gone to charge my phone only for the screen to briefly flash and fizzle out in my hand.

That's when I realized my phone had been in my pocket when I'd fallen into the pool and it was beyond repair now.

Still, I just added it to my mental to-do list and decided to send her an email instead. The screen had just started to load when they announced the weather had cleared and we were boarding immediately. So the laptop got shoved in the bag and I settled into my seat to read the copy of *Sense and Sensibility* I'd borrowed from Brianna.

I spent the rest of that first day exploring the convention hall. Finalizing my registration, signing up for different lectures or panels to attend. I'd even met a philanthropic billionaire at the registration table who I'd chatted up over dinner about the humanitarian possibilities of our product. From that point, everything had quickly gone horribly wrong.

My suitcase on the bed, I stood in my undershirt and slacks. My maroon shirt haphazardly tossed over a chair. I'd planned to pull out my toiletries, take a hot shower and try emailing Brianna again. I really needed her cell number. If I could just get to the project tracker... A knock at my door interrupted my plotting. The clock on the nightstand said eight pm. Who the *feck* could that be? Could Brianna have changed her mind? That thought brought a smile back to my face and some energy into my step as I rushed to open the door.

Instead of the curvy brunette I expected, a slim blond with a suitcase stood in the hall. Rachel bit her crimson lip provocatively as she eyed my bare arms.

The smile fell immediately as I ground my teeth. "You have the wrong room." I started to slam the door in her face, but Rachel pushed her arm in to stop me.

"Don't be like that. There is no other room." She boldly stepped forward until her breasts pressed against my chest, peering up at me through her fake lashes. My stomach twisted and my nostrils flared in disgust. "Come on, Colin, you shared a bed with Brianna so easily. Time to trade up to a real woman." She lifted her hand to trail her fingers down my arm.

I caught her wrist and shoved it firmly away from me, rage curling in my stomach. "You aren't even half the woman Brianna is."

"Oh, so you like 'em chubby? I promise you I've never gotten any complaints before. Let me in and I'll show you what you've been missing."

"Get the *feck* out of here, Rachel. I don't know how to be more clear. I'm not interested," I yelled, stepping further away as if burned.

For a moment, her pretty face twisted with rage before she smoothed her expression. She was *fecking* mental. "Come on, I don't have anywhere else to go. This is the only room and Richard sent me to help you network. If I go back now, he'll probably fire me."

Her eyes turned glassy with unshed tears and her lips trembled. As much as I disliked this woman, it didn't feel right to get her fired. If I said no, she'd probably just camp out in the hall all night, making things even worse. God, I wouldn't put it past her to call the cops and accuse me of kicking her out or hitting her. I had to tread carefully.

"Fine, you can stay here."

Her tears dried in a moment as triumph filled her eyes. I grabbed my suitcase off the bed. Rachel sauntered over and laid herself across the foot of the bed, stroking the coverlet provocatively. I turned on my heel and strode towards the door with my suitcase in tow.

"Where are you going?" Her voice rose as she scrambled back off the bed to follow me.

"I said you can stay here. I'll find another room." Without looking back at her, I opened the door and stepped into the hall.

"What am I supposed to do here all alone?" Gone was the genteel seductress mask. She was livid and did not hide it well.

"Whatever you want. It's not my problem. If you don't want to be alone, go down to the bar and pick up some john for all I care."

She'd still been yelling after me as I'd headed back to the lobby. The hotel had been full for the conference, so I'd had to find another hotel further away. Then I hadn't even gotten to fully enjoy the conference because Joe from legal began blowing up my phone as soon as I got it replaced. Then the media got word, and the stocks took a dive. Even Duncan had called me in Las Vegas asking me to fly back to Florida.

That's why I'm now rushing back to Brianna's at eleven at night, three days early. It took an encounter with a surly ticket agent and three flights, but I finally made it back. Tomorrow, I will be stuck in a conference room with a team of lawyers and executives, but tonight I just want to hold my girl.

Pulling into Brianna's driveway, the darkness surprises me. There isn't a single light on in the house. I'd texted her my updated itinerary. Maybe she went to bed already, it is rather late. I fight back the disappointment that she didn't wait for me. I guess she didn't miss me as much as I missed her.

Why didn't she leave the front light on, though? That's not like her.

I approach the door, carefully picking my way across the dark walkway after almost falling into a bush. Cursing under my breath, I dig out my keys from my bag and try to unlock the door, but it won't budge. I lean back, confused, eyebrows knitted. Trying the lock a second time doesn't make a difference.

Am I that tired that I'm at the wrong house? Arching backwards, I check the house number. Nope, this is the right place.

As I think, the quiet of the house hits me. Riley would have been barking at the door by now. Tromping back over the walkway, I peek in the garage. Strange, her car isn't there. Guess that explains the lack of barking. Maybe she's at Pop? Or a girls' night at Nic's apartment?

On a Wednesday though? Did Brianna just not get my message?

Deciding to try the front door one more time, I pull out my cell phone and activate the flashlight feature. Last thing I need is to roll an ankle on this damn walkway. This time, I easily see the white envelope taped to the front door with my name on it. Opening it, a white key card falls into my hand.

> Hey asshole—As Brianna is no longer employed at C.A.E., you have no reason to stay here. Room 1266 has been booked for you at the address below. Do not attempt to contact Brianna again—your number is blocked. Thought you were different.
>
> N

What the hell happened while I was gone? How did everything get so *fecked* up in only three days?

Did I scare her away when I said I loved her? Was she just looking for a good time and I was the only one catching feelings? If Brianna didn't have feelings for me, why was Nic calling me an asshole, though?

I try calling Brianna for the hundredth time. No clue why. Maybe I'm hoping this is just a bad joke? The call goes straight to voicemail, like every other time I'd tried her over the past few days.

As much as I don't want to admit it, nothing is getting solved today. I'll just corner her at the office tomorrow. Wait a minute... I double-check the note. 'No longer employed at C.A.E.'. What does that mean? Brianna is the most dedicated employee I've ever met. None of this makes any sense.

Shoulders stooped and chest tight, I head back to my car with the note and key card. I need a shower and some sleep. Tomorrow I'll get to the bottom of this mess.

Where are you, Brianna?

Chapter Forty

Pissing Contest

Colin

I toss and turn most of the night, worrying about Brianna and trying to think of a logical explanation for her cutting me off so completely. It's just after lunch now, and I haven't accomplished a goddamn thing. I'm no closer to saving my product or finding my girl. Despite being in the same room as Stan for hours, ten other men surround us, leaving me no opportunity to question him.

The only positive in the past twenty-four hours has been finding the few belongings I'd left at Brianna's safely, if haphazardly, packed up and waiting in my hotel room. Also, the lawyers feel they have enough evidence proving our designs are original to stop the competing patent. They also have evidence of sabotage.

We just aren't sure who the fuck is responsible.

Everyone keeps talking in circles in the war room. My skin is crawling and my head is pounding from listening to so many voices yelling over each other for hours on end. I am so grateful for our lunch break that I practically sprint to the men's room to calm down. A flush somewhere behind me breaks my concentration. I shake the last thoughts from my mind as I turn on the water to wash my hands and attempt to not look like I am having a breakdown in the jacks.

Brown eyes meet mine in the mirror. Fuck me, not this maggot again.

"Well, well. If it isn't big time McLeary. Would have thought you'd be long gone by now." Chris swaggers from the stall and washes his hands. The entire time, his weaselly eyes hold mine in the mirror.

I clench my jaw to keep quiet—God only knows what I'll say to the maggot. What is that breathing technique Brianna always does to calm down? Package breathing? That's not it. Box breathing!

"First," Chris says, "you lose the edge on your world-changing device. Got scooped by some nothing startup. That's got to hurt. You came all the way out here just to make sure this project is a success. How's that going for you? You hiding out here in the States because you can't go home?"

My teeth squeak from the force of grinding them. Come on, Colin. Brianna wouldn't lose her temper, and she wouldn't want me to. Come on. BREATHE, dammit. In through the nose... two, three, four. Out, through the mouth... Slowly my jaw loosens until I am no longer in danger of cracking a tooth. I'm still pissed, but the red haze over my vision is fading a bit.

A smug smile spreads on Chris's face. "Seriously, why are you still here? Even the *Ice Queen* abandoned you."

Anger pops like a balloon and my stomach twists with despair. Brianna didn't abandon me. I still have no idea where she is or what happened, but she wouldn't betray me. Where the hell is she, though? "You keep Brianna out of this."

"All that effort and what do you have to show for it? No legacy. No profits. And no girl." As Chris talks, he keeps getting closer.

I stand to my full height and turn to meet him straight on. He doesn't stop until we are almost chest to chest.

I will give it to the bastard. He has balls. I easily have three inches and fifty pounds of muscle on the guy, but he just keeps coming. "Watch it, lad."

Ignoring my warning, Chris's eyes turn hard and his smirk more sinister. "You should be thanking me, *mate.*" Chris emphasized the word with a terrible imitation of a British accent and taps me on the chest. Does the guy not realize I'm fucking Irish? "Brianna really is a crappy lay. More of a robot than a woman. I know—I've had her plenty of times."

With a roar, the last threads of my self-control snap. My fist connects with his cheek with a satisfying snap of his head. I barely hear the thud of him hitting the tile floor over the rushing in my ears. Panting, I try to rein my temper back in. The sound of laughter finally breaks through my harsh breaths. Why the fuck is this guy laughing after I punched him?

"You're so fucked." Chris touches his cheek and examines the blood on his fingers. "I'm going to get you fired, just like I got Brianna out. And her stupid mentor. You should have let me in when I approached you."

I look down at him, completely lost. "What the fuck are you talking about?"

"God, really? They all said you were so smart, too. You really haven't figured it out yet? The leaked plans to Synergenics. The stock shifts. It was all me and Rachel. She got the documents off your laptop and I brokered the deal and the trades. I'm going to be one rich bastard and you're going to be blacklisted at every engineering firm just like Brianna when I'm done with you."

"I wouldn't be so sure of that." A voice startles me. I turn to see Johnson just over my shoulder, holding a cell phone out. He must have been in the far stall when I came in. His smile is smug as he stares down at Chris. "Got your whole villain monologue on video, dipshit."

All the color drains from Chris's face and his eyes widen as he looks at Johnson behind me. His mouth opens and closes a few times before he finally manages to reply. "Then you also got this bastard punching me! You report me and I'll sue him."

Johnson steps forward to stand next to me. "I don't know what you're talking about, Chris. I was still in the stall. Didn't see any punch. When I started recording, you were already on the floor." Johnson taps on his phone a few times. My phone buzzes loudly from my pocket, the sound harsh in the sudden silence. "And now that video is with both CEOs and the in-house counsel. How did you put it? Oh yea. You're so fucked."

Without breaking his stare down with Chris, Johnson holds his fist up to me. Chuckling slightly, I return the fist bump. Chris is still sitting on the floor sputtering as we leave the bathroom and head to the executive suite.

CHAPTER FORTY-ONE

Begging the Bestie

COLIN

It's been a week since I last saw Brianna, and I'm going out of my mind. I called her dozens of times since getting my phone replaced. I even camped out at her house until a neighbor called the police on me. No one at C.A.E. knows where she is, just that she doesn't work there anymore. She's completely disappeared. I'm confused, worried as hell, and desperate to find her.

That's why I am now standing in front of Pop. I have no idea what sort of reception I'll get, but I bet Anna knows where she is. I just need to convince her to tell me. With one more deep breath, I open the doors and walk in, looking for a familiar face.

It is early; the restaurant has barely opened and the lunch crowd hasn't arrived yet. I immediately see a familiar blond head behind the bar talking to a man seated at a stool and head over. My long, determined strides eat up the distance. Halfway across the room, Anna looks up and sees me. Her chocolate eyes—usually warm with humor—burn like hellfire. If looks could kill, I'd be a dead man. I can't imagine Nic looking more pissed. *Fecking* hell, I really hope Nic is nowhere around here.

Throwing a bar rag on the top, Anna plants her hand on her cocked hip. "What in the Sam Hill do you think you're doing here?"

"Anna, please. I just want to talk. I don't know what happened."

"We all trusted you, and you turned out to be a snake." She practically spits the last word in my face in her rage.

The man on the bar stool to my left stands, and I spare him a side glance. He's in green slacks and shirt with a badge on his chest. As he eases closer, he moves his hand to a holster and gives me a calculating look. "This man giving you trouble, Anna?"

"Don't you worry, Billy, the only one in trouble here is him." She continues to glare me down.

Ignoring Officer Billy, I lay my hands on the bar top and lean towards her. "Anna, I'm begging you. Is Brianna ok? Where is she? I just want to talk to her."

She slams her hands on the bar top and leans into my face. "People in hell want ice water, but that don't mean they get it."

I close my eyes and my shoulders droop in defeat. Anna had been my last hope. My throat constricts as I realize it truly is over. My eyes burn and my heart aches. After a shaky breath, I look back up to meet Anna's glare with my beseeching gaze. "A week ago, I told her I love her. I leave on a business trip, come back planning on telling her I want to move here for her and the locks are changed! She's not at home. She's not at work. No one has spoken to her. I've been so worried that I even called local hospitals!" Something besides unrelenting anger flickers in Anna's eyes.

Clinging to that last bit of hope, I take another shaky breath before laying it all on the table. "Brianna is it for me, Anna. If she doesn't feel the same way, I completely respect that. If she wants me to go back to Ireland and never see her again, I will." I swallow as my voice cracks. "I just want to hear it from her."

She looks unsure. Her lips purse and her eyes narrow as she studies my face. I just hope she sees how genuine I am. "Ok. I'll give you fifteen minutes to convince me." She walks over to the kitchen doors and props one open with her hip, calling for someone to take over the bar service before turning back to me. "Well, you coming?"

"Are you sure you are ok, Anna?" Billy is still standing guard and eying me like a threat.

"Yea, Billy. Thanks, though darlin'. Enjoy your lunch."

I follow Anna through the industrial kitchen. Four individuals in white coats nod as she passes. We approach an office at the back, but instead of entering, Anna bypasses it and approaches the back doors. As we draw closer, I notice a stairway behind the office and follow Anna as she ascends. At the top is a small landing and a plain door, which she opens.

I step over the threshold and realize this is an apartment over the restaurant. Small, but tidy and well decorated. Standing in a sitting area which abuts an open kitchen, I can see a hallway with a couple of closed doors beyond. Before I can take in more details, a yipping at my ankles draws my attention.

Looking down, I see a familiar black fur-ball and eagerly scoop him up. I cuddle him to my chest and scratch his head as he happily licks my chin and whips my chest with his tail. "I missed you too, buddy."

Anna is giving me a calculating look as she watches my reunion with Brianna's dog. She sucks on her teeth once and, evidently coming to some conclusion, strides off to the kitchen. Glasses appear on the massive island. After filling each with a brown liquid from a pitcher in the fridge, she picks one up and leans back against the sink. "Ok, Casanova. You have until I finish my sweet tea to plead your case. You really want me to believe you have no idea why she's pissed?"

I sit on a stool across from her, still holding Riley against my chest, one armed. "I really don't! Yea, we got in a fight about work stuff before I left, but we talked it out and things were amazing. My cell broke before I left, so I couldn't call her when I got to Las Vegas, but I emailed her to let her know!"

Anna stills. "Emailed her work or personal account?"

The question is obviously important, but I can't figure out why. "Work—that's all I had. We work and live together, Anna. We usually just talk."

"What happened at the conference?"

I rake my fingers through my already standing-up hair. What the hell does the conference have to do with Brianna? I'm wasting my time. "Not much. I networked a bit with potential buyers. Gave a presentation to a few government officials. I ended up leaving early because of the legal issues back at the office. When I got back, Brianna's desk was cleared out and her house was empty."

Anna takes a big sip of her iced tea as she studies me. It feels like she is examining my soul. I lean towards her as I beg her with my eyes to help me. "Anything interesting happen at the hotel?"

"Which hotel?" I snort with disdain. "That *slag*, Rachel, *fecked* the reservations. I left the convention center and booked my own room in some disgusting motel."

"Then why did Brianna find Rachel in your hotel room? Wearing your shirt."

My jaw drops and my eyebrows move to my hairline. Suddenly, it all makes sense.

"Jesus, Mary, and Joseph. That's it. She warned me that cheating was a deal breaker but I swear, Anna, Rachel showed up at my room but I didn't sleep with her. Even if I wasn't in love with Brianna, I wouldn't touch that woman. I will tell Brianna every detail... if she'll just talk to me."

The silence stretches as Anna tilts her head, probably debating if she believes me. Slowly, she lifts her glass, draining the last of her drink.

I deflate in my seat. My time is up and I'm not sure if I've made my case. I run my fingers through Riley's silky fur, preparing to say goodbye to him. The clink of the glass on the counter might as well be a door slamming.

"She probably would have talked to you if it hadn't been Rachel." Anna's voice is soft, and a little sad.

I jerk my head up to look at her. "How does Rachel make a difference?"

With a lift of her eyebrows, a tilt of her head, and pursed lips, Anna gives me a look that clearly says I'm an idiot. What am I missing, though? Yea, Rachel is horrible, but why is cheating with her so much worse than anyone else?

Slowly, the pieces fall together. "Chris cheated on her with Rachel, didn't he?"

"Not as dumb as you look, sugar."

Red hot rage spears my chest. My breath releases in a hiss and Riley turns his head in my arms to lick my chin again, sensing my distress. "*Fecking eejit*. I should have punched him harder."

Anna's eyes widen, and she leans forward slightly. "You punched Chris?"

"Yea. He and Rachel were the ones behind the issues at work. He was saying *shite* about Brianna and I decked him." I hold up my bruised knuckles as proof.

The side of Anna's mouth slowly lifts into a slight smile. "Maybe we weren't wrong about you after all, Irish. Nic took Brianna with her on a shoot in Bermuda while I dog sit. She's heartbroken, but Brianna is safe."

Feeling the first burst of hope in days, I rush around the counter and pull her in for an awkward hug, Riley still in my arm between us. "Thank you, Anna. What changed your mind?"

"Riley. That dog hates Chris. He barely tolerates Brianna's mom for that matter, but he likes you. No man that loves that dog as much as you do could be all bad." With a joyous laugh, I hug her closer to my side. "Ok, Irish, don't make me regret this. How are you going to get your girl back?"

Anna refills our glasses, and we get down to making a plan together.

CHAPTER FORTY-TWO

Face the Music

BRIANNA

I hate to admit when I'm wrong, but I have to give it to the girls. It is really hard to be sad in the tropics with gorgeous views. And gorgeous men. Can't remember the last time I just sat for a week with no responsibilities. I feel refreshed and ready to plan the next phase of my life.

After opening up to the girls, I feel like a burden has been lifted. While Nic was busy working, I did some more self-reflecting. I also had a few video sessions with my therapist to discuss how my neurotic planning tendencies are just my anxiety and abandonment trauma working overtime. It will take years to fully believe it. But intellectually, I understand that it wasn't my job to make my parents love me.

At almost thirty, it's time to live for myself. There will most likely never be a day that I don't overthink things—that's my job after all—but I am done planning my life to fit anyone's expectations besides my own. So far, my new philosophy is going remarkably well. I've even gotten on board with this speed dating event Anna came up with while Nic and I were away.

Serves us right for not taking her with us.

It won't be all bad, I get to spend more time at the restaurant. If this is successful, we can branch out to other events. Maybe even a book club. I smile to myself as I sit by my pool, curled up with my dog and *Persuasion* by Jane Austen. I've already refreshed my resume and reached out to a few head hunters I trust. With the income from Pop, though, I can take my time finding the perfect opportunity.

Miss Musgrove is just about to jump from the rocks when my cell buzzes on the table by my lounger. Sighing at the interruption, I place my bookmark before answering the phone.

"Is this Brianna Chance?" a woman's voice asks, prim and professional.

"Yes, it is. What is this regarding?"

"This is Miranda Barker from C.A.E. Human Resources department." I sit up straighter and swing my legs off the lounger, suddenly at attention. "Mr. Stone informed us of your resignation but there is some paperwork we need you to fill out. There's also the matter of your exit interview. Can you come in this afternoon? Say two o'clock?"

I glance at my watch, it's only eleven am now. "Yes, I can make that work. Should I ask for you at reception?"

"Just give them your name and someone will direct you. Thank you for your cooperation, Ms. Chance." With a chipper farewell, the line disconnects.

Heaving myself off the lounger with a sigh, I head back into the house for a shower. As I walk, I shoot off a group message.

Breehive

I need to push our lunch to happy hour. HR called and I need to sign forms at C.A.E.

LettyGo

What do you think that's about? Happy hour sounds great though - I'll be at Pop whenever you get done.

Annabanana

No worries, sugar. I'll be here - I mean, I live here. Literally.

Breehive

Probably should have expected this sooner. Exit interviews are standard. Plus I technically never handed in my badge.

LettyGo

Boo. We'll have a drink waiting for you at the bar.

Annabanana

Chuckling at my friends' antics, I set about making a quick lunch and getting ready for my meeting with HR.

Taking a deep, steadying breath, I pull the handle on the front doors to C.A.E. and stare down at the elevator bank. It's time to face the music. Rage-quitting had felt amazing, but it hadn't been the most professional choice. R and D is not as big of an industry as you'd think, and word gets around about difficult employees.

Let's do this. Shoulders back, I walk to reception with my head held high, relieved to see a familiar face. "Hi, Wendy. Ms. Barker asked me to come in for some paperwork."

Wendy looks up from her computer screen for a second, her eyes widening. "Ms. Chance, of course, have a seat and someone will escort you shortly." She is already picking up the phone before I turn to the waiting area.

The office seems eerily subdued today. Glancing around, I don't see anyone I recognize. Should I text Stan while I'm here? Not that they'll let me wander around alone, but maybe he could meet me in the parking lot after or go grab a drink.

No sooner has my ass hit the chair than a middle-aged woman in a dress and cardigan strides up to reception. She spots me and changes directions. Her assessing brown eyes scan my appearance before landing on my face. I opted for black cigarette pants and a black silk blouse with ruby red pumps and a chunky red bib necklace. There's no need to play down my personality anymore since I don't work here, but I'm still going to dress professionally for a meeting.

The woman approaches me and sticks out her hand. "Brianna, thanks for coming in. I'm Miranda, if you'll just come with me."

I return her firm handshake and follow her down the hall to one of the smaller, more private conference rooms. At the door, she gestures for me to go first. One step into the room, I freeze.

Sitting there at the center of the conference table is Stefan Cullingford, CEO of C.A.E.

Looking up, Mr. Cullingford smiles at me, further taking me aback. He stands and waves me to the chair opposite him. As my mind reels trying to figure out what's going on, Miranda shuts the door behind me, blocking my exit. She sits further down the table, facing us both.

"Ms. Chance, good to see you. Can we get you anything? Water? Coffee?" The CEO is all smiles as he retakes his seat.

"Water would be fine, Mr. Cullingford."

"Oh, please, call me Stefan." He reaches into the mini-fridge behind him and passes me a bottle of sparkling water.

"Thank you, Mr.... Stefan. I will admit I am rather confused. I thought this was an exit interview with HR?" I shoot a frantic look at Miranda, who nods slightly at me with a firm but encouraging look.

"In a way, yes." His eyes sparkle with mischief. "I've told you before, Ms. Chance, you are an appreciated employee within my company. When a top performer like you quits, I want to know why. I'd also like to discuss this." He picks up a thick manila folder and slides it across to me.

Flipping open the cover, I find the note I'd given to Gabe and various documents providing proof of the leak's source. I swallow harshly, thinking of the best way to word this. "Mr. Stone asked me to compromise my integrity, and I refused. I did not feel staying an additional two weeks prudent after that."

Stefan nods knowingly. "I see. Would this have anything to do with the file you are now holding?"

"Mostly, sir. Mr. Stone asked me to accuse someone without sufficient proof. I refused, gave my resignation, and then packed up my desk. It was at that point I received the file from IT and asked them to forward the findings to you and Mr. O'Toole."

"You realize if you'd already quit, you had no legal obligation to come forward?" He scrutinizes me.

I hold his intense gaze as I answer candidly. "Moral integrity does not depend on employment status, sir. I only wish I had the same opportunity to prove Barry's innocence."

At the mention of my mentor, Stefan's head jerks back, eyes wide. "Barry? Whatever does this have to do with him?"

"He was not guilty of making those bribes. If I had the contacts then I do now, he might still be here." My eyes sting slightly as guilt twists my stomach.

"Oh, child, no." He leans forward and lays his hand on mine. "Barry had been thinking of retiring for years. He was waiting for you to be ready to succeed him. He took advantage of that situation to retire with a substantial package and has been cruising the Caribbean with his wife for the last year. It had nothing to do with you or that project."

I release the breath I'd been holding in a rush. It's not my fault? I'd felt so guilty for so long.

My eyebrows furrow. "If you had the files tracing the internal leak, then I really don't understand why I'm here. Is it because I threatened the merger by sending the file to both companies?"

Releasing my hand, Stefan leans back in his chair and smiles again. With that twinkle of mischief, he looks like Santa's corporate brother. "Quite the opposite. You impressed Mr. O'Toole with your integrity and he has agreed to move forward. With certain stipulations. We'd like to appoint you Chief Product Officer, reporting directly to me."

Blinking, I lean forward, sure I misheard. "I'm sorry. It sounded like you just offered me a job."

"You have a gift and I can use you on my board. I'd like you to head up a covert team to run all confidential product developments. With Innovative Solutions's engineering and our production skills, we expect to crank out more world-changing products over the next few years. You are exactly who we need to make that happen. I'll triple your salary."

It takes all my willpower to keep my face blank. "While I appreciate the offer, I'm not quite sure what to say."

"You would operate as an insulated team. Completely separate from the rest of research and development. Bottom line, what is it going to take to get you to say yes?" Stefan leans forward and grows serious.

Might as well shoot for the moon. "I want to choose my team. I need to be able to trust the people I work with. That will include an IT expert who will create a secure server with restricted access."

"Done." The twinkle in his eye intensifies.

"I'd like complete autonomy in how I run my team. Work schedules, assignments, bonus structure."

He turns to Miranda, who dips her chin before returning to her notes. Stefan turns back to me. "As long as it complies with labor laws, yes. Anything else?"

I swallow. This is the big one. Acting more confident than I feel, I meet Stefan's gaze. "I want those that were found responsible for the leak terminated and evidence turned over to the authorities."

Stefan smiles and pride shines in his eyes. "Already done. Thanks to the evidence provided by your team, those three are going away for a long time. Do we have a deal?" He reaches a hand across the table.

I give his hand a single pump. "We do."

"Fantastic. You can tell Miranda who you would like on your team and a list of any roles you need to hire for."

"Thank you, Stefan, for this opportunity."

"You earned it." With a proud smile and nod, he leaves me in the conference room with the intimidating Miranda Barker.

A half hour later, I've signed employment contracts and discussed my dream team. A stack of resumes will be on my desk tomorrow for the remaining roles. We are about to discuss office arrangements when Miranda's cell phone vibrates. She clicks onto a text and sighs, before putting the phone back down with a clatter on the surface.

"I'm so sorry, I need to see to an urgent matter. As you are again an employee, you no longer need an escort. I trust you can see yourself out?" At my nod, she stands and heads for the door, pausing as she reaches me. "He's right, Brianna, you earned this. I look forward to seeing what you do here."

Before I can think of a response, she is already out the door with her cell to her ear. In a daze, I wander back towards the elevators.

At reception, I stop short. Richard and Rachel are standing together in a crowd of people. Rachel's arms are behind her back. Her normally perfect hair sticks to her sweaty face and her blouse is half untucked. Richard's face is red and his hair stands up in places. Confused, I look closer at the crowd standing around them. The men and women in suits sport FBI badges.

As an agent pulls Rachel into the elevator, her eyes land on me. Her face twists into a hateful sneer and her cheeks flame. "You!"

The elevator doors close before she can screech another word.

Chapter Forty-Three

Boss Lady

Brianna

The drive to Pop is a complete blur. I blindly stumble into the bar area, not quite believing the past few hours really happened.

"Finally! Where the hell have you been?" Nic turns towards me from where she and Anna sit at the bar, chatting with Asher. She already has a martini in her hand.

My red heels clack against the flooring as I approach, saying nothing. Pop is busy tonight, and the sounds all jumble together in my head.

"You ok, suga'? You look like you saw a ghost." Anna tilts her head in concern.

I look at Asher. "Give me a shot of something." Without breaking eye contact, he fills a shot glass from a nearby bottle and pushes it across the bar top. I shoot the liquor back, letting the burn clear my mind.

"Girl, what happened? Are they trying to hold you in breach of contract or something? I thought it was just an exit interview." Martini forgotten, Nic leans towards me as I sit on the stool next to her.

"They offered me a promotion." I push the empty shot glass away. Magically, a glass of amber liquid with black cherries takes its place. Asher truly is an amazing bartender.

"Really? The director job you've been wanting?" Anna sounds confused, like she doesn't know if she should be happy or not.

"No, Chief Product Officer, reporting directly to the CEO." I gulp down half my drink and turn to my friends with wide eyes. "They tripled my salary."

"Seriously? Are they trying to buy your silence on Dick?" Nic sounds suspicious.

"No. Dick and Rachel were being hauled off by the FBI when I left." Rachel's angry face flashes in my mind and I throw back the rest of the drink.

Nic's mouth is hanging open. "Holy shit! That's insane. Did you take it?"

"Yea, I start tomorrow. I'm sorry Anna." I turn to her.

She looks surprised, but not mad. "Don't worry about it, darlin'. It would have been nice to have you here more often, but I knew it was only temporary. You're still on the hook for speed dating, though!"

A hiss followed by a loud pop makes me jump. I look back to the bar, where Asher holds an open bottle of pink champagne. "This calls for a celebration."

We smile and laugh as Asher fills flutes and hands them out. Excitedly, we talk about the future ahead. Nic wants to overhaul my entire closet with a new 'badass boss bitch' wardrobe. Her words. Anna is more concerned about finalizing plans for speed dating this week. All three of us end up sharing a late night of champagne and chatting. It's perfect. The next phase of my life is falling into place.

I look around the small conference table in my new office. Six faces look back at me. The large screen on the wall shows a similar table surrounded by people and a few individual faces on the web meeting. They're all waiting for me to speak.

No pressure.

The rest of the week has been a marathon of interviews and discussions with HR. Today is our first team meeting. This is the moment. Time to show everyone the boss I plan to be.

"Good morning and good afternoon. I'm thrilled to have you all here. As I've told each of you one to one, I personally selected this team. You are the best C.A.E. has to offer, and together we're going to develop products that change the world."

Looking around the room, I pause on each face. Stan, Gabe, and Johnson's familiar faces are all smiling at me encouragingly. With them sit two women—Tina Williams, who is a top-notch electrical engineer, and Laura Davis, who is a genius marketing lead. Rounding out the team of Dublin engineers on screen are Joe Fuentes from legal, and Jasmine Singh from data analytics. To my right sits my new assistant, Jay Smith, taking notes.

"We'll start each week with a quick call to set priorities. At the end of the Dublin day, we'll convene for a quick status check to review any issues. I expect full transparency. I can't help if I don't know where the problems are. You can expect the same from me. We will function as a separate organization from the rest of C.A.E. I care more about getting quality product out the door than dress codes and formalities. Recognizing hard work is important to me, so I created a bonus program based on the success of our products. Think of it like commissions or profit sharing. Any questions?"

Smiles and shaking heads meet my question. I take a deep breath to calm my pounding heart. So far, so good. "Excellent. Johnson, run us through the product proposals. Let's pick our next winner."

The next hour flies by as we review the ideas submitted by the Dublin team. We narrow it down to two potential products, and I break the group into two teams to create a more detailed pitch on each idea. "Thanks, team. Enjoy your weekend."

The screen goes blank and everyone at the table packs up their things. I stand and bring my tablet back to my desk. Jay offers to get me a coffee and scoots out the door. I can easily get used to having an assistant. Gabe gives me a smile and a nod as he leaves, already discussing ideas with Tina. Johnson gives a little wave as he exits with Laura.

When Stan is the last one remaining, he steps closer. "Terrific meeting, boss lady. You made it where you belong."

I perch on the edge of my desk with a heavy exhale. My bravado evaporates in an instant. "Thanks for taking this journey with me, Stan. You sure it doesn't feel like a demotion?"

"Hell no. I'm making more money, get a flexible schedule so I can catch more of the kids' school stuff, and less whiny staff. Wins all around. Plus, when we get the new location, I get to build my dream production line from scratch. Bree, this is my dream job." With one more affectionate smile, he pats my arm and heads out the door.

I survey my new office in the executive wing. The operations staff worked fast, decorating to my tastes. A large modern painting of aquas and gold centers one wall over a large white credenza. Two aqua upholstered chairs create a conversation zone on the opposite side of the mini conference area. I take in the entire effect and smile.

After the initial shock of the offer wore off, I worried I'd made the wrong decision. Walking into C.A.E. Tuesday morning had been shockingly easy. I received warm welcomes and congratulations from everyone I passed. My work friends—because let's be honest, they'd become more than just coworkers—had jumped at the chance to join me. When word of my new team got out, the resume pile had exploded, and I had to turn away candidates. Everyone wants to be a part of the innovation department, but I have a vision.

There's been no sign of Colin. That particular complication hadn't occurred to me in the heat of the moment. I don't mention him, and neither does anyone else. He's apparently gone back to Ireland now that his mistress is behind bars. With a sigh, I close my eyes as my heart aches.

I miss him. The house feels colder, lonelier. Even Riley has been mopey lately. I'm still pissed as hell and hurt that he chose Rachel. It's almost like he exists as two people in my mind. Colin the cheating asshole, and Colin the thoughtful live-in boyfriend.

I still have no idea how we got here. Maybe my no explanation policy wasn't my best idea—it leaves no room for closure.

Jay comes bustling back into my office, a steaming ceramic tumbler in one hand. "Ms. Chance, you have a meeting with the board in ten minutes. The agenda is in your inbox."

I smile at the man. He is extremely organized and comes highly recommended, but we are still breaking each other in a bit. "Thanks, Jay. Please call me Brianna, though. Can you please set up meetings with both pitch groups on Monday and Tuesday, and a call with the whole team on Wednesday? Hour each should be sufficient."

"Of course. I'll get the notes from today out and set everything up while you're in your meeting."

Thanking him, I grab my tablet and coffee and head down the hall to the executive boardroom. Soon, the rest of the board gathers around the table, with Stefan at the head. "First, I'm happy to welcome Brianna Chance to her first board meeting. I'm looking forward to hearing how our new team is getting on. Second item, Terry plans to retire, and we are searching for a new Chief Technology Officer from within I.S.'s organization as we move forward with this merger. Now, let's begin."

CHAPTER FORTY-FOUR

Speed Dating

BRIANNA

I look around Pop to make sure everything is perfect for Anna's speed dating event. I've closed the back section and arranged ten mini tables in two lines of five, each with two seats. Each table has a laminated card of icebreaker questions, a votive candle, and a small bell. A long table for the snacks, drink tickets, registration list, and feedback forms sits to one side as you enter the space. Just one more inspection to make sure everything is perfect.

An arm drapes around my shoulders, and I turn to find Nic. "Looks awesome, Bree. This is going to be fabulous." Nic's voice is full of pride and excitement.

"Yea, Anna had a great idea."

"What did I do?" Anna comes through the kitchen doors, carrying a large tray of snacks.

Nic eyes the snacks for a minute. "Girl, are you sure snacks are a smart idea for a dating event? Can you imagine if someone has spinach in their teeth? Or garlic breath." She grimaces and fake gags, making me chuckle under my breath.

Snacks safely placed on the waiting table, Anna turns back, hand on a hip cocked at a saucy angle. "Pa-lease, who do you take me for? There are no onions, garlic, or green leafy vegetables in any of this. Teeth and breath are secure. The guys will blow these dates all on their own."

Leaning closer to my ear, Nic stage-whispers, "I still think we should stick to the booze, get everyone loose."

I laugh, the antics of my two best friends a welcome comfort. "Come on, Nic, think of our insurance premiums! Plus, the law says if you serve drinks, you need food to soak it up." Dropping my voice, I turn back into Nic. "Though I agree that the number of matches would increase."

Nic chuckles and gives me a side hug. Anna fusses with the other items on the table, not changing my layout so much as ensuring everything is in place. She picks up the registration list and gives it a quick scan before squinting slightly and running her tongue over her teeth. Uh oh, that's her thinking face.

"What's wrong, Anna?" I ask.

"The count is off. We have more bachelors than bachelorettes." She looks up at me, her gaze calculating.

"Let me see that." I march over to look for myself. "I handled the registration myself and we had even numbers." Taking the clipboard from her, I scan the names. Sure enough, one of the girls' names has a line through it with a handwritten note that she canceled. "Fuck. Well, I guess one guy will just have to sit out every rotation—gives them a chance to get some snacks." I look up at my friends to gauge their reactions.

Nic comes over to look at the list over my shoulder. "Nope, won't work. The girls will bitch they don't get a break for snacks. Plus, it just complicates things. One of us will have to be a bachelorette."

Anna holds her hands up, palms out. "Well, I can't do it! I have more snacks to bring out and the rest of the restaurant to oversee."

"And I can't do it, I'm the MC." In unison, they turn towards me, heads tilted and eyes sharp.

"Hell no! I just got my heart broken, remember? I'm not ready for one date, let alone ten!" I slowly back away from them, feeling outnumbered.

"Bree darlin', when you get thrown, you just gotta get back on that horse." Anna's eyes are soft, but her tone is firm.

"Daisy Duke is right." Anna smacks Nic's arm playfully at the nickname. "Think of it as a practice run! Just rip off the Band-Aid and get ten crap dates out of the way!"

"Oh yea," I roll my eyes, "because that sounds way better. How about I MC and Nic can do it? I'm not dressed for a date, anyway." I sweep a hand over my standard restaurant uniform of black dress slacks and blouse.

"I have something in my car that will be perfect on you. Plus... you know I love you... you are the best planner in the world, but you're not exactly the best at working a crowd. You can't MC if we want this to be successful." Nic has the grace to wince, but she is never shy to tell you the brutal truth.

With a sigh, I deflate. "Yea, you're probably right. Do you have a makeup bag with that outfit? And for the love of God, someone get me an Old-Fashioned."

Nic and Anna share a look that instantly makes me regret agreeing to this. Before I can say a word, they rush me up to Anna's apartment to change and glam up my makeup a bit. I'm caught up in a whirlwind, unsure of what's happening. Feels like I blink and find myself seated at a candlelit table for two, decked out in a shimmery cobalt halter, smoky eyes, and raspberry lips.

I end up at the corner table, back to the rest of the attendees. Around me, nine other women ranging from twenty-three to forty-five sit at identical tables, doing last makeup checks or reviewing the suggested topics cards. I fidget in my seat, wishing I was safely behind the organizer table instead of in the middle of the event.

"Here you go, old-fashioned with extra cherries." Asher arrives at my elbow with a drink.

I grab the drink out of his hand and take a big swig, moaning in appreciation.

"Thank you." I grab his arm, desperation clear in my voice. "Keep them coming. I need the liquid courage."

Asher smiles down at me and pats my hand on his arm. His eyes are warm with humor and a sprinkle of pity at my predicament. The man must rake in the tips—and phone numbers—with that smile. It's no wonder ladies' night is so good for business here. The man is objectively gorgeous, but he's having no effect on me. My stomach twists as I realize I'm comparing him to Colin, and I take another swig of my drink.

"Don't worry, Bree. You're the prettiest bachelorette here. All ten of those guys are going to want another date," Asher says.

Letting go of his arm, I bury my face in my palms to muffle a groan. "Not better! More dates is so not the goal here." After a deep breath, I look back up at the confused-looking Asher. "But thanks for the compliment." He heads back to the bar, shaking his head.

"Ok, ladies, it's about time to begin!" Nic holds a portable mic and beams at the crowd, completely in her element. She is right, she's way better at this. "Welcome to Pop's first speed dating event! Ten lucky bachelors are waiting just around the corner to meet you.

You'll have six minutes to chat and decide if you'd like to exchange numbers. There will be no ending a date early—just smile and nod for six minutes, ladies. We're all pros at it."

Nic pauses for effect, and I hear a smattering of giggles. She is so good with people, so charismatic. "During your date, if you have an insta-connection you can both agree to bypass the rest of the candidates by ringing the bell. Any questions?"

Soft murmurs and gentle head shakes come from the crowd. I turn back to face my table, concentrating on slow breaths to calm my racing heart. Shit, what do I even talk about?

Wait, this isn't real. I'm just filling an empty chair. I can just say no to all ten. No harm, no foul.

Feeling a little better after my self-pep talk, I square my shoulders and take another sip of my drink.

"Bachelors, find your first table number on the card in your hand. Let's begin!" Nic's voice rings out in the quiet space.

A familiar face sits down across from me and I feel myself relax further. A genuine smile crosses my face as I look up at Johnson, who smiles back down at me.

Nic plays some sound effect on her phone like harp strings. "That's going to be the sound to switch partners. Have fun, everyone, your six minutes starts... NOW."

"Hey, sorry if this is weird, since you're my boss now. I won't suggest a match. Not that you're not great! You're great, just not appropriate." Johnson's cheeks blush as he stumbles through his greeting.

Seeing the typically so-cool man frazzled breaks my remaining nerves. The stress releases in gales of laughter. I clutch my hand to my chest as my shoulders shake.

"Somebody is enjoying herself," a voice mutters behind me.

Reining in my amusement with a sigh, I look up. My eyes are wide as I wipe the tears from the corners. "Shit, I probably look like a raccoon now." Still smiling, I meet Johnson's shocked gaze and pat his hand on the table. "Absolutely no offense taken. Honestly, I'm glad you're the first bachelor. I'm just filling an empty seat and I was freaking out a bit before you sat down. But yes, I agree that dating is a bad idea. We can still chat a bit, though."

Johnson looks relieved. "You said you were filling in? How'd that happen?"

"I actually own this restaurant with my two best friends and helped plan the event. There was a cancellation, and I got stuck in the hot seat." The bourbon is kicking in.

Warmth spreads in my stomach and my frazzled nerves calm. Clearly my tongue loosens too. I even manage a self-deprecating smile.

"Wow, how do you have the time?"

"Well, obviously I'm single." I chuckle dryly. "Honestly, Pop isn't *work*. I get to enjoy delicious food I don't have to make and spend time with my friends. If I have to do some paperwork for that, I'll happily take the trade. What about you? Any hobbies?"

He smiles slightly and blushes again before clearing his throat. "Promise not to laugh?"

"Of course!" I find myself leaning forward, so curious to hear the answer. With his cleft chin, square jaw, and perfectly tousled black waves, he looks like a walking GQ cover model. What could he possibly be embarrassed about?

"I'm a gamer—fantasy co-ops mostly, like World of Warcraft." He nervously plays with the beer glass in front of him, shooting glances at me to gauge my reaction.

Huh, didn't see that coming. "I've never met a gamer. Is it good stress relief?"

His eyes widen, as if that wasn't the reaction he expected. "Yea! It's very immersive, so you tend to stop stressing about real life. It's actually a lot more complicated than most people think. There's a lot of strategy and planning that goes into a campaign. You meet some interesting people too." Johnson gets more animated as he speaks, clearly enthused about the topic.

"That's probably why you're so good at your job. Planning, strategy, communication... all key aspects of project management. Well, you've convinced me. Maybe we could find a shorter game to play as a team builder."

As Johnson opens his mouth to reply, the harp timer sounds. We wish each other luck as he moves to the next table. Maybe I should try some video games. Eviscerating orcs sounds more cathartic than Jane Austen or smutty novels about now. I'll have to ask Johnson for some entry level suggestions on Monday.

Taking another giant swig, I finish my drink and wave at Asher, who salutes me back. My next date sits down as I'm fishing out one of the delicious cherries from my glass. As I finally free the fruit and pop it in my mouth, I look up and choke.

Sitting across from me is none other than Colin McLeary.

Eyes wide with concern, Colin jumps up to tap my back until the cherry dislodges. "Brianna, are you ok?"

Through a wheezing breath, I hold up my hand and wave him away. "What the fuck are you doing here? You know what? Nope, I'm not doing this. This date is over."

As I push my chair back, Anna appears behind me. "Sorry, darling, rules are rules. No skipping a date. You only have to hear him out for another five and a half minutes." With a comforting squeeze of my shoulder and a meaningful look at Colin, she escapes back to the kitchen.

This is starting to smell like a setup.

"Traitor," I mutter at her retreating figure. Crossing my arms, I sink back in my seat and glare boldly at the man who just broke my heart. A man I'd somehow greatly misjudged.

CHAPTER FORTY-FIVE

End of the Line

COLIN

I lean forward with my hands clasped on the table. Brianna has shuttered her expression, her emotionless mask firmly in place. Although I've studied the nuances of her moods over the last three months, I have no idea what she's thinking. My stomach in my throat, I take a deep breath as I try to pour every ounce of emotion and sincerity into the speech I prepared.

"My name is Colin Andrew McLeary. Thirty years old, originally from Dublin, Ireland, but I have been looking to move here. I like dogs, especially small black ones who are fiercely protective of their owners. I've only been in love once, but she thinks I did something unforgivable and won't talk to me."

Brianna's eyes flicker with an analytical gleam, but give away no emotion. At least she's listening. I can work with that. "You have less than five minutes left."

"Nothing happened at the conference! I didn't even know Rachel was going to be there until she showed up at my door. She was in the hotel room booked for me because she manipulated the bookings, but I wasn't there. After I repacked my bags, I stayed at a terrible motel near the conference center. I can show you the invoices. I never cheated. I've never even lied to you once since we've met."

My heart feels like it's going to explode and my lungs burn. Desperately, I search her eyes for some flicker of emotion. Some sign that she believes me. Just as I start to think I may be too late, I see it. The briefest flicker in her cobalt eyes.

Pain.

It breaks me that I've hurt her so much, but it proves she isn't indifferent.

Brianna's emotions break through her usual placid façade, causing her cheeks to turn red with anger. "She was wearing your shirt, in your room, with a man in the shower."

"I swear on my mother's life it wasn't me. The shirt got missed as I threw my shit in a bag, trying to get the hell out of there. Rachel tried to get me to sleep with her before I even met you, and I turned her down. Every chance I got, I avoided her while we were in the office. Why would I do all that just to sleep with her now?" I beg her to believe me with my eyes.

She pauses as she thinks through my words. "That doesn't explain you ignoring my phone calls. If you are innocent, why didn't I hear from you for a week?"

A flicker of hope blooms in my chest and I lean further, reaching out and stopping just short of touching her hand. "My phone was in my pants when I fell into the pool. I didn't realize it was dead until I got to the airport. I didn't know your number, but I sent you an email at your work account as soon as I landed. By the time I got a new phone, you must have already blocked me. I tried calling you dozens of times." I search her eyes for any sign she believes me. A kaleidoscope of emotions flickers across her face. My six minutes have to be almost up.

This is it, now or never. Time to lay it all on the line.

"Brianna Chase, from the moment I saw the fire in your eyes in that conference room, you've captured me. These last few months of living together have been the happiest of my life. I love you so much. Even if I have to spend the rest of my life proving to you how much it will be worth it. Because you are undoubtedly the only woman for me."

I take a deep breath as I push my chair back and fall to one knee beside her, a blue velvet box in my hand. My eyes lock on hers as I open the box to reveal a white gold Claddagh ring with a blue sapphire heart. Her eyes widen as they dart between the ring and me. Confusion and shock clear on her face as her emotionless mask falls away entirely.

With my free hand, I clasp her limp fingers before continuing. "I know this seems impulsive, but I've never been more sure of anything in my life. Will you marry me?"

The room has gone eerily silent. I hold my breath as I wait for her answer.

"I can't."

Her voice is barely a broken whisper, but it shatters me. She bites her lip and her eyes glimmer brightly, red around the edges.

My breath rushes out, all traces of hope gone. My eyes burn as I hold back tears of my own. This is it, the end of the line.

I nod absently, drowning in emotion. Sniffling slightly, I stand and start to walk away. The room around me fades away as I concentrate on putting one foot in front of the other, away from the love of my life. Grief and regret overwhelm me. I did nothing wrong, but there's so much I could have done better.

I could have tried harder to get a message to her, or call the number at Pop. Instead of running away, I could have stayed in my room and filed a formal complaint against Rachel. Brianna had been crystal clear about her hard limit. She was with Chris for years but still severed all ties. I can't expect her to go out on a limb for a man she's known for three months.

Ding-a-ling.

In a daze, I look back at the sound of a bell. Brianna still holds the silver bell aloft, her eyes bright, as a lone tear trickles down her cheek. Her lips curve in a tremulous smile as she watches me.

"I can't... yet." She stands, and her smile grows. "I mean, we never really *dated,* so it's a bit premature to get married. But you can move back in and I'll think about it." Her shoulders shrug slightly, and a beautiful blush spreads across her cheeks.

Long strides eat up the distance between us as I rush to embrace her. My lips capture hers in a drugging kiss. I pour all the love and joy I feel into it. Her arms circle my shoulders as I lift her and spin. The crowd bursts into applause as we hold each other, and I don't give a *feck.* The woman of my dreams is in my arms and she didn't say no.

"I love you." I whisper as I break the kiss, using my thumb to dry the tears on her cheeks.

Her smile is bright and wide as she cups my face in her palms. "I love you, too."

Epilogue – Three Months Later

BRIANNA

The afternoon light glows as I stare out the window of my office in thought. I can't believe it's been three months since speed dating. In that time, Colin has proved himself over and over again. He's stayed true to his word. Every day, he shows me how much he loves me.

We just got back from Dublin, where we packed up his apartment to make the move permanent. I met his family, and they are absolutely wonderful. So welcoming and supportive. His sisters and I even have a group chat going and we are already planning Christmas together on the family farm. Seeing him with his niece and nephew was adorable. My ovaries nearly combusted, picturing him with a child of our own.

Thinking back to how I almost wrote him off, my smile falters. When I saw the sincerity in his eyes, I believed him. Honestly, I felt a little silly when the full truth came out. I should have just talked to Colin in the first place. After everything with Chris, when the evidence was so damning, I thought I was protecting myself by not listening to excuses or explanations. But I was letting my past haunt me, and I almost lost everything.

We fill our days working together to deliver world-changing tech. The lawyers finally made headway on the patent issues. Turns out Rachel took a plea deal, turning on Chris and Stone and giving a full confession for reduced jail time in a white collar prison. The trial made national news. They featured me as a pioneer of women in R and D. The story of how I brought down corporate espionage from within and still got the product to testing on time has brought C.A.E. into the limelight. Companies are lining up to work with my special innovation team.

Business at the restaurant is booming, too. Anna is talking about expanding again, and I've been rerunning the numbers. Colin's proposal made it to social media. Speed dating is now a bi-weekly event, and we have a waiting list to join. When I have to fill in at Pop, Colin either stays home with Riley or hangs out at the bar with Asher and Johnson. Those three are thick as thieves now. Colin and Johnson even have a weekly game night.

A knock at my door draws my attention. I swivel my chair back to my desk and call for the person to enter. Colin opens the door and my heart swells. No matter how many times I see him, his handsome face takes my breath away. He is wearing his typical happy grin as he walks in, coming close to perch on my desk by my elbow.

"Hey, Brianna girl. I was thinking we could head out a little early. How do you feel about dinner at Pop to celebrate six months together?"

A smile spreads across my face, and I eagerly tilt my head back for a chaste kiss on the lips. We maintain clear boundaries between work and home, but the occasional display of affection behind office doors occurs. I rest my hand on his thigh as he pulls back. The sapphire on my engagement ring sparkles in the golden glow of the sun, catching his attention. Confusion lights his green eyes as he looks at the ring and then back up at me.

Standing slowly, I smooth my favorite pencil skirt and step between his spread legs. Taking his hands in mine, I look deep into his eyes. "Colin Andrew McLeary, I think I've loved you since the first time I saw you with my crazy dog. You are the most caring, intelligent, and loyal man I've ever met. I want nothing more than to spend my life with you. *An bpósfaidh tú mé*?" I spent weeks practicing the Gaelic translation of 'Will you marry me'. It was totally worth it for the look of complete joy on his face.

With the biggest grin I've ever seen, Colin rushes to his feet. He tenderly cups my jaw with his large hands and kisses me so sweetly my heart melts all over again. He rests his forehead against mine as he keeps me in his embrace. "Of course, *a ghrá*, nothing would make me happier."

Giving him one more kiss, I pull back. "Now we can go celebrate at Pop with some champagne."

Colin is already heading to the door in long strides. Instead of heading to his office to get his bag, though, he shuts the door and locks it.

"What are you doing?" My voice shakes with confused laughter.

As Colin turns back to me, his eyes burn with intense hunger. He stalks back to me by the desk. "There's something I've been dreaming of doing for months." His hands grip my hips as he backs me up until I sit heavily on the desk's surface. As his lips descend to my throat and his hands stroke up my thighs, I give him a sultry laugh.

This man can never stick to the plan, and that is fine by me.

Want more Brianna and Colin?

Catch up with them as they appear in their friends' stories—starting with Annabel in *Stick to the Recipe*. Keep reading for a preview!

How about a short story from Riley's POV where he saves Halloween?

Sign up for my newsletter for bonus content!

Also by

Want more Friendship Springs?
Friendship Springs Romance:
Stick to the Plan (Brianna & Colin)
Stick to the Recipe (Annabel & David)
Stick to the Deal (Nicolette & Reginald)
One More Chapter (Gabby & Asher)

Stick to the Recipe

SNEAK PEAK

My palms are sweating, for Christ's sake. I wipe them on my jeans, hoping the dark wash hides the wet marks. This is the most nervous I've been in my entire life—and I've stood on an active land mine for thirty minutes while someone disabled it.

I look up at the building before me. I can't quite motivate myself to enter. The bright lettering says Pop, and the bold pink logo taunts me. Big scary marine can't walk into a restaurant and talk to a girl. But Annabel Bennet isn't just any girl, is she?

Buck up, marine. This is the whole reason you moved to this town. You are not a nineteen-year-old idiot anymore. You served through two contracts, saw a lot of shit, saved a bunch of people.

I absently touch my back pocket, hoping the lucky charm in my wallet will lend me courage. With one more deep breath, I ready myself for war, and open the damn door.

My eyes squint as they adjust to the dimmer indoor light. It is three in the afternoon and the restaurant is empty. The lunch crowd has moved on with their lives and the happy hour crowd is still counting down the time at work.

I scan the room, looking for threats and my target. Some habits die hard. Three exits—the one I just entered, another to the rear by the bathrooms, and doors that likely lead to the kitchen. The walls and tables are monochrome and modern, with bright splashes of art dominating the space. The plaques hanging by the hostess stand brag to customers that this place was voted best restaurant in the city three years in a row. Looking around, I can believe it.

My Bella's done good.

My heart clenches at that thought. My Bella.

She isn't really my anything anymore. I'm not sure if I deserve to be anything to her, but I am making it my mission to try—and a Marine always finishes his mission. Turning back, I find my target standing behind the bar, wiping a glass.

She doesn't look up as I approach, and I can study her uninterrupted. Her blond hair is in a bun on top of her head. The chef coat she wears is crisp and clean. Bella seems lost in thought as she inspects the glass and hums along to the music playing over the speakers. Off-tune, of course. Her face has lost the roundness of youth, her cheekbones more sharp. Those adorable freckles still sit across her nose, though. Somehow she's even more beautiful after ten years.

Great start to the plan. I'm staring at her like a creep.

I know I should say something, but it's impossible around the lump in my throat. This could go so many different ways, most of them badly. I take a painful breath through tight lungs and will my heart rate to slow as I take the last few steps to the bar.

"Hey, Hell's Bells." My voice is low and gravely to my ears.

Her head jerks up, and her gorgeous chocolate eyes widen. Her lips part as her grip on the glass falters. It plummets, the side of the glass hits the edge of the counter and smashes. The sound echoes in the empty space.

"Davy..."

I barely hear her whisper. We just stand there. Staring into each other's eyes. A million emotions cross her face. I read them all. The time apart doesn't matter. I know this woman better than I know myself.

So far, so good. At least she didn't throw the glass at my head.

The doors by the bar swing open, and a man strides out, heading behind the bar. "Anna, love, are you okay? I heard a crash."

Pain slashes through my chest as I watch him wrap his arm around my Bella. The motion is intimate and caring. My gaze locks in on him as I assess my enemy. Shorter than me, but tall for a man—around six feet. His chiseled jaw and green eyes are annoyingly attractive. Women probably go nuts for the accent too.

Bella—or maybe it's Anna now? That's what he called her—is frozen still, staring at me. He rubs her arm soothingly and I feel the muscle in my jaw spasm. An annoying squeaking sound pierces my ear, and I realize I'm grinding my molars.

The touch must snap her shock. Her brown eyes narrow, and I swear I can feel electricity in the air as her anger builds. "What are you doing here?"

He follows her gaze and jerks back slightly in surprise. His intelligent eyes sharpen as they assess me, then look back at her. Trying to gauge the situation.

"It's good to see you, Annabel." I tuck my hands in my pockets, unsure what to do with them.

"Why are you in my restaurant? Shouldn't you be off playing hero? Or back in Hitchcock?" The hellfire I named her for burns in her eyes.

"My contract ended last year. A buddy from the corps and I started a security business nearby. I live here now."

Her mouth opens and closes, but no words come out. It isn't easy to make my Bella speechless—the girl was always chattier than a magpie in May. Somehow I've managed it, though.

The silence drones on in the uncomfortably charged air—then the pretty boy breaks it. "Hey, we haven't met. I'm Colin. How do you and our Anna know each other?"

My gut drops at the casual possessiveness in his statement. He carefully steps around the broken glass and reaches over the bar to give my hand a firm pump.

"David. We grew up next door to each other back in Georgia." I nod my chin at her while I maintain eye contact with him.

"David is friends with my brother," her tone is all Southern belle. Ouch. That hurt, guess all those pinky promises meant nothing.

"Well now, isn't that grand. What a nice reunion. You should come by the house."

"What?" Bella's head jerks towards him, and his arm tightens around her back. He seems immune to the daggers she's shooting at him.

"The little woman and I just got back from a trip to Ireland and we're having friends over for a get together this weekend. I think you'd call it a cookout?"

What the hell? Is this a power play or is the guy just dense? I immediately don't like how he's ignoring her wishes—or the clear 'shut the hell up' signals she's throwing. "That's a mighty kind offer—but I wouldn't want to intrude." See, I can hide behind Southern charm too.

"Nonsense. Any family friend of Anna's is a friend of mine. You should come by and meet some locals. Right, love?" He turns to her and squeezes her tighter. I clench my fist as I see his fingers dig slightly into her bicep as he stares her down.

"Yea, sure. More the merrier." She sounds meek.

I hate it. I named her Hell's Bells because she was a tenacious wild cat when we were kids. This woman in front of me is starting to feel like a stranger, and it's breaking what's left of my heart.

"Grand!" Colin releases his hold on Bella to grab a bar napkin and pen. He jots an address and time down and hands it to me. Woodenly, I reach out and take it, eyes still on the silent but fuming woman next to him. I mumble my thanks and goodbyes and hightail it the hell out of there.

It's my first retreat in my long military career, and it sucks.

Read It Now

Acknowlegements

I first started Brianna's story over a decade ago. It was my first week as an IT project manager at a new company. I had little work to do yet and my boss told me, "I don't care if you write your memoir, just look busy." So I started plucking away at a novel. In the years since, I've picked up and put away this project countless times. My dream had always been to be an author, but life and responsibilities kept getting in the way.

Then my world changed. Within six months, I unexpectantly lost both my grandmother and my mother. These were two women who turned me into the reader I am today. Although I'm a mood reader, and bounce between multiple genres, I've always had a special relationship with romance. My mother bought me *I Thee Wed* by Amanda Quick at the airport after I'd run out of reading material (these were the pre-Kindle or free Wi-Fi days). I was instantly hooked. After that, both my mother and grandmother handed over shopping bags full of Harlequin novels. It was something special I shared with them.

Losing them, especially so close together, made me take an honest look in the mirror and reassess my priorities. Sure, my nine-to-five paid the bills, but did it feed my soul? What about my dreams? What kind of example was I setting for my daughter? Things had to change. So I made space for myself in my life. I stopped working fifty-plus hour weeks and wrote in every spare moment I could carve out, and rewrote that original draft into the book it is today.

To my husband, Jay (yes, I named Brianna's assistant after him). He has been a one man hype team and a major reason I could do this. Keeping the kids in line during my writing sessions. Kicking my ass when I was doubting myself. Talking through business decisions when my ADHD got stuck in research mode. Even debating plot lines! He has truly been a partner through this process. Thank you!

To my girl squad. Thank you for being my cheerleaders, therapists, and beta readers through this journey. I am so lucky to have all y'all in my life.

Lastly, to you, the reader. Thank you so much for reading my debut novel and taking this journey with me. I wish you joy and many happily ever afters.

Life is short. Eat the damn cake.

About the Author

R.S. Barry, a resident of Central Florida, shares her life with her loving husband and their two kids. A dedicated and passionate reader for many years, R.S. Barry now makes the voices in her head work for her.

Drawing inspiration from life's experiences, R.S. Barry weaves contemporary tales of love, connection, and self-discovery. As a long-time reader and working professional, she brings a unique perspective to her writing, infusing her work with a genuine understanding of the complexities of human emotions.

When she's not writing, R.S. Barry is probably curled up with a novel by the pool, over-analyzing a fictional couple's chemistry, or debating whether to buy just one more book.

Find out more and see her complete book list at www.RSBarry.com
And find her on Facebook, Instagram, and TikTok.

facebook.com/profile.php?id=61555639000320

instagram.com/authorrsbarry

tiktok.com/@authorrsbarry